# THE FRACTAL PRINCE

Also by Hannu Rajaniemi from Tom Doherty Associates

*The Quantum Thief*

# *The* FRACTAL PRINCE

Hannu Rajaniemi

**TOR**®

A TOM DOHERTY ASSOCIATES BOOK

NEW YORK

THE FRACTAL PRINCE

Copyright © 2012 by Hannu Rajaniemi

First published in Great Britain by Gollancz, an imprint of the Orion Publishing Group, an Hachette UK Company

All rights reserved.

A Tor Book
Published by Tom Doherty Associates, LLC
175 Fifth Avenue
New York, NY 10010

www.tor-forge.com

Tor® is a registered trademark of Tom Doherty Associates, LLC.

ISBN 978-0-7653-2950-9

First U.S. Edition: November 2012

Printed in the United States of America

0  9  8  7  6  5  4  3  2  1

This is for Tomi, who lives in our stories.

'His likeness? How can I trace it? I have seen Arsène Lupin a score of times, and each time a different being has stood before me ... or rather the same being under twenty distorted images reflected by as many mirrors ...'

Maurice Leblanc, *The Arrest of Arsène Lupin*

'When we gaze upon a fractal, we must peer at a one-way mirror, unaware of the other mirror, standing somewhere far behind us.'

Christian Bök, *Crystallography*

# THE FRACTAL PRINCE

# Prologue
# THE DREAMING PRINCE

That night, Matjek sneaks out of his dream to visit the thief again.

In the dream, he is in a bookshop. It is a dark, filthy place, with a low ceiling and a drooping staircase that leads up to a small attic. The shelves bend their backs under the weight of dusty volumes. A heady smell of incense from the back room mingles with a whiff of dust and mould in the air.

Matjek squints at the handwritten shelf labels in the dim light. They have changed since the last time, and list esoteric topics. *Fire-eaters. Human Cannonballs. Poison Resisters. Wall of Death Riders. Multiple Mental Marvels. Escapologists.*

His pulse quickens, and he reaches for a small volume whose back says *The Secret History of the Zacchini Cannon*, in curly, golden letters. He loves the stories in his dreams, although he can never quite remember them when he wakes up. He opens the book and starts reading.

*The cannonball man never loved her, even though he told her so many times. His only true love was flying, that sensation of being blasted out of the mouth of the great iron thing that his grandfather cast out of metal that was said to come from a rock*

*that fell from the sky. He wanted a wife like a thing he should*
*have, another tool to keep the great mechanism he and the cannon*
*formed together in working order, but love was the wrong word*
*for it—*

Matjek blinks. It's not the right story. It does not lead to
the thief.

He jumps when someone coughs behind him, and he
slams the book shut. If he turns around, he will see the lanky
shopkeeper sitting behind the counter, looking at him dis-
approvingly, eyes wild, grey chest hairs peeking out from the
buttonhole of a stained shirt, unshaven face full of malice.
Then he will wake up.

Matjek shakes his head. Tonight, he is not just a dreamer.
He is on a mission. Carefully, he replaces the book in the
shelf and starts walking up the stairs.

The wood groans under his weight with each step. He
feels heavy. The handrail suddenly feels soft in his grip. If he
is not careful, he will sink into another, deeper dream. But
then he sees it: a flash of blue amongst the grey volumes, up
in the corner shelf ahead, just where the stairway ends.

Below, the shopkeeper coughs again, a mucous, jagged
sound.

Matjek reaches for the book, standing up on his toes and
pulling at the blue binding with his fingertips. The book
falls, and a cascade of others comes toppling down with it.
Dust stings his eyes and throat. He starts coughing.

'What are you doing up there, boy?' says a creaking voice,
followed by sudden, shuffling steps, and the groaning of
floorboards.

Matjek gets down on his knees, tosses aside books on flea
circuses and singing mice, and uncovers the blue volume.
There are tears and dents on the cover, with brown paper

peeking out, but the silver cover design with its minarets, stars and moon is still bright.

Something comes up the stairs, something that smells of incense and dust, not the shopkeeper anymore but something far worse, something papery and whispering and old—

Matjek fixes his eyes on the book and flings it open. The words leap out at him, black insects moving on the yellowed page.

*Among the histories of past peoples a story is told that in the old days in the islands of India and China there was a Sasanian king, a master of armies, guards, servants and retainers, who had two sons, an elder and a younger—*

The words swirl. The paper and the letters bulge out, form the shape of a hand, fingers of black and white, reaching out from the book.

The dust thing coughs and whispers, and something brushes Matjek's shoulder, tickling sharply. He grabs the hand as hard as he can, and the razor edges of the word-fingers cut his palm. But he holds on, and the hand pulls him in, into the suddenly vast sea of language in front of him. The words roll over him like—

—waves, a gentle, teasing pull and push of cold foam around his bare feet. A warm evening sun above, a beach of white sand like a smile.

'For a while there, I thought you weren't going to make it,' the thief says. He holds Matjek's hand in a warm, tight grip, a slight man in shorts and a white shirt, eyes hidden behind sunglasses, blue like the book of nights.

The thief has laid a towel on the sand, close to a cluster of abandoned parasols and lounge chairs. They sit together and watch the slow descent of the sun into the sea.

'I used to come here,' Matjek says. 'You know, before.'

'I know. I took it from your memories,' the thief says.

And suddenly, the empty beach is full of Saturday afternoons. Matjek and his father would go to the tech bazaars first, spread the loot on the sand, test little swimming drones in the waves, or just sit and watch the ferries and jetskis. But even with the soft sand between his toes, the smell of sun and sweat and salt on his skin, and the red curve of the rocks at the other end of the beach, it does not feel quite right, not entirely his.

'You mean you stole it,' Matjek says.

'You didn't seem to need it. Besides, I hoped you'd like it.'

'It's okay, I suppose,' Matjek says. 'Some details are wrong.'

'Blame your memory, not me,' the thief says.

That bothers Matjek. 'You look different, too,' he says, just to say something else.

'It helps with not getting caught,' the thief says. He takes off his sunglasses and puts them in his breast pocket. He does look a little different, somehow, although Matjek could swear the heavy eyelids and the eyebrows and the little twist in the corner of his mouth are the same as before.

'You never told me how they caught you,' Matjek says. 'Just about the prison, and how Mieli got you out. And how she took you to Mars, to look for your memories. So you could steal something for her boss, and then she would let you go.'

'And then?' The thief smiles, like he sometimes does, as if at some joke only he knows.

'You found the memories. But there was another you who tried to take them. So you trapped him in a prison, and only got out with a box with a god in it. And a memory that said that you needed to go to Earth.'

4

'You *do* have a good memory.'

A sudden current of anger rushes through Matjek's temples.

'Don't make fun of me. I don't like it when people make fun of me. And you are not even people, just something I made up.'

'I thought you went to school. Don't they teach you about the importance of made-up things?'

Matjek snorts. 'Only to chitraguptas. The Great Common Task is about reality. Death is real. The enemy is real.'

'I see you are a quick learner, too. So what are you doing here?'

Matjek gets up and walks a few angry steps towards the sea. 'I could tell them about you, you know. The other chens. They would cut you out.'

'If they caught me,' the thief says.

Matjek turns around. The thief is looking up at him, squinting his eyes at the sun, head cocked to one side, grinning.

'Tell me about the last time,' Matjek says.

'Ask me nicely.'

Matjek is about to tell the thief what he thinks, that he is a figment of Matjek's imagination and Matjek does not have to ask him anything. But the thief is so full of mirth, like a little Buddha that Matjek's mother used to have in her garden, that the words die on his lips and he takes a deep breath instead. Slowly, he walks back to the towel and sits down, hugging his knees.

'All right,' he says. 'Tell me about how they caught you the last time. Please.'

'That's better,' the thief says. The sun is barely more than a golden wink in the horizon now, but he still puts his sunglasses on. The sunset spreads out in the sea, like flowing watercolours. 'Well. It's a story told against death, like I am, like you are, like we all are. Did anyone ever teach you that?'

Matjek gives him an impatient look. The thief leans back and grins at him.

'Here's how it goes,' he says. 'On the day the Hunter came for me, I was killing ghost cats from the Schrödinger Box.'

All around them, the dream vir begins to paint the thief's words with the sunset, sand and sea.

# 1

# THE THIEF AND THE BOX

On the day the Hunter comes for me, I am killing ghost cats from the Schrödinger Box.

Q-dot tendrils like sparks from a Tesla coil trail from my fingers into the little box of lacquered wood floating in the middle of my cabin. Behind it, displayed on one gently curving wall, is the Highway – a constantly flowing river of spaceships and thoughtwisps, a starry brushstroke in the dark. A branch of the gravitational artery through the Solar System our ship, *Perhonen*, is following from Mars to Earth. But today, I'm blind to its glory. My world is the size of a black box, just big enough to hold a wedding ring, the mind of a god – or the key to my freedom.

I lick sweat from my lips. My field of vision is a spider-web of quantum protocol diagrams. *Perhonen*'s mathematics gogols whisper and mutter in my head. To help my all-too-human senses and brain, they translate the problem into yosegi: opening a Japanese trick box. The quantum protocols are sensations, imperfections and valleys in the marquetry, pressure points inside the wood like tense muscles, faint grins of sliding sections. I need to find the right sequence that opens it.

Except that here, the trick is *not* opening it too early, the wood patterns are hidden in the countless qubits inside – each zero and one at the same time – and the moves are quantum logic operations, executed by the arrays of lasers and interferometers the gogols have built in the ship's wings. It all amounts to what the ancients called quantum process tomography: trying to figure out what the Box does to the probe states we ease into it, gently, like lockpicks. It feels like trying to juggle eight-side Rubik's cubes while trying to solve them at the same time.

And every time I drop one, God kills a billion kittens.

The gogols light up a section of the diagram, red threads in the tangle. Immediately, I can see another section that is linked. If we rotate *this* arrow and *that* state and apply a Hadamard gate and *measure*—

The imaginary wood beneath my fingers groans and clicks.

'Sesame,' I whisper.

Drathdor the zoku elder liked to talk, and it wasn't that hard to get him to explain what a Box was (without letting on that I had stolen one from their zoku twenty years ago, of course).

Imagine a box, he said. Now put a cat in it. Along with a death machine: a bottle of poison, cyanide, say, connected to a mechanism with a hammer and a single atom of a radio-active element. In the next hour, the atom either decays or not, either triggering or not triggering the hammer. So, in the next hour, the cat is either alive or dead.

Quantum mechanics claims that there is no definite cat in the box, only a ghost, a superposition of a live cat and a dead cat. That is, until we open it and look. A measurement will collapse the system into one state or the other. So goes Schrödinger's thought experiment.

It is completely wrong, of course. A cat is a macroscopic system, and there is no mysterious intervention by a magical observer needed to make it live or die: just its interaction with the rest of the Universe, a phenomenon called decoherence, provides the collapse into one macrostate. But in the microscopic world – for qubits, quantum-mechanical equivalents of ones and zeroes – the Schrödinger's cat is real.

The Box contains trillions of ghost cats. The live cat states encode information. A mind, even, a living, thinking mind. The Box qubits have been rotated into a limbo state between nothingness and existence. The mind inside would not notice anything – a set of quantum gates can let it continue thinking, feeling, dreaming. If it stays inside, all is well. But if it tries to get out, any interaction with the environment will bring the Universe down on it like a ton of bricks and collapse it into nothingness. Bad kitty, dead kitty.

'So what do you put in a Box like that?' I asked Drathdor.

'Something very, very dangerous,' he said.

A section of the Box in the qubit map we have created over the last week lights up like a city at night. I can feel it: the unknotting that always comes with a job when you discover the flaw in a lock or a security system or a con mark's mind. Eagerly, I close my eyes and follow the flow of moves. The wood panels slide beneath my fingers. The gogols sing with the joy of the orgasmic jolts of pleasure they receive from computing spectral sequences of Hilbert space operators. More light in the map. The lid moves, ever so slightly—

And snaps shut. The next register dies, for good. The protocol network ties itself into a knot. The last measurement shows only death. I have destroyed another fragment of the contents of the Box.

I swear and throw the accursed thing across the cabin. The q-dot tendrils tear and dissolve. The Box bounces from the starry field of the wall and spins in the air.

The words that have been ringing in my head for days come back to me.

*I am not Jean le Flambeur.*

A small white butterfly lands deftly on the Box and brings its spin to a halt, fluttering its wings.

'Before you break anything,' the ship says in its soothing, feminine voice, 'I would like to point out that this was all your idea.'

The ship is right: it *was* my idea. Or, rather, my earlier self's idea. The original Jean le Flambeur, a thief and mind burglar of legend, an all around nice guy. Who left me with nothing apart from a few fragmented memories, old enemies, a prison sentence – and the thing inside the Box.

'Touché,' I say.

'That's three days straight now, Jean. Maybe you should leave it alone for a while.'

'There is no time. You told me it's decohering.'

Fatigue stings my eyes like sand. A reminder that, in spite of appearances, I am not free. *Perhonen*'s captain Mieli stubbornly refuses to give me root access to my Sobornost-made body, keeping it firmly within baseline human operating parameters in spite of my assurances that my previous attempts to escape our involuntary partnership were misunderstandings and that I am firmly committed to paying my debt of honour to her and her elusive Sobornost employer. Honest.

But I can't give up. When the ship first examined the Box,

it found that the quantum information inside is short-lived. In a few days, the kittens will die of old age.

'Almost as if the designer deliberately wanted to introduce a time limit. Like a game,' *Perhonen* says.

'As you say, it's a zoku device. What do you expect?' There is a great variety of zokus out there, but they are universally game-obsessed. Not that the Sobornost are immune to the lure. A memory of their Dilemma Prison and its deadly games makes me shiver – not to mention its resident monster, the All-Defector: the shapeshifting nightmare who wore my own face to beat me. Whatever job Mieli's boss got me out for has to be better than that.

'I don't know *what* to expect. Neither Mieli nor you have told me what's inside it. Or what it has to do with our destination. Which I'm less than keen to visit, by the way.'

'Earth isn't *that* bad,' I say.

'Have you been there since the Collapse?'

'I don't know. But I know we have to go there.' I spread my hands. 'Look, I just steal things to earn my keep. If you have a problem with the big picture, take it up with Mieli.'

'Not with the mood she's in,' the ship says. The butterfly avatar makes a circuit around my head. 'But maybe *you* should talk to her. About the big picture.'

Mieli *has* been acting strangely. She is not the life of the party at the best of times, but she has been even quieter than usual during the slow weeks of our journey from Mars, spending most of her time in the pilot's crèche or in the main cabin, meditating.

'That,' I say, 'seems like an exceptionally bad idea. Usually, I'm the last person in the world she wants to talk to.' *What is the ship talking about?*

'You could be surprised.'

'Fine. Right after I get this thing open.' I frown at the Box. The butterfly avatar settles on my nose, making me blink furiously until I have to brush it away.

'It sounds to me like you are trying to distract yourself from something,' it says. 'Is there something *you* are not telling me?'

'Not a thing. I'm an open book.' I sigh. 'Don't you have better things to do? They created the first psychotherapist bots about four hundred years ago.'

'What makes you think you are not talking to one?' The avatar dissolves into a bubble of q-dots, leaving behind a faint ozone smell. 'Get some sleep, Jean.'

I touch the Box, feel the solid shape of the warm wood, make it spin in the air again until its edges become a blur. The movement makes me drowsy. The ship is right. It is easier to think about it than about Mars and the castle and the goddess. And as soon as I close my eyes, they all come back.

The memory castle on Mars could have been mine: all its rooms with their wax and brass statues, the treasures and zoku jewels, stolen from diamond minds and gods. It's all gone now, my whole life, eaten by an Archon who turned it into a prison. The only thing left is the Box, and the memories that came with it.

I could have reached out and taken it all back, but I didn't. Why not?

*I am not Jean le Flambeur.*

I walk down the gold-and-marble corridor of the castle in my mind and look through the open doors, into the rooms of stolen memories.

There is the time I did not *want* to be Jean le Flambeur.

I lived on Mars, in a place of forgetting, the Oubliette. I made a new face. I made a new life. I found a woman called Raymonde. I hid my secrets, even from myself.

There is the Spike, a Singularity both in technology and spacetime. A bright flash in the Martian night, a dying Jupiter raining quantum dreams down on the people of the Oubliette.

There is the Hallway of Birth and Death, the building I made to remind immortals of how things end.

There is the lover of an Oubliette artist whose memories I ... sought inspiration from. He was touched by the Spike. In his mind, I saw the fire of the gods. And I had to have it.

There is the Martian zoku. They brought the Box with them, from the Protocol War. Inside, a captured Sobornost Founder gogol, one of the rulers of the Inner System. A trapped god.

There is the girl called Gilbertine – another thing I could not help but want, even when I shouldn't – whose memories I hid the Box in. I wore a face filled with a cold purpose that feels alien now. *Being Prometheus, that sort of thing,* the old me told her. That's what the goddess with the serpent smile who Mieli serves wants me to be.

There is the woman Xuexue from the robot garden who was an uploader on Earth. She turned children into deathless software slaves in the sky, in the time before the Collapse, before Sobornost. That is what pulls me to the home of humanity now, the knowledge that this memory has a purpose, that there is something in the world of ghosts that I need.

And then there is the closed door.

I open my eyes. The Box is still spinning. I *have* been

distracting myself. Earth is where the answers lie – and inside the locked room in my head.

*What would Jean le Flambeur do?*

I take the Box and hum a few notes of Stan Getz. A circular opening appears in the curving surface of one of the walls. Much of the ship's structure is made from Oortian smartcoral – or väki, as they call it – and it responds to music. I have had enough time to watch Mieli to figure that out. No doubt the ship knows what I'm doing, but I like the modicum of privacy that comes from having a hiding place.

I put the Box inside and make an inventory of the contents. A couple of zoku jewels – tiny dark amber ovals the size of quail eggs – stolen on Mars when the detective Isidore Beautrelet and I went to his girlfriend Pixil's reincarnation party. There is also her Realmspace sword, which I brought with me from the battle with my other self, Jean le Roi.

It's not much, but it's a start.

I put a zoku jewel in my pocket for good luck, lock the rest of my paltry secrets away and go looking for Mieli.

Mieli prays to the Dark Man in the main cabin of the ship. The songs come to her haltingly at first but, after a while, the sculptures in the walls start moving to the sound of her voice, twisting into the dark countenance of the god of the void. It is a song Grandmother Brihane taught her, only to be sung in dark places, on dark journeys. But as she slips into meditation, the images become her reflections: many Mielis looking at her in the walls, their faces the colour of dirty comet ice.

She stops, staring at them. The spherical candles floating in the air, their tiny heart-flames emanating light and a soft cinnamon smell, the song – none of that matters. The hollow feeling inside her is back.

There are things she should be doing. Preparing cover identities for the approach to Earth. Reviewing Sobornost databases about the home of mankind – and the place that her people, the Oortians, fled, centuries ago. Instead, she sighs, pulls herself to the comfortably ordered axis of zero-g furniture and spherical bonsai trees in the centre of the cabin, and fabs herself a bulb of liquorice tea.

She cradles the rough warm coral of the bulb in her hands. The song to make it comes to her, suddenly: a few simple notes a child could learn. She hums it as she takes a sip. A dark taste, liquorice and bitterness. She has forgotten how foul the stuff could be. But a memory comes with the mouthful, a morning in the koto when the blinds were opened and the Little Sun shone in, turning the thousand scars and cracks of the ice sky into bright winks, the Grandmother pressing the bulb into her hands and giving her a kiss with her withered lips, her dry, sweet smell mingling with the tea, the pumptrees opening, the little anansi catching the morning thermals in their diamond web gliders—

Even that memory is not hers anymore. It belongs to her mistress, the pellegrini.

It should not feel any different from everything else she has already given. Her flesh, shaped into a container for fusion and death. Her mind, augmented with a metacortex that kills fear, figures out what her enemies are going to do before they know, turns the world into vectors and forces and probabilities. All that for Sydän. So why does the last thing she gave up – uniqueness, the right for the goddess to copy her, to create gogols that think they are Mieli, daughter of Karhu – feel so precious?

Perhaps because it was not for Sydän, but for the thief.

She brushes aside the old, habitual anger at the thought

of his face, features that have become familiar over the last few months: bright eyes beneath heavy eyelids, an easy smile, high eyebrows as if sketched with a sharp pen. For a moment, she almost misses the biot link that her mistress used to bind them together, feeling what he feels. It made him easier to understand.

He made her sing, on Mars. Like everything he does, it was a trick, meant to cover up something he was doing behind her back. But through the biot link, she could feel his joy at her song. She had forgotten what it was like.

And there was honour. She could not abandon him to die in another prison, discarded by the pellegrini like a broken tool. How could she have done anything else? She touches the jewelled chain around her leg. Precious gems in a chain, one after another, irrevocable choices.

She lets go and continues to pray, slowly. The candlelight dances on the faces of the statues, and they start to become Sydän's face, the wide mouth and high cheekbones, the arrogant pixie smile.

'Why is it that you never pray to me, I wonder?' the pellegrini says. 'Gods are so old-fashioned. Memetic noise inside monkey heads. You should pray to me.'

The goddess stands in front of Mieli, a shadow framed by the zero-g candles, arms folded. As always, it is as if she is standing in normal gravity: her auburn hair is open and falls across shoulders left bare by a white summer dress.

'I serve and obey,' Mieli says. 'But my prayers are my own.'

'Whatever. I am generous. Prayers are overrated anyway.' She waves a red-nailed hand. 'You can keep them. I have your body, your loyalty and your mind. Remember what you promised me.'

Mieli bows her head. 'I have not forgotten. What you ask is yours.'

'Who is to say I haven't already taken it?'

Mieli's mouth goes dry, and there is a cold fist in her stomach. But the pellegrini laughs, a sound like tinkling of glass.

'Not yet. Not yet.' She sighs. 'You are so amusing, my dear. But unfortunately, there is little time for amusement. I do, in fact, need your body, if not your soul. My Jean and I need to have a conversation. Circumstances have forced my other selves to set certain things in motion. Something is coming for you. You need to be ready.'

The pellegrini steps into Mieli's body. It feels like plunging into freezing cold water. And then the cabin and the candle-light and the goddess are gone and Mieli is in the spimescape, a ghost among the tangled threads of the Highway.

# 2

# TAWADDUD AND DUNYAZAD

Before Tawaddud makes love to Mr Sen the jinn, she feeds him grapes.

She takes one from the bowl in her lap, peels it carefully and holds it between her lips, kissing the sweet moist flesh. When she bites, there is a faint, metallic sigh from the jinn jar that is attached to the fine sensor net of the beemee in her hair by a thin white cable.

Tawaddud smiles and slowly eats another grape. She lets other sensations mingle with the taste this time. The feel of the silk of her robe on her skin. The luxurious weight of the mascara in her eyelashes. The jasmine scent of her perfume. Her former master Kafur taught her that embodiment is a fragile thing, made from the whispers and silences of the flesh.

She gets up, walks to the keyhole-shaped window with slow, careful steps. The delicate dance of the embodiment slave: moving so that the jinn bottle always stays out of sight. It took two hours to place the embroidered pillows and mirrors and low tables in the narrow room just right.

She allows the sun to warm her face for a moment and

draws the soft curtains, and the light in the room takes on the hue of dark honey. Then she returns to her pillow seat at the round, low table in the centre of the room and opens the small jewelled casket that sits on top of it.

Inside, there is a book, hand-bound in cloth and leather. She takes it out slowly, to let Mr Sen enjoy the forbidden thrill that comes with it. The story within is a true story, of course, the only kind you are allowed to tell in Sirr. She knows it by heart but looks at the words anyway as she reads aloud, running her fingers along the rough texture of the paper before turning a page.

'There was a young woman in Sirr,' she begins, 'not long after the coming of Sobornost and the Cry of Wrath, who was married to a treasure-hunter.'

## The Story of the Mutalibun's Wife

Her father married her off when she was still very young. Her husband the mutalibun was old beyond his years. His first wife was possessed and went to the City of the Dead to live as a ghul. After that, he went on long journeys to dig up old heavens in the desert, to mine gogols for the Sobornost.

He bore the scars of his work: troubled wildcode dreams and sapphire growths that felt rough and sharp against her skin when they lay together. That was seldom: as mutalibun do, he had long since given up desire to survive in the desert, and touched her only because it was his duty as a husband. And so her days were lonely, in their fine house up on the Uzeda Shard.

One day, she decided to build a garden on the roof of their house. She hired Fast Ones to fly up loam from the greenhouses by the sea, planted seeds, told green jinni to make her seeds for flowers of all colours, and trees to provide shade. She worked hard for days and weeks, and asked her sister the muhtasib to protect the garden from wildcode with Seals. At night, she whispered to her garden, to make it grow: she had studied athar magic with jinn tutors in her father's house, and knew many Secret Names.

The jinn-made seeds grew quickly, and when the little garden was in full bloom, she spent long evenings sitting there, enjoying the smell of the earth and the fragrance of the flowers and the sun on her skin.

One evening, a strong wind came from the desert. It blew over the Shard and through the garden. It brought a cloud of old nanites with it that settled in the garden like thick, heavy fog. The little machines condensed into glittering droplets on the leaves and petals of her flowers. They were as fresh and pure as some of the ancient utility foglets from the Sirr-in-the-Sky that her father kept in a bottle in his study.

The mutalibun's wife started whispering and thinking at the fog, like she had been taught. She lay down on the soft grass and asked the fog to make the hands and lips of a lover.

The fog obeyed. It swirled around her and ran soft, cool fingers down her spine. It tickled her neck and collarbone with a tongue of mist.

Tawaddud pauses, slowly removes her robe and whispers to activate the mirrors she has carefully set around the room. Mr Sen used to be a man, and men need to see. In that way, her once-female clients are easier – but far more demanding in other ways, of course.

So she lies down on the pillows, looks at herself in the mirror, rolls her head so that her thick dark curls hide the beemee cable, and smiles. The amber light brings out her cheekbones and hides the fact that – so unlike Dunyazad's – her mouth is slightly too large and her body not as slender as her sister's. But her skin is as dark and smooth, and her muscles firm from the long climbs on the Shards.

Remembering the fog, running her fingertips across her breasts and down her belly, she continues.

'But with the second kiss, and the third, she found that the fog was not just responding to her thoughts, was not just an extension of her own hands and lips, but a living thing from the desert, just as alone and hungry as she was. Fog-tendrils wove themselves into her hair playfully. As she reached for the fog, it made smooth, warm curves and planes for her to touch. Gently, it pushed her down to the grass—'

Her heartbeat quickens. This is how Mr Sen likes to finish. She touches herself harder, lets the book fall shut. As always, as the heat under her fingers builds up and her hips buck against her hand, shuddering with hot and cold earthquakes, she finds herself thinking of the Axolotl—

But before she can cross the edge and take Mr Sen with her, the visitor chime rings, the brass sound sharp and sudden.

'Good morning, dear Tawaddud!' says a voice. 'Do you have a moment for your sister?'

Dunyazad's sense of timing is impeccable, as always.

Tawaddud leaps up, face burning with arousal and embarrassment. She pulls her robe around her and disconnects the beemee cable from the jinn jar.

There are muffled footsteps outside. The assignation room is next to her study, down the corridor from the entrance hall.

'Tawaddud!' says her sister's clear voice again. 'Are you still asleep?'

'That ... was exquisite, as always, my dear. Although, towards the end, you seemed ... distracted.' Mr Sen says in his dry, tinny voice.

'A thousand apologies,' Tawaddud says, digging for the jinn bottle from under the pillows. 'No compensation will be required.' Tawaddud swears under her breath. The ancient jinn purchased her services with a new Secret Name that she had been searching for a long time.

'I promise I will arrange a new assignation at your earliest convenience. A simple family matter has come up that I have to deal with.' She lifts the heavy bottle. A precious pre-Collapse bioprocessor within allows the jinn to maintain a temporary localised presence in her quarters. The outer shell is the work of Sirr craftsmen, simple ceramics and circuitry, decorated with blue glass.

'In my experience,' the jinn says, 'family matters are never simple.'

'Tawaddud! What are you doing?'

'I'm afraid that I really have to ask you to leave,' says Tawaddud.

'Of course, if you will just lend me a hand. Until next time.'

Tawaddud takes the bottle to the windowsill. There is a rush of heat that makes the curtains flap, a barely visible shimmering in the air, and then the jinn is gone. She hides the jar behind the pillows, covers the mirrors again and takes a moment to arrange her hair.

There is a knock on the door. Just as Tawaddud is about to touch the unlocking symbol, her heart misses a beat: her book is still lying on the floor. Hastily, she replaces it in the casket and slams the lid shut.

The door opens. Dunyazad looks at her with a mischievous smile on her lips, one hand resting delicately on the qarin bottle around her neck. The Secret Names written on her fingernails are bright against her dark skin. Tawaddud's sister is dressed for a walk in the town: blue robes, slippers and a jewelled cap covering her braided, beaded hair. As usual, she looks perfect.

'Am I disturbing you, dear sister?'

'As a matter of fact, you are.'

Dunyazad sits down on one of the pillows. 'What a *lovely* room. Smells wonderful. Have you been ... entertaining?'

I know what you are doing, her smile says. And that's why you are going to do whatever I ask you to.

'No,' Tawaddud says.

'Excellent. That is exactly what I wanted to talk to you about.' Duny lowers her voice to a conspiratorial whisper. 'There is a young man I want you to meet. He is wealthy, handsome and a wit to boot – and free this afternoon. What do you say?'

'I'm perfectly capable of arranging my own social schedule, sister,' Tawaddud says. She walks to the window and closes the curtains with a jerk.

'Oh, I'm well aware of that. That is why you associate with street entertainers and riff-raff.'

'I have work to do this afternoon. Charity work, healing work. The Banu Sasan – *entertainers and riff-raff* – need doctors.'

'I'm sure the young gentleman would be curious to see what it is that you do, down there.'

'Yes, I imagine it's difficult to see how the Banu Sasan live, up from a muhtasib tower.'

There is a dangerous glint in Dunyazad's eyes. 'Oh, I assure you that we see *everything*.'

'My work is more important than a date with some perfumed boy you met at a Council party. I appreciate the effort, Duny, but you really don't have to keep trying.' She walks towards the door to her study, with steps that she hopes are determined.

'Oh, I agree entirely. It is like washing wildcode off a mutalibun's cock, and about as rewarding. Father feels differently, however.'

Tawaddud stops, a chill in her belly.

'I spoke to him this morning. I told him that you had repented your actions, that you wanted nothing but to restore the good name of our family, to become an honourable woman again.'

Tawaddud turns around. Duny looks straight at her, with blue and earnest eyes.

'Do you want to turn me into a liar, dear sister? Into a teller of tales, like you?'

Tawaddud pulls her robe tighter around her and grits her teeth. *A teller of tales. A lover of monsters. Not my daughter anymore.* That's what her father said on the day the Repentants found her and brought her back from the Palace of Stories, three years ago.

'Who is it, then?'

'Abu Nuwas,' Dunyazad says. 'I think Father would be very pleased if you two became ... friends.'

'Duny, if you want to punish me, there are easier ways to it. What does Father want from him?'

Duny sighs. 'What could he possibly want from the richest gogol merchant in the city?'

'I am not stupid, sister.' *And Repentant jinni like Mr Sen like to tell me things, afterwards.* 'Father has all the support in the Council he needs: he does not have to buy it. Why him and why now?'

Dunyazad narrows her eyes and runs one of her rings along her lips, back and forth. 'I suppose I should be glad that you follow at least the rudiments of city politics,' she says slowly. 'There have been recent developments that have made our position … unstable. A Council member died this morning, very suddenly. Councilwoman Alile, of House Soarez: I think you remember her.'

Alile: a dour-faced woman at her father's table, with a wildcode-eaten bald patch in her dark hair, a brass hawk on her shoulder. *You should rather shovel shit for a living than become a mutalibun, little girl.* I guess this is why, Tawaddud thinks, brushing away the memory. Her chest feels hollow, but she keeps her face blank.

'Let me guess,' she says. 'She was the biggest supporter of Father's proposal to modify the Cry of Wrath Accords. How did she die?'

'A far too convenient suicide. The Repentants think it was a possession. It could be the masrurs, but so far they haven't claimed responsibility. We are looking into it. Father even contacted the Sobornost: the hsien-kus are sending somebody to investigate. The vote on the Accords is in three days. If we want to win it, we need to buy it. Abu Nuwas knows that, and that's why you, dear sister, are going to try your best to make him very happy.'

'I am surprised that Father would entrust such an important task to me.' *To a lover of monsters.*

'Lord Nuwas specifically requested Father's permission to court you. Then again, rumour has it that his tastes are … unusual. In any case, I am going to be busy looking after the Sobornost envoy – a dull babysitting job, but somebody has to do it – so it is up to you, I'm afraid.'

'How convenient.' You are the one he trusts, and I am the one he sells to the merchant like a gogol from the desert.

It was not always like that. She remembers a sizzling pan, the rich heat on her face, her father's soft hands on her shoulders. *Go on, Tawa, taste it, you made it. Add some more marjoram if you feel like. Food should tell a story.*

'Dear sister, this is me trying to *help* you. Our father is merciful, but he has not forgotten what you did. I'm offering you a chance to show him who you really are.'

Duny takes Tawaddud's hand. The jinn rings in her fingers are cold. 'It's not just about you, Tawaddud. You talk about your Banu Sasan. If we win the vote, we'll have the power to change things, for all the people of Sirr. If you help me.' Duny's eyes are sincere, just like they always were when she tried to convince Tawaddud to run away to the sukh or hide from Chaeremon the jinn.

'Promises? I thought you would try threats,' Tawaddud says quietly.

'Very well,' Duny says. 'Perhaps there are some things Father really *should* know about.'

Tawaddud squeezes her eyes shut. Her temples throb. *It's the Aun punishing me. Maybe I deserve it.*

*Maybe Father will look at me again.*

'Fine,' she says slowly. She feels weak and cold. 'I only hope I'm unusual enough.'

'Wonderful!' Duny gets up and claps her hands. Her jewellery and jinn rings tingle. 'Don't look so glum. It's going to be fun!'

She looks at Tawaddud, up and down, and frowns. 'But we *are* going to have to do something about your hair.'

# 3

# THE THIEF AND THE ARREST

I enter the main cabin hesitantly. If the ship is worried, Mieli might really be in a bad mood, and I hate getting beaten up by an Oortian warrior when I'm tired.

I don't have to look far. She floats in the middle of the cabin, eyes closed, dark, almond-shaped face illuminated by soft candlelight, wrapped in her usual dark toga-like garment like a caterpillar in her cocoon.

'Mieli, we need to talk,' I say. No response.

I pull myself along the cabin axis and orient myself to face her. Her eyes are closed, and she barely seems to be breathing. *Great*. She must be in some sort of Oortian trance. Figures: live on berries in a hollowed-out comet lit by artificial suns long enough, and you start to have delusions about achieving enlightenment

'This is important. I need to have a word with your boss.' Maybe she's in a piloting trance. I once got her out of it by exploiting our biot link, but it took pushing a sapphire dagger through my hand. I have no desire to repeat the experience – and besides, the link is gone. I snap my fingers in front of her face. Then I touch her shoulder.

'*Perhonen*, is she all right?' I ask the ship. But there is no reply.

'Mieli, this isn't funny.'

She starts laughing, a soft, musical sound. She opens her eyes and smiles like a serpent.

'Oh, but it is,' she says. In my mind, a prison door opens and closes. Not the Dilemma Prison, but another one, a long time ago.

Maybe I should have stayed inside.

'Hello, Joséphine.'

'You never called,' she says. 'I'm hurt.'

'Well, on Mars, you seemed to be a little short on time,' I say. Her eyes narrow dangerously. Perhaps it's not a good strategy to remind her that I ended our last night together by having her thrown off the planet by Oubliette authorities.

Then again, perhaps it is.

'Joséphine Pellegrini,' I repeat her name. There should be memories that come with it, but they, too, are behind the closed door. That is not surprising: she has probably done some careful editing of my memories herself. If you are a Sobornost Founder, you can do that sort of thing.

'So you figured it out,' she says.

'Why didn't you tell me?'

'Oh, that was for your own good, my sweet,' she says. 'You've spent a couple of centuries running away from me. I didn't want you to be distracted.' She touches the middle finger of her left hand, as if adjusting a ring. 'And do you know what happens when you try to escape your fate?'

'What would that be?'

She leans closer.

'You lose yourself. You become a petty thief, a magpie, chasing after shiny things. You need me to be something more.' She touches my face. Her hand is smooth and cold.

'I gave you a chance to steal yourself back. You failed. You are still the little thing from the Dilemma Prison, good for nothing except guns and games. I thought you could be a seed for something greater. I was wrong.' Her eyes are hard. 'You are not Jean le Flambeur.'

That stings, but I swallow it. Her tone is soft, but there is a glint of genuine anger in her eyes. *Good.*

I brush her hand away.

'Then we are two,' I say, 'because I don't think you are Joséphine Pellegrini. You are just a gogol. Maybe from one of the older branches, sure. But you are not a Prime. You would never send an important part of yourself to do a job like this. You are just a low-level Founder ghost, running a rogue operation. I want to talk to the Prime.'

'And what makes you think you deserve *that*?' she says.

'Because you need me to steal a Spike fragment from Matjek Chen. I know how to do it. And I want a better deal.'

She laughs. 'Oh, Jean. You *failed*, last time. All you were— Oh my, I can't even tell you— Cognitive architectures stolen from the zoku and us alike. Machines made with a sunlifting factory. The perfect disguise. And still you were like a child compared to him, the father of Dragons. And you are telling me you know how to do it *now*? Oh, my sweetheart, my little prince, you *are* amusing.'

'Not as amusing as watching the other Founders eat you. It'll be the vasilevs and hsien-kus, right? They never liked you. You need a weapon against them. That's why you got me out.'

Her eyes are two green pearls, cold and hard. I take a deep breath. *Almost there.* I must not forget that she can read at least my surface thoughts. There are ways to obfuscate them.

Associative images. Pearls and planets and eyes and tigers. She frowns. Better distract her.

'And I *do* wonder how they caught me in the first place, if I was *that* good,' I say. 'Could it be that you had something to do with it, lover?'

She stands up in front of me. Her mouth is a straight line. Her chest is heaving. She opens Mieli's wings. They quiver in the candlelight like two giant flames.

'Maybe I've been running away from you,' I say. 'But when *you* get desperate, you always find a way to catch me.'

'*Desperate?*' she hisses. 'You little bastard.'

She grabs my head and squeezes so hard that it feels like a yosegi box about to pop open, pulls me up so our faces are close together. Her breath is warm. It smells of liquorice. 'I'm going to show you desperate,' she says.

'No.' *Yes.*

Her eyes are pale green at first, then impossibly bright, like looking right into the Sun. The world goes white. My face flows like wax beneath her fingers.

'*This* is how they caught you,' she says.


*The Story of the Inspector and Jean le Flambeur*

The inspector catches that bastard Jean le Flambeur in the photosphere of the Sun.

Before he begins, he takes his time to look at them, the Founders aboard the good ship *Immortaliser*. The bearded engineer-of-souls rocks slowly back and forth in his chair. The pellegrini in her white-and-gold naval uniform stares at him intently, waiting. The vasilev leans back in his chair, swirling the golden wine in his glass. The two hsien-kus, inscrutable. The chen, still and quiet, looking at the sea. The chitragupta pokes holes in the structure of the vir with its finger, making tiny, glowing singularities that vanish with a popping sound as soon as they appear.

The inspector frowns at the chitragupta. The *Immortaliser* is a knotted configuration of electromagnetic fields around a nugget of smartmatter the size of a pinhead. It floats five hundred kilometres above the solar north pole, in the temperature minimum region of the photosphere. He went into a lot of trouble to get the vir to run on that kind of hardware.

The vir is a little restaurant in the crook of a rocky harbour's arm. They sit around tables set out on the uneven sunlit rock in a cool breeze, glasses of white wine and plates of seafood in front of them, full of rich, subtle smells. The rigging of the sailboats in the water makes a tinkling sound in the wind, like improvised music. To remind them where they are, the jewelled orrery of the Experiment looms in the sky, larger than clouds or worlds, against the blazing white curve of the Sun. It's a patchwork reality, put together from the memories of the Founders, as these things should be. To show respect, to have consensus. Or so the theory goes.

The vasilev is the first to speak.

'What are we doing here?' he says. 'We have already answered all your questions.'

The inspector's fingers find the ridges and valleys of scar tissue on his cheeks. The touch awakens the dull ache that is always there, not because the wounds have not healed but because it is part of him, a show of respect to the Prime.

*Good*, he thinks. It is good to meet the others in a vir where they can feel pain. These are gogols from branches deep within the *guberniyas*, used to abstraction, with a tendency to forget that the physical reality is still there, raw and painful and devious and messy, like a razor blade hidden inside an apple.

'One of you is Jean le Flambeur,' he tells them. 'One of you is here to steal.'

The Founders look at him in stunned silence. The chitragupta giggles. The engineer stares at the coils of purple octopi on his plate. The pellegrini flashes the inspector a smile. He feels a strange warmth in his chest. That was something he did not expect. High-fidelity virs and embodiment have their advantages and disadvantages. He stops himself from smiling back.

'I don't understand any of this,' he says, gesturing upwards.

The sky is full of neutrino winks of other raion ships like the *Immortaliser*, millions of them, moving in tight, orderly orbits, interwoven like threads in a tapestry. Somewhere, far away, echoes the thrumming song of a *guberniya*, an artificial brain the size of a planet, watching over its children from the shadow of Mercury, coordinating, guiding, planning.

The Sun wears a belt made from tiny points of light: sunlifting machinery that pumps heavy elements from the fusion depths and feeds it to smartmatter factories in stationary orbits. An entire ecology of constructor gogols in plasma bodies churns the solar corona, creating pockets of order that will be used as the lasing medium for solar lasers.

'But I know it is to serve the Great Common Task. Our brother the engineer tried to explain thread theory to me, about quantum gravity scattering, about the Planck locks and how God is not a gambler but a cryptographer. I don't care. My branch deals with simpler things. You all know what I do.'

It is a little dishonest. Of *course* he knows what is about to happen. But it is better if they think of him as a barbarian.

Solar lasers will focus on a constellation of points until the concentration of energy tears the fabric of spacetime itself and gives birth to singularities, fed with the particle stream that the sunlifting system kicks up from the pole. Countless gogols will be cast into them, their minds encoded in thread states in the event horizons. Seventeen black holes will pull together long tails of plasma from the Sun like orange peels, coming together. A many-fingered hand of God will close into a fist. A violent Hawking decay will convert several Earth masses into energy.

And, perhaps, within that inferno, there will be an *answer*. An answer someone wants to steal.

'So, where is this fabled creature, then?' asks the vasilev. 'This is madness. Nine seconds in the Experiment frame, and we are wasting cycles in this fancy vir. Out there, our brothers and sisters are getting ready for the most glorious of tasks. And what are we doing? Jumping at shadows.' He looks at the pellegrini. 'Sister pellegrini here has decided that we should dance for the monkey.'

The inspector lays his large hands on the table and gets up. His sudden movement and his bulk make the glasses shudder and sing.

'Brother vasilev should reconsider his words,' he says, quietly. He will have to deal with this one soon. And possibly the hsien-kus: there are two of them, an older and a younger, one in an elaborate avatar from the Deep Time – a hsien-ku face embedded in a blue, many-angled body and a forest of limbs – the other an unassuming young woman a plain grey uniform. He is almost certain they sent the core vampire that tried to kill him in the ship's Library.

'Sister pellegrini here detected an anomaly in the mathematics gogols,' the inspector says. 'She brought me from the Library to investigate, and cut off communications from the rest of the fleet. It was the right thing to do. I found traces. In virs, in gogol memories. Le Flambeur is here.'

He looks at the chen from the corner of his eye, trying to see a reaction. The grey-haired Founder is the only one who is not looking at the inspector. His eyes are fixed on the sky, and a smile plays on his lips.

The older hsien-ku rises.

'This creature you are talking about is a myth,' she says. 'In our ancestor sims, he is little more than a story. A bogeyman.'

She is impressively ancient. The instinctive *xiao* – the in-built respect for a gogol closer to a Prime than he is – makes the inspector feel like a child for a moment. *The inspector was the sword of Sobornost*, his metaself rewrites his thoughts. *He stayed strong. He knew his cause was true and pure.*

'Is sister saying that the Prime memories are flawed?' he says, clinging to the metaself's reassuring voice, gritting his teeth.

'Not flawed,' she says. 'Merely … distant.'

'We are wasting time,' the vasilev says. 'If there is an anomaly here, if the ship has been infected, then sister pellegrini should self-destruct and so our deaths will serve the Task. But then, she has always been a little too fond of her continuity to do what is necessary.'

The inspector smiles. 'My investigation was thorough. It seems that our brother vasilev and sister hsien-ku tried to manipulate the balance of test gogols used in the Experiment. But I'm not here to accuse them. I'm here to find Jean le Flambeur.'

The vasilev stares at him. 'Of all the outrageous accusations—'

'Enough,' says the chen. There is a sudden silence. The

chen is the only gogol on the ship not branched for the Experiment: fourth generation, Battle-with-the-Conway-Angel branch. Even the metaself cannot silence the heavy rush of *xiao* that the inspector feels when he speaks.

'Our brother has performed his task well. If anyone questions his recommendations, it is surely not out of guilt, but merely out of desire to see the Great Common Task performed well, am I not right? If it is a question of identity, then the answer is simple. The Primes, in their wisdom, have provided us with the means to tell the world who we are.'

The chen turns to face them, a beatific smile on his face. 'Let us draw forth our Founder Codes, and pray.'

The inspector takes a deep breath. He knew this was coming, but he has no desire to touch his Code, the thing that grants Founders root access to the meta-laws of the firmament that govern all virs. The Code derives from passwords in the same way that nuclear weapons descend from flint axes: not just a string of characters, but a state of mind, a defining moment, the innermost self. And his isn't pretty.

Nevertheless, he grins at the vasilev as they all get up. The golden-haired gogol takes a drink from his glass, spilling a few drops as he puts it back on the table: his hands are shaking. *I would really like it to be this one.*

'Come, now,' the chen says. 'Let's all do this together, like brothers and sisters.' He closes his eyes. An expression of bliss spreads across his face, as if he was watching something indescribably beautiful. The vir dissolves around them, absorbed by the firmament, disappearing into empty whiteness like the vasilev's wine into the cotton tablecloth.

One by one, the other Founders follow. The chitragupta's face is full of serenity. The pellegrini looks afraid. The engineer's forehead is furrowed by furious concentration. The plain faces of the hsien-kus are made beautiful by expressions of wonder and awe. The vasilev is pale and sweating. He gives the inspector one more look full of hate and closes his eyes.

And then it is the inspector's turn.

In the firmament, closing your eyes does not bring darkness, only white. The Founders are stark silhouettes against it. Hesitantly, the inspector touches his Code. It aches like his scars, only a hundred times worse, an unhealed gash inside him that reeks and oozes pus like a

*bedsore. It opens when the gunfire wakes him up. His sister lies next to him. Flies walk on her open eyes. He tears out the wires in his scalp. There is a squelching sound and a lightning bolt of pain. Blood runs down his face. He touches her forehead. Under his fingers, the skin is clammy and soft.*

He casts it at the firmament, eager to be rid of it. The hungry whiteness claims it and swallows. Suddenly, it is no longer white but a mirror that shows him six reflections.

He touches his face to feel the scars and sees the others do the same. The scars are not there: his cheeks are smooth. His mirror images are young men with coal-black hair and pencil-stroke eyebrows, dimpled temples and heavy eyelids. They wear slim velvet jackets and white shirts and look like they are on their way to a party. They brush invisible dust from their lapels, look at each other, blinking, as if they had just woken up from a dream.

As he watches them, there is a sharp *crack* inside him. Another self hatches like a bird from an egg. I smile at the confusion in my other selves' eyes as we shake off the heavy shell of the inspector.

\*

Next to me, the chen starts clapping.

'Wonderful!' he says, grinning like an excited child. 'Wonderful!'

We all look at him. He alone is unchanged, a small grey figure against the firmament white. Something is wrong. I look for his Code in the vir trap we have created and find nothing.

The chen wipes his eyes and his expression becomes a serious mask again. Now that the *xiao* of my Sobornost disguise is gone, it is easier to look at him. A short, stocky Asian man with unevenly cut grey hair, barefoot, wearing a monkish robe. His face is younger than his eyes.

'A vir that emulates the firmament,' he says. 'I did not think such a thing possible. And all this drama, just for me, just to steal my Codes. Better than going to the theatre. Very entertaining.'

The six of us take a bow, all together. 'Surely you can figure out how I did it,' we chorus. I can see it in my other selves' eyes: trying to find a way out. But the vir is sealed around us, tight as a bottle.

'Of course,' he says, looking us up and down, hands behind his back. 'I remember the first sunlifter factory you broke into, a century ago. So you did it again. The old compiler backdoor trick. Basic cleptography. The only part I can't figure out is where you got my old friend's Codes. From Joséphine? I will need to have a word with her.'

I *am* rather proud of it: hacking the ultimate trusted computing platform, by inserting a few choice things into the hardware of the *Immortaliser* when the sunlifter factory compiled it and its sister ships, four minutes or so ago in the Experiment reference frame.

So of course, I also made an escape route.

'A gentleman never tells. And there is a reason why classics are called classics,' we say, a slight disharmony in our chorus now as we diverge.

*There. The vir is sealed tight like a bottle, but he missed one of my firmament back doors. Just have to keep him talking.*

'Indeed. And *betrayal* is one of them, isn't it? The oldest of them all.' He smiles a thin smile. 'You should have known better than to trust her.'

*I didn't.* But we only shrug.

'It was always a gamble. That's what I do.' We gesture at the whiteness. 'But you are gambling, too. This whole thing, the Experiment. It's just to distract the others, isn't it? You don't need it. You already have the Kaminari jewel. The key to Planck locks.'

He raises his eyebrows. 'And can you think of anyone else who deserves to have it?'

We laugh. 'With all due respect, Matjek,' we say, 'you should really leave jewels and locks and keys to the professionals.'

'Respect. I see.' He crosses his arms. 'You treat this as a game. Do you remember the first time we met? I told you it was not a game to me.'

*That was not the first time we met. But it's good you don't remember that.*

'Then why is it,' we ask, 'that I always won?'

One of us – I'm no longer sure who – activates the escape protocol. The others self-destruct, flooding the white vir with noise. The software shell that contains my mind dumps its contents into thoughtwisps, launches them from the *Immortaliser* at other raion ships.

I jump from node to node in the Sobornost communications network, splitting, merging, sending out self-sacrificing partials. The chens come after me, tenacious, relentless. But it doesn't matter. A few milliseconds and I will reach one of my getaway ships, beautiful *Leblancs* built by the Gun Club zoku, with their warm Hawking drives, ready to make my getaway at the speed of light—

Then the raions start self-destructing. The photosphere is full of antimatter blooms as they burn my bridges, sacrifice billions of gogols to contain me like a virus. The destruction spreads like a wildfire, until there is only one of me left.

I try to hide in the firmament processes, become a slow, reversible computation. But in vain: they hunt me down. The chens and the engineers come, swarm over me like lilliputs over Gulliver, trapping me.

Then the mind-blades come, invisible and hot.

They take me apart. The metacortex goes first: the ability to self-modify to sculpt my neural matter. Fixed, dead, no longer changing personalities at will, imprisoned. But they make sure to leave the knowledge that something is gone.

A voice asks questions.

I don't answer and die.

A voice asks questions.

I don't answer and die.

A voice asks questions.

I don't answer and die.

Finally, the blades touch a trap I built inside myself a long time ago. My secrets catch fire and consume themselves in my head.

In the end, I am naked, in a cell made of glass. There are phantom pains in my mind where the god parts have been cut away. There is a gun in my hand. Behind each of the four walls, there is somebody else, waiting.

*Cooperate or defect?*

# 4

# TAWADDUD AND ABU NUWAS

While Duny waits, Tawaddud puts on a new face in her bedroom.

She looks at her image in the mirror. The fantasy she created for Mr Sen is gone, replaced by a plain woman in a white body stocking that does not flatter her broad hips. *Unusual? Not today.* She runs her fingers through her unruly hair, refuses to do anything about it and chooses a short, hooded cloak to hide it. After a moment's hesitation, she puts on her mother's old athar glasses. Somehow, it is easier to look at the world from behind the round golden lenses.

She picks up her doctor's bag and joins Dunyazad at the balcony of the palace's apartment wing, to wait for the elevator. Her sister gives the glasses a disapproving look.

'They do not really suit the shape of your face,' she says. 'Mother never had much taste, poor woman. I trust you will be extra charming to make up for the lack of style.'

*You never knew Mother at all,* Tawaddud thinks. *And you do not know me.*

She decides to ignore Duny's barb. She has spent the

whole day indoors, and it is good to feel the breeze and the heat of the afternoon sun.

Her father's palace is like a hand sticking out of the Gomelez Shard, resembling a climbing plant on a giant wall: five tall buildings that were once vertical but are now horizontal, overgrown with walkways, joined together with extensions, balconies and hanging gardens. Somewhere above, there are faint echoes of moaning jinn music. Heavy smells of food drift up from Takht the gogol merchant's palace, mingling with the warm wind. Below, overhanging minarets, snaking platforms and vertical streets cling to the Gomelez Shard like ivy. The city itself is lost in haze far below, glints of purple, gold and blue within a shroud of white mist.

The Shard is a cylinder segment almost two kilometres high, a piece of the orbital O'Neill colony where her ancestors lived, until it fell from the heavens. The impact broke its hull – millions of tons of diamond and metal and strange pre-Collapse materials – into pieces like an eggshell, into five Shards sticking out of the bedrock. They reach towards the sky that was lost, guarding Sirr the hidden, Sirr the blessed; the last human city on Earth.

There is a cough behind her.

'Please excuse my sister,' Dunyazad says. 'She is a dreamer, and sometimes I have to be firm to get her to notice the real world.'

'The Aun know Sirr needs more dreamers, in these hard times,' says a male voice, low and soft.

Tawaddud turns around. A man stands on the balcony with them. He is small and slight, shorter than Tawaddud, and looks tired: his skin is pale and tallowy. He is dressed in rich black-and-silver robes that emulate a mutalibun's traditional garb but are made from strange Sobornost fabrics that flutter in the breeze. He has long flowing hair, a narrow face – and a jinn jar for an eye. A leather strap across his face supports an ornate brass device where his left eye should be. His human eye is bright and green.

'I am a dreamer myself,' he says haltingly, as if reciting lines. 'Sometimes I am a blind beggar dreaming that I am Abu Nuwas, and the morning wine I had and such beautiful ladies as you are just fantasies. But I'm quite sure that I would never dream of anything quite as hideous as my reflection in your eyes, so you must be real, thank the Aun.'

Abu Nuwas kisses Tawaddud's hand, and sunlight glints in his brass eye. His lips are cool and dry and barely brush her skin, like the tickling touch of a jinn. His hand shakes a little and he lets go quickly.

'Lord Nuwas, this is my sister Tawaddud. We are most grateful that you have agreed to escort her. She is so diligent with her charitable duties, you see: otherwise she would have arranged to meet you in a more dignified setting.'

Tawaddud studies Abu Nuwas, looking at him longer than is strictly proper. His smile wavers. She straightens her back. Suddenly, she is not Tawaddud, the black sheep of the Gomelez family. She is Tawaddud, the pride of the Palace of Stories, the lover of the Axolotl. *No, sister, you do not know me at all.*

'My sister jests,' Tawaddud says in a low voice. 'I have no intention of being dignified.' She removes her athar glasses and smiles, giving Abu Nuwas the same look she shared with Mr Sen and her mirror image. 'But I would be delighted if you were to escort me, and say more such beautiful things. I did not know you were a poet.'

She offers Abu Nuwas her arm. He steps forward and

takes it, puffing his chest. 'Merely a dabbler, my lady, just words that come to a mutalibun's mind while walking the desert, pale shadows of beauty like yours.'

Tawaddud laughs and rewards him with another smile, just a little warmer than the last one. 'I would happily let a blind beggar accompany me for such words, Lord Nuwas,' she says.

'Please, call me Abu.'

Dunyazad gives Tawaddud an astonished look. Tawaddud purses her lips. 'Dear sister, did you not have some Council duties to attend to? I'm sure they are terribly important. And we must both serve our Father and our city, in whatever way we can.'

The elevator is a clunky, analog thing with a flexible frame, a metal centipede that crawls along rails protruding from the Shard. The descent creates a pleasant breeze. For a time, Abu Nuwas seems content to hold on to her arm and watch the city unfolding before them. An idea is hatching in Tawaddud's mind, and she welcomes the quiet to let it grow. *You are going to regret this, Duny, you really are.*

To the east, there are the hills and greenhouses, and beyond them the sea. In the north lies the City of the Dead, with its row upon row of grey featureless buildings. Tawaddud quickly turns her gaze away from it.

The city proper is dominated by the spire of the Sobornost Station: a massive diamond tower, bristling with heroic statues higher than the Shards. It looms above the morass of the gogol markets that slowly give way to the wide streets and low buildings in the shadow of the Ugarte and Uzeda Shards. The sunlight flashing off its upper segments makes it seem like it's made of gold. It changes, sometimes slowly, sometimes even as you watch, new spires rising and falling, surfaces and statues rotating. Every few seconds, there are booms and flashes, streaks of light from thoughtwisps carrying Sobornost minds, fired towards the Gourd that the masters of the Inner System are building in the sky.

'Makes you feel small, doesn't it?' Abu says.

Abu Nuwas has a reputation: grand gestures in the gogol markets, investment decisions that sometimes look like madness. Yet her more influential clients speak of Abu with reluctant respect. *Small men need to feel powerful.* Tawaddud keeps her eyes downcast.

'I prefer the grandeur of the Shards to the undead creations of the Sobornost,' she says. 'And the wildcode desert taught them in the Cry of Wrath how small they can be.'

'Yes, well,' Abu says. 'At least for a time.'

Another elevator passes them. A swarm of Fast Ones flashes past, trying to catch up with it, buzzing. They are tiny humanoids the size of Tawaddud's forefinger, with black bodies and humming wings, who hitching rides to the top of the Shards on elevators, to soak up solar energy and potential energy on the way down, selling it to the cities of the little people like Qush and Misr and a hundred others in central Sirr whose names slow baseline humans will never know. The passengers are trying to shoo them away. They dodge flailing hands effortlessly, buzzing around the elevator like a cloud of flies.

'I envy them, sometimes,' Abu says, looking at the creatures. 'To live in a world of giant statues, live fast lives, fight fast wars, fit centuries and dynasties in a day. Our lives are far too short, don't you think?'

'They also say,' Tawaddud says, leaning closer to him, 'that the Fast Ones and the jinni know pleasures that are lost to us, and once a human has tasted them, it is far too easy to lose interest in the flesh.'

'I see,' Abu says, turning his brass eye towards her, cocking his head like a bird. 'And do you speak from experience, Lady Tawaddud?' His expression is stiff.

After his initial shyness, Abu Nuwas is hard to read, like mutalibun often are. At the pretext of shielding her eyes against the sun, Tawaddud lifts up her athar glasses and looks at the gogol merchant's aura in the Shadow. His entwined jinn is a fiery serpent, coiled protectively around him. *I need to be more subtle with this one.*

Tawaddud follows the receding elevator with her gaze. 'I am just an innocent girl from the Gomelez family.'

'That's not what the stories say.'

'The stories say many things, and that's why the Repentants hunt them down before the body thieves steal our minds with them. I care for stories less than poetry, dear Abu: and you promised me more of it. I'm afraid the only thing I have to offer in return is an evening of hard work amongst the Banu Sasan.' She touches Abu's hand. 'But then you are no stranger to hard work. My sister and I both appreciate the help you have offered my father.'

'It is nothing. I would rather you appreciated my wit. Or my handsome features.' He smiles ironically and touches his eye.

Foolish girl. Kafur's first lesson. Make it like a dream, and never let them wake.

'There is no greater honour in Sirr than the touch of the entwiner, and honour is greater than beauty,' Tawadudd says. 'What is it that you see with your eye?' She smiles mischievously. 'Anything you like?'

'Would you like to see?' He holds out his hand.

Wordlessly, she hands over her athar glasses, blinking at the bright sunlight. Abu turns them around in his hands. He whispers a Secret Name that Tawaddud does not know.

'Try now.'

Tawaddud accepts the glasses uneasily and puts them on. She blinks, expecting to see the usual chaos of the local athar, the digital shadow of reality. The Seals of the palaces keep the worst of the wildcode away from the Shard, but even here the athar is always full of old spimes and noise.

She sees a different Sirr.

It is a vast, shifting spiderweb of light. The Sobornost Station is still there, a glowing star in the centre, but everything else is replaced by an intricate, constantly shifting network: bright braids that flash into being and disappear, dense glowing currents that stretch from horizon to horizon, sudden blooms of activity that look like nests of fiery insects. After a moment, Tawaddud has to close her eyes. It is like watching the surface of the Sun.

'*This* is what we see, muhtasib and mutalibun,' Abu says. 'This is what the Repentants gather for us, the blood of Sirr. Gogol trade. Sobortech trade. Jinni labour. Even,' he lowers his voice, 'embodiment trade.

'It's like a garden, and we are gardeners. We need to decide where to plant and where to cut and where to grow, to keep Sirr alive. That is why I help your father. That's what makes me feel small.'

Tawaddud blinks, and the vision is gone, replaced by athar, the broken scrawls it writes on people and buildings, defaced by the white noise of wildcode. She removes her glasses.

'Then I'm glad I'm taking you to see the Banu Sasan,' she says slowly. 'One often feels small when looking at things from too far above.'

'Your sister did say that we would get along,' Abu says, taking Tawaddud's arm again, and try as she might, she cannot read his smile. *This is going to be harder than I thought.*

Clanking and rattling, the elevator takes them down to the base of the Shard, and, with even more noise, reconfigures itself into a tram. It carries them through the wide streets of the Shade quarters towards the city centre, along the narrow channels of water that lead towards the sea, the Station and the Banu Sasan.

# 5

# THE THIEF AND THE HUNTER

Mieli floats in the spimescape, a ghost within the ghost of the ship. It is a representation of the worldlines all smart-matter leaves behind, from every nut and bolt of *Perhonen* to the System-wide machinery of the Highway. Reality overlaid with interpretation and explanation, cold physics caught in a cobweb of meaning.

Even when she is not piloting, she likes it here. The ship is made from her words, and here, she can see them. With a thought, she can look through walls, zoom in to the pseudo-living sapphire nanomachinery of the ship – or grow into a giant and hold the impossibly complex clockwork of the System in the palm of her hand. She can even turn back and look at her own body as if from some strange afterlife.

Except now: the central cabin of the ship is closed to her spime vision. She has been banished here like an ancestor spirit, while the pellegrini plays with the thief. At least the dreamy feel of the spimescape makes the disgust easier to bear.

'Don't worry,' *Perhonen* says. 'As far as I can tell, they are just talking this time.'

'I don't want to know,' Mieli says. 'In any case, we have better things to do. She said something is coming.'

She interrogates the gogols in the ship's sensor array who spend their bodiless existence watching the ship's ghost imagers, neutrino detectors and other sensors. They are on one of the lesser Highway branches, engineered by Sobornost to provide pathways for their thoughtwisp traffic. Apart from old, scattered zoku routers – remnants of the Protocol War – and relativistic worldlines of the wisps, there is not much within millions of kilometres of the ship.

Still, just to be sure, she tells the ship to start activating the hidden Sobornost technology in its hull. Like Mieli, the ship is an uneasy amalgam of Oortian and Sobornost, remade on Venus, hidden weapons and quantum armour and virs and gogols and antimatter, embedded in *väki* smartcoral like diamond insects in amber.

'I was wondering,' *Perhonen* says. Its voice is different here, not just coming from a butterfly avatar but from everywhere, even from within Mieli herself. 'Are you going to tell him about the gogol you gave to the pellegrini?'

'No,' Mieli says.

'I think it might help him. He doesn't really understand you.'

'That's his problem,' Mieli says. It feels safe to be here, among the stars and inside the ship, inside a song. She wants to forget about the thief and the pellegrini and wars and gods and quests. Maybe she could even forget about Sydän. Why does the ship has to spoil it?

'I have been thinking,' the ship says. 'He could help us. He wants to be free, too. If you told him the truth—'

'There is nothing to tell,' Mieli says.

'But don't you see what the pellegrini is doing to you?

Promises and vows and servitude, and where did that ever get us? Why should we—'

'Enough,' Mieli says. 'You have no right to question her. I am her servant, and I am no traitor. Don't make me regret making you.' Here, without the steady breath of meditation or candlelight to anchor her, the words and anger come out easily. 'I am not your child. I am your maker. You have no idea what—'

And then, neutrino rain, gentle as a breeze. Anomalous.

She stops. The ship says nothing. The spimescape is silent.

Mieli scans the sky again. Synthbio seeds, thoughtwisp shells, and much further away, a lonely Sobornost raion in the main vein of this Highway branch. Still, her neck bristles.

*Maybe I should apologise*, she thinks. *Perhonen* is trying its best to watch over her. That's what it has been doing ever since she brought its spirit up from the alinen—

A bright line splits the spimescape in two like lightning. The ship and her words vanish in white noise. The scape goes down.

Mieli comes back to her body with a force like a thunderclap. Around her, *Perhonen* rings like a bell. A ragged tear in the hull shows blackness and stars. Air rushes out.

In the middle of the cabin, there is a bright, dancing dot. White beams flash from it in all directions, like from a lighthouse gone mad. The bonsai trees next to Mieli burst into flame.

*Never pray to the Dark Man*, Mieli thinks.

It takes me a long, long time to come back from the memory of the arrest.

There is blood in my mouth. I have been biting my tongue, and it hurts. The taste of failure is worse. I spit. Droplets of spittle and blood float in front of me like a string of glistening, white and dark red.

It was dangerous to play the pellegrini like that. A high roller's luck. She had to be in Mieli's body, like last time. Sobornost gogols get confused in the flesh, easy to read, easy to manipulate, no matter how godlike they are in the virs. She gave me exactly what I needed. The door in the memory castle is open. I remember Earth. I remember the prince in the jannah. And in spite of the pain, the plan is now whole in my head.

And that's when the diamond policeman from space hits me in the face.

Mieli is still holding the coral drinking bulb in her hand when the beam sweeps over her. The liquid inside boils, and the bulb shatters with a mournful note, swallowed by the roar of the vacuum. For a moment, the heat is almost gentle, welcome after the chill of the spimescape. Then it comes down on her like the fiercest *löyly* steam in an Oortian sauna.

Her metacortex reacts. Her subdermal smartmatter armour kicks in. Third-degree burns become damage statistics. Quicktime freezes the world into a slideshow of still frames.

In the combat autism, the world always makes sense.

*Zoom in.*

In the heart of whiteness, there is a machine, a fraction of a millimetre long: a sleek thing like a dagger, with delicate petals protruding from its hilt. Faces, carved around the needlelike tip. A Sobornost device—

The knife-flower moves. Even in quicktime, it is like a wasp, dancing a deadly dance amongst *Perhonen*'s butterfly avatars. Its strobing beam sweeps along the cabin's wall, dancing in a random pattern, leaving behind a fiery scrawl. It turns towards Mieli.

*Perhonen* slams a q-dot bubble around it and pumps the binding energies of the artificial atoms up. The mirrored sphere bounces around the cabin and starts to glow.

*Lasers*, Mieli thinks at the ship, arming her own weapons. *Get ready to throw it out and burn it.* She positions herself between the knife-thing and the thief, who is floating motionless, eyes closed, puts up another q-dot wall to keep him safe.

Tactical gogols feed analysis results into her metacortex. The thing's beam is *scanning*, like an aggressive version of a zoku Realmgate, capturing information but destroying the source, sending the results to someone. The heat is *bandwidth*.

*Killing it all, letting the gods sort it out.*

'Mieli,' the ship says. 'It's not going to—'

The bubble shatters. The thing comes straight at Mieli like a bullet. She fires her ghostgun at it, a thick cloud of nanomissiles, but already knows she is too slow. The thing is a bright serpent, dodging the tiny projectiles.

Its scanning beam rakes across Mieli's torso like a claw. Her armour goes mad and deploys active countermeasures. Her skin erupts in tiny fireworks. It doesn't do much good. Her intestines boil and burst – *pressures and temperatures and recovery times* – and the beam comes up, towards her head, swinging from side to side to a staccato rhythm of damage reports.

She expected a kind of detachment from the battle, with the knowledge that another Mieli will survive her death. Instead, a keen edge of fear presses down on her mind even through the blanket of combat autism.

She welcomes it.

The knife from the void changes direction, brushes her cheekbone, swings around her, towards the helpless thief. The metacortex Nash engine gives her three options, all of them bad.

Mieli ignores them and lets the thief loose from his chains.

Between one eyeblink and the next, just before the diamond thing hits, I become a god. A small god, but still: with an omniscient awareness of the contents of my smartmatter shell that pretends to be a human body, and the raion computer that is its brain.

It is only the second time that I have had root access to it. I wonder at the intricacies of its synthbio cells in a diamonoid frame, the fusion power source at the base of the spine and the nifty q-dot emitters. I get lost in the brain for a while. My mind is a tiny thing in its vast labyrinth, and for a time, it is good just to wander through the cool corridors of logic and to think. The plan that the pellegrini unwittingly gave me is there, too, a mosaic of interlocking pieces. I study it from every angle, humming to myself. Something is missing.

Then I hear the zoku jewel, an eager receptacle for thought and desire. I tell it what I need and it makes itself into something that completes the pattern, clicking into place. A part of me says that it is wrong, that I should feel guilty, but it fits too well. Surely there can be no harm in something so beautiful?

I feel like a little boy who has found pretty rocks on a beach. I hum to myself. I could happily stay inside my mind forever.

Except that there is a distant voice shouting that my flesh

is boiling away and the bright, bright light weaving back and forth in front of me like a hypnotist's watch has something to do with it.

I start moving. It feels like I'm wearing an oversized robot costume, huge and clumsy and slow. My mind is racing much faster than the body can react. My left hand disappears in white flame: fake skin, bones and flesh, consumed. The metaself informs me calmly how long it will take to grow it back. It puts together a picture of the tiny machine that is burning me alive: a hungry Sobornost creation, with a zigzag trajectory through the wreckage of *Perhonen*'s central cabin, now aimed straight at my brain.

*Cops. No matter how much things change, they always stay the same.*

And then it happens. I'm not much of a chess player, but there is an aspect of the game that I find fascinating. After a while, you can almost see lines of force between the pieces. Areas of danger where it is physically impossible to move pieces into. Clouds of possibility, forbidden zones.

That's what it's like, watching the diamond cop. Suddenly, it is as if there is a mirror image of the thing inside me, full of single-mindedness and purpose—

*Good hunter fast hunter nice hunter if you find it there will be a treat—*

That's it. *Mirrors.* Silently, I shout commands at my alien body. It obeys.

The q-dot layer beneath my burning skin turns into metamaterials. An improvised invisibility cloak. I become a quicksilver statue. The hungry white light is bent around me. It takes out a set of tribal statues in Mieli's gallery of comet ice. The cop keeps blasting, confused, stationary just long enough for me to tell *Perhonen* what to do—

54

A q-dot bubble blinks into being around it, a shiny billiard ball that shows a distorted reflection of my face. Sudden electromagnetic fields make my skin tingle. And then *Perhonen* blasts the intruder into space along the cabin's axis like a bullet from a gun, leaving a streak of ionized air behind.

The ship's lasers flash. There is a blinding antimatter explosion in the distance. A torrent of gamma rays and pions gives me a headache.

The locks of my Sobornost body snap back to place. Mieli floats next to me, tendrils of black blood around her like Medusa's hair. Then the pain of the hand comes, and I scream.

Mieli takes care of the thief's hand as the fires die away and the ship seals the tears in the hull. The cabin is full of the sickly sweet smell of burnt synthbio flesh, mixed with ozone and smoke and ashes from the bonsai trees. A bubble of liquorice tea floats near Mieli like a grey, stinking ghost.

'That *hurt*,' says the thief, looking at his stump with distaste as the tissue seals itself. 'What the hell was that? It was *not* made by gogols who deal with cuddly slowtime monkey people.'

He is a miserable sight. The left side of his face is a red ruin, and burn craters make his upper torso look like a planetary surface. Mieli does not feel much better. She is drenched in sweat and her stomach and head throb as the repair nanites of her body work overtime. Except for her brain, her biological parts are almost redundant, but they are a part of her, and she's not going to let them rot.

'Whatever it was,' *Perhonen* says, 'I'm afraid there is more. It dumped a *lot* of bandwidth. I traced the vector. There is something else out there. Something that does not follow the

Highway protocols. Something big. A whole swarm of the little bastard's brothers, thousands of them, and by the looks of it they plan to intercept us.'

'How long?' the thief asks.

'A day or two, maybe three if we really push it,' *Perhonen* says. 'They are *fast*.'

'Damn,' Mieli whispers. 'The pellegrini warned me. I need to talk to her.' She reaches for the goddess in her mind, but finds nothing.

The thief looks at her with his one good eye.

'My guess is that she is going to be hiding until we get rid of our tail,' he says. 'This is big, bigger than either of us. Maybe even bigger than I used to be. To be completely honest, if I were you, I'd be looking for another line of work. It's going to get ugly.'

Mieli raises an eyebrow. They both look like broken dolls. Her garment is in tatters and stained in blood. The thief's face is still red and raw. Only clumps of white medfoam excreted by his body's repair systems hide the terrible burns on his torso, legs and arms.

'Well, uglier,' the thief says. The undamaged side of his face grows serious. 'I've got something to tell you. I know who your boss is, and what she wants. The stakes are high enough for the Founders and Primes to take notice. This whole affair – it's part of some conflict between them. And we are right in the middle of it.'

'Thanks to you,' Mieli says.

'Touché,' the thief says. 'So. Can we run?'

The damage from the battle with the knife-flower is superficial, and *Perhonen* is already fixing it. But she knows exactly what her ship can and cannot do. The fear needles of the battle are still in her belly. She finds herself clinging on to their sting.

'No,' she says. 'But we can fight.' *Perhaps this will be a good way to end things. Fight an unbeatable enemy, hope for a honourable death.*

The thief looks at her incredulously. 'As much as I have come to respect your ability to kill things,' he says, 'I'm starting to wonder if Oortian schools teach basic mathematics. Just one of these things nearly killed us. Are you *sure* fighting a few thousand is a good idea?'

'This is my ship,' Mieli says. The jewelled chain around her leg feels like it's burning. *Sydän. Could it not be another me who gets her back?* She closes her eyes. 'It's my decision.'

*Mieli*, whispers *Perhonen. That was really tough sobortech. I expended a lot of weaponry on Mars. We are good, but we are not that good. What are you doing?*

'Mieli?' the thief says. 'Are you all right?'

Mieli takes a deep breath of the stinking air. She opens her eyes. The thief is staring at her with a look of concern. 'Come on,' he says with a soft voice. 'Let's think about this. There is always a way out.'

'Fine,' Mieli says finally. 'What do you suggest?'

The thief is quiet for a moment. 'It seemed to want me pretty badly,' he says. 'Maybe we can use that.'

'Make a gogol of you and sacrifice it?' Mieli says in disgust.

A cloud passes over the thief's face. 'No, that's not possible. Looks like Joséphine does not want more than one of me running around. There must be something else—' His good eye flashes. 'Of course. I'm an idiot. That's what it's for. If the cop thing wants me, I need to become someone else. I need a new face.' The thief tries to scratch the red ruin with his missing hand, then looks at the stump in dismay.

'Not to mention some other bits and pieces. But I think I know where to find one. If *Perhonen* is right, we have less than two days to open the Box.'

'And how are we going to do that?' Mieli asks.

'How is anything really important ever done? With smoke and mirrors.'

'No games, Jean. Please.'

The thief gives her a broken smile and takes out a small amber egg from his pocket. A zoku jewel.

'How quickly can you find us a zoku router?'

# 6

# TAWADDUD AND THE GHUL

The district of the Banu Sasan lies around the Sobornost Station. It used to be the Sobornost model city: high, heavy buildings, squares, statues, upload temples. But ever since the Cry of Wrath, they have stood mostly empty, apart from the logistics hubs where the otherworldly goods Sobornost trades for gogols are distributed to those who can afford them. And it is here that the small and the weak of the city hide from wildcode.

Tawaddud watches Abu carefully. She would have expected the gogol merchant to turn his nose up at the dirt and the poverty but, instead, he wears a look of detached fascination, even when they pass the Takht al'Qala'a square, where the spider woman lives. She has spun a huge tent of spider silk from the glands the wildcode has grown in her breasts. Little statuettes and jinn bottles hang from the wispy strands, like strange fruit.

The air is dry, with the faint smell of ozone everywhere, mixing with the pungent odour of unwashed bodies. There is music, shadow-players who create images on the sides of high pillars, cafés with old men with faces marked by wildcode playing chess. Chimera acrobats in silk robes, sapphire-enhanced muscles gleaming.

Abu stops to give a few sobors to a man who has a chimera beast in a cage, a fetus-like pink thing the size of a dog, with a blue transparent shell and sharp spider legs. The man bows to him many times, loudly proclaiming to his audience that the creature is a prince of Fast New York, transformed into this shape by the Aun, and that it understands holy texts. It spells out answers to questions with a sharp tap-tap-tap of its legs on concrete. In the athar, Tawaddud sees the chains that make the creature an extension of the handler's mind.

'You should be careful, Abu dear,' she says. 'I don't want you to become one of my patients.' *And no doubt you have jinni bodyguards following us that would stop you if you tried to do anything stupid.*

'What a terrible fate that would be. I'm sure there are those who go to the desert just so they can be treated by you.'

'I warn you: my medicines can be bitter.' She pats her doctor's bag.

Abu looks at her curiously. 'Why do you do it? Come here, I mean.'

'Perhaps you will see, before the day is over. What do you make of the Banu Sasan?'

Abu smiles. 'I grew up here.'

Tawaddud blinks. 'That is a story I would like to hear.'

'Too long to be told on an afternoon walk, I'm afraid. I do not speak of it often: it is difficult enough for me to deal with the muhtasib families without being a Soarez, Ugarte, Gomelez or Uzeda.' Abu spreads his hands. 'No matter how many gogols my mutalibun bring back from the desert.'

'So, in your position, a wise man would be looking for the

hand of a younger daughter of a muhtasib House? Even one with a … less than perfect reputation?'

Abu looks down. 'I had hoped to spend a pleasant afternoon with a beautiful woman without discussing such things.'

There is such sadness in his human eye that Tawaddud almost tells him the truth: that he should never marry a girl who loves only monsters. Then the wound left by Duny's smile stings again. *I am going to show Father who I really am. But not like she thinks.*

Tawaddud touches Abu's shoulder lightly.

'You are right. Let us leave marriages and Houses up on the Shards, where they belong. Here, no one cares who we are. And that is one reason why I come here.'

As always, Tawaddud sets up her practice next to a defaced Sobornost statue – a bearded man with a machinist's tools, now covered in athar scrawls and patches of wildcode.

As Abu watches, Tawaddud unfolds her stall from her bag: components that open up into spindly structures like giant insect legs. She turns them into a tent with a small table and a bed. She spreads out her gear and the jinni bottles. Almost as soon as she is finished, the patients start coming.

They line up outside the tent and, one by one, Tawaddud does the best she can. Most are simple hauntings, easily dispelled. Actual wildcode infections are more difficult but, fortunately, the ones today are not too bad. Merely a boy who has glowing v-shaped dashes all over his skin, chasing each other, moving in flocks like birds. He claims they are ancient symbols of victory and would like to keep them, but Tawaddud points out that they will grow and take over his skin entirely.

She studies the boy with athar vision, gently cupping his face.

'You have been in the desert again,' Tawaddud chides. The boy twitches, but Tawaddud grips his face firmly. 'Let me see.'

She takes one of the little jinn bottles from her belt, opens it and lets the software creature out, a cloud of sharp triangles in the athar.

'I thought I told you not to go there,' she says.

'A man needs to have a dream, my lady, and the dreams are in the desert,' the boy says.

'I see you are going to be a poet next. Hold still.' The little jinn eats the wildcode in the boy's frontal lobe. 'This might hurt a little. But if you don't stay out of the way of the mutalibun, you are not going to be much use to anyone.'

'I'm too fast for them to catch me,' the boy says, wincing. 'Like Mercury Ali.'

'He wasn't fast enough in the end: no one runs away from the Destroyer of Delights for ever.'

'Except the flower prince,' the boy says. 'The thief who never dies.'


In the afternoon they bring her the ghul.

It is the wife of one of the sapphire acrobats, a lean, muscled woman with dark curls in a tight sobor-fabbed dress. The acrobat leads her by the hand. She follows him like a child, an empty look in her eyes.

Tawaddud sits her down in the tent. 'Can you tell me your name?' she asks gently.

'Chanya,' the girl says.

'Her name is Mari,' says the acrobat gruffly.

Tawaddud nods. 'Do you know where she got it from?'

The acrobat spits and hands Tawaddud a smooth, transparent sheet. 'Found them in her tent,' he says. 'Burned them. Kept one to show you.'

Tawaddud glances at the page of dense text. The words dance in her eyes, and pull her in.


## The Story of the Wirer Boy and the Jannah of the Cannon

Before the Cry of Wrath rattled the Earth and Sobornost sank its claws into its soil, there lived a young man in the city of Sirr. He was a wirer's son, with a back and chest burnt brown by the sun, nimble in his trade; but when the night fell he would go to taverns and listen to the tales of the mutalibun – the treasure-hunters. Eyes aglow, he sighed and listened and breathed in the stories of hissing sands and rukh ships and the dark deeds that greed summons out of the hearts of men.

The story he loved best was the story of the Lost Jannah of the Cannon, the sacred place guarded by the Aun, the underground city where the first uploaded souls dreamt and turned in their sleep.

'Take me with you,' he would say. 'I will carry your burdens. I will rake through sand for jinn jars. No task will be too low for me if you will only let me be a mutalibun.'

But the old mutalibun scratched their beards and shook their heads and said no, never explaining why. One night, he got an ancient one to talk by spending a day's pay on honey wine.

'You want too much,' the old man said, a sad smile on dried lips. 'A mutalibun does not want. He finds, he takes, but he does not want. Jinni and lost jannahs are less to him than dust. Cast asides your desires, boy, and maybe then you will be a mutalibun.'

By day, the boy wired, made paths for the jinni to travel – the cable reel a constant burden on his back, his arms and shoulders aching – but he also thought. Surely, the old men were tired, tired of the sapphire roughness of their skin, lost in the desert dreams that the wildcode brings. Even his father with his small dreams had taken him to the spiderwoman of al'Qala'a to receive her gifts so he could climb higher, clinging to walls with the tiny spikes in his palms and feet.

Surely you had to *want* to succeed, to climb higher than others? The more he thought about the old man's words, the more the desert burned in his mind, like the sun up on the Shards, beating on his brow.

He bedded a tavern girl with promises and the hungry gaze of his dark eyes and promised her jinn rings and thinking dust that would glitter in her hair like stars. And so she became his accomplice: she slipped a spiderwoman's drug into the drink of a tired mutalibun, took his Seal armour and rukh stick and gave them to the young man. And so, in the dawn, he donned the garments of the mutalibun and joined a group of the treasure-hunters at the gate of Bab in the dawn, heading out to the desert.

Now, back then, even more so than now, the mutalibun were a taciturn lot. They save their voices and speak with signs, if at all. Even their hunter jinni are silent, shadows that come out of their bottles and pursue dead dreams at night, like dark gusts of wind with teeth. So the young man was taken as one of their comrades, just another hunched figure in the long walk to the mountains of the rukh. But he almost gave himself away when they stopped to rest on the first night, in a glade of windmill trees: he tried to open his water flask before the leader did. A dark look from another mutalibun saved him.

But his dreams drove him onward, and all around the wildcode desert listened.

The city he had been searching was there, suddenly, the Jannah of the Cannon, shining like a jewelled dream. But it seemed that the mutalibun would simply pass it by, and so he made signs to the leader to change direction. The old man just shook his head. And so the young man strode out on his own, leaving the column, and entered the city, certain that only he had the courage to lay claim to the secrets within.

Walking the streets alone, he felt like a king. There were jinn machines from a lost age, virtual worlds you could enter with a thought; machine bodies that jinni used to wear, more beautiful than any love-slave he had ever seen. They called out to him and he took his mutalibun's tools to cut out and bottle their souls.

And then the Aun came to him in their glory. The Chimney Princess. The Kraken of Light. The Green Soldier. The Flower Prince.

Tell us a true story or we will take your life, they said.

But the boy only knew one true story.

*Before the Cry of Wrath rattled the Earth and Sobornost sank its claws into its soil, there lived a young man in the city of Sirr—*

Tawaddud looks away. How did the ancients deal with this? Ghosts in their heads, made by others, everywhere they looked, ready to possess them and to do their bidding. But in Sirr, the ghosts are real, and they hide themselves in stories.

'I think I know this one,' Tawaddud says. She puts on her glasses, summons her athar vision again, speaks the words the Axolotl taught her. And there, two entwined loops in the girl's head, clearly visible.

'Ahmad,' she says harshly, looking at the girl. 'Ahmad the Sickness.' A filament of neurons lights up in the girl's brain. *Got you.*

'Ahmad, I know it's you. Do you know who I am?'

The girl snickers, suddenly, an odd, high-pitched sound. 'Oh yes, baby, I know you, the Axolotl's whore, long time, no see,' she says, in a hissing voice.

Next to her, Abu Nuwas draws a sharp breath. *Damn it. Not now. So much for the plan at getting back at Duny, so much for seduction.* Tawaddud shakes her head and bites down on the disappointment. Muhtasib plots or not, she has a patient to treat.

'So you know what I can do?' She lowers her voice. 'I know Secret Names that will root you out. If I speak them, they will find you and eat you. Is that what you want?'

'Mahmud, what is she saying?' says the girl, suddenly. 'Where am I? Don't let her hurt me.'

The acrobat takes a step forward, but Tawaddud holds up one hand. 'Don't listen to her, it's a trick.' She looks into the girl's eyes. 'Go away, Ahmad. Let this girl's self-loop swallow you. Go back to the City, and I won't tell the Repentants where your lair is. What do you say?'

The girl tears herself from the acrobat's grip and leaps up. 'Bitch! I will eat your—'

Tawaddud speaks the first syllables of the Thirty-Seventh Secret Name. The girl hesitates. Then she lays down on the mat on the floor. 'You win,' she says. 'I'll give your regards to the Axolotl. I hear he has a new squeeze.'

Then the girl goes limp, closes her eyes and starts breathing steadily. Tawaddud watches her brain for a few moments to make sure that the thing called Ahmad is letting its self – sneaked into the poor girl's mind through words and athar – dissolve into nothingness. The girl's eyes start fluttering behind closed eyelids.

'She is going to sleep for a day or two,' Tawaddud tells Mahmud the acrobat. 'Surround her with familiar things. When she wakes up, she should be fine.'

She shoos away Mahmud's excessive thanks, suddenly tired but triumphant. She looks at Abu and nods. *See? That's the other reason I come.* She looks for signs of disgust or horror on the gogol merchant's face, but sees only his brass eye, glittering with a strange hunger.

The patients finally thin out by nightfall. Abu Nuwas buys two shawarma wraps from a street vendor, and they eat together, sitting cross-legged on the inflatable mattress inside the tent. Outside are the noises of Banu Sasan, the constant rattle of the soul trains, flashes and booms of the Station, the chill of the Sobornost buildings slowly eaten by wildcode.

'You know, I don't come back here very often,' Abu says. 'Perhaps I should. To remind myself how much there is to fix. How much wildcode there is.'

'Without wildcode we would all be Sobornost slaves already.'

Abu says nothing.

Tawaddud cradles the hot wrap in her hands for warmth.

'So, what do you think about the stories they tell about the girl from House Gomelez now?' she asks. *No point in pretending anymore.*

'What the body thief called you,' Abu says. 'Is it true?'

Tawaddud sighs.

'Yes, the stories are true. I ran away from my first husband to the City of the Dead. A jinn there took care of me. We became close.'

'A jinn. The Axolotl?'

'Some call him that. His name is Zaybak.'

'He really exists?'

That's what Tawaddud first thought as well: a story come to life, the Father of Body Thieves, who came to Sirr a hundred years ago and became half the city.

'Yes. But not everything they say about him is true. He did not mean to do what he did.' She puts the remains of her food away. 'But if you want a reason to give to my father, *Axolotl's whore* is as good as any.' Tawaddud closes her eyes and tugs at her hair, hard. 'But thank you for a pleasant afternoon, and for showing me the city. The other city, I mean. That was nice.'

Abu turns and looks away. With his brass eye hidden, he looks terribly young, all of a sudden: for all his wealth, he must be younger than she is.

'Do not trouble yourself,' Tawaddud says. 'I'm used to it.'

'It's not that,' Abu says. 'There is a reason I don't come here.' He touches his brass eye. 'You asked for my story. Do you still want to hear it?' His voice is flat, and his human eye is closed.

Tawaddud nods.

'My parents died in the Cry of Wrath. I stayed with a Banu woman who let me sleep in her tent, for a while. When she found out I could hear the Aun, she sold me to an entwiner. I was six. It wasn't like what the Council entwiners do. It was forced.

'I was put in a tank, warm water, no sound, nothing else. Then there was another voice in my head, a thing that had once been a man, a jinn, screaming in pain. Its name was Pacheco. It swallowed me. Or I swallowed it. I don't know how long it took, but when they let me – us – out, I was thin like a stick. I couldn't stand. My eye ached. But I could see athar, touch athar. I couldn't find my way around at first because I got lost in the ghost buildings in the Shadow.

'And I could hear the desert, the jannahs and the heavens, old machines from the other side of the world, calling.

'The entwiner was happy. He sold me to a mutalibun party. They took me to the desert to find gogols.' Abu smiles. 'Fortunately, I turned out to be rather good at it. Don't get me wrong, it was not all bad. The mutalibuns' rukh ship was the most beautiful thing I had ever seen, white-hulled, curved like a chip of wood, and as light; the rukh birds carried it lightly and the hunter jinni rode with it like bright clouds. And the desert, I don't know why they still call it the desert, there are roads and cities and wonders, herds of von Neumann machines, dark seas of the dead, sand that listens to you and makes your dreams come true—'

Abu shakes his head. 'I'm sorry. I'm babbling. None of it matters. I am an ill-made muhtasib, a thing, only half a man. So I cannot love as a man. I wanted to find someone who could understand both the jinn and the man. I thought—' He squeezes his temples with his wrists.

'It's not about that, not just that, you understand. I … believe in what your father is trying to do. We can't just keep pretending the Sobornost is going to go away, and the hsien-kus are much more sane than some of the other ones, so no matter what you feel or want, I'm going to help him.'

Tawaddud swallows. *This is not how it was supposed to go.* Twin snakes of guilt and pity chase each other inside her chest.

'Maybe I should go,' Abu says.

'Ssh,' Tawaddud says and kisses him.

His brass eye is cold and hard against her eyelid. His lips are dry, his tongue unpractised. She caresses his cheek, nuzzles his neck. He sits still like a statue. Then she pulls away, opens her bag, takes out the beemee net and carefully weaves it in her hair.

'What are you doing?' he whispers.

'This is not how it usually goes,' she says, laughing. 'Kafur would kill me if he knew.' She opens her bodystocking at the neck, pulls it open all the way to her navel. She takes his hands and places them on her breasts. She whispers the Secret Name of al-Latif the Gentle, sees its shape before her eyes, focuses on its spirals and recursive twists like she was taught, and the tingle of a beemee connection comes in an instant.

'You thought to court a woman who has lain with both jinni and men,' she whispers. 'You would find that Kafur's Palace of Stories drives a cheaper bargain than Cassar Gomelez.'

'I know I shouldn't have,' he says haltingly. His hand shakes slightly as he traces the shape of the aureola of her left breast with a finger, gently, uncertainly. The promise of the touch makes her tingle all over.

'But when I heard the stories—'

'Stories are things of the evening, not the night, and the night is here,' she chides, kissing him again, drawing him close, opening his robes.

'Is there anything I can give you to—'

'You can tell my father that this is not all I am good for,' she hisses in his ear. 'Tell him that I want to serve him like my sister does.'

The beemee hums around her temples. His hands wander down her belly, caress her back.

Abu's brass eye lights up like a star in the athar. Fire pours out of it and into her, incandescent tongues that tease and burn. She sees her own face, like in a mirror, her lips a circle, her eyes squeezed shut. And then she loses herself in the entwining of Shadow, flesh and flame.

# 7

# THE THIEF AND THE ROUTER

'What are you going to do when this is over?' I ask *Perhonen* through our neutrino link.

From our orbit around 90 Antiope, the zoku router looked like a tree with mirror leaves, two kilometres in diameter, floating in space. But inside it is sheer Escherian madness. The processing nodes are blue glowing spheroids, ranging in size from hot-air ballons to dust motes, moving and tumbling in spirals around each other. Polygon-shaped silver mirrors that reflect each other, opening into infinite corridors. But like a vampire, I have no reflection.

*I'm going to find a job that does not involve breaking into giant machines full of lesbian dragon sex,* the ship says. Its white-winged butterfly avatar flutters around my helmet. I blow at it to get it away from my field of vision: I'm in the middle of hacking into yet another processing node, a giant amoeba the size of my head. It is a rippling, transparent bubble, with an irregular crystalline structure within. Much of zoku q-tech is alive, and so is this thing – constantly hungry, eating quantum states from the photon stream through the router and encoding them into complex organic molecules. I'm about to feed it a treat.

'That's very narrow-minded of you – the zoku can do whatever they want in the Realms. But another job? Come on. Crime is the only way to make the world make sense. Besides, you are a natural.'

I approach the node with gentle nudges from my quick-suit's ion drives. I have to move slowly: there is enough band-width here to fry an unprotected human many times over. A constant photon storm of fantasy, bent around me by the metamaterials of the quicksuit. I'm invisible and undetect-able, a ghost in the machine – as long as the suit keeps up.

At my command, the quicksuit extends invisible tendrils that englobe the node. Far away, *Perhonen*'s mathematics gogols work hard to inject a tiny piece of quantum software into the node's memory, to allow us to monitor the traffic through it. We need to find the scale-free patterns in the traffic flow, to detect when a quiet period is coming, to allow us to use the router's quantum brain for our own purposes—

The traffic spike hits. Even through the faceplate of the helmet, the node becomes a bright, hot sun. The suit's gogol processors – customised upload minds – literally scream. The sudden heat scalds my arms, face and chest. *Not again.* There are needles in my eyes, and suddenly I only see white noise. I fight the urge to curl up into a ball, reach for the suit's tiny ion drives through the neural interface and fire them.

The thrust pushes me out of the boiling current of data, and the world goes blissfully dark: we are back within the suit's operating regime. I fire the drives again to stabilise, and they die as well, leaving me in a disorienting spin.

—*going too fast*, shouts *Perhonen* in my ear through the neutrino link. The butterfly avatar of the ship beats its wings frantically inside my helmet, a delayed reflection of the ship's distress.

'I would be going *faster* if somebody had updated their traffic models!' I yell at it. I straighten my arms to slow the spin, praying that I'm not going to collide with a processing node. Too much disturbance inside the router and it's going to call the zoku sysadmins. Although if I don't get the Box open in a few hours, angry zoku computer nerds are going to be the least of our worries.

*Hold on. Just stay put. It's settling down.*

I start healing again. It feels like needle-legged ants crawling all over me, accompanied by a sudden light-headedness. I'm still in a bad shape: my hand has not grown back properly, and the body's synthbio cells are riddled with mutations and cancer analogues from being exposed to hard radiation. At least Mieli now allows me enough control to turn the pain off at will. The only problem is the detachment that comes with the numbness, and I can't really afford it in a job like this.

The suit vents heat and hisses. The gogols' complaints in my head settle down into a soft murmur as the suit systems recover. I lick sweat from my lips and take deep breaths, squeezing the Box in my hand, hard. There should be easier ways to break into something that small.

'And by the way, I'm all right here, thank you for asking,' I mutter.

*Do you want to update a simulation model of a quantum system with about three million unknown parameters? No? Then shut up and let me and the gogols do our job.*

I can't blame the ship for being slightly cranky. We turned her wings – her pride and joy – from something resembling trapped aurora borealis into rigid grids of quantum logic, the closest thing we have to proper quantum processors. Which also means that if something does go wrong, it's going to be difficult to run.

And then there is Mieli, who seems awfully keen to die a heroic death.

'I would like to point out that I'm still the one going in,' I say testily.

*I would like to point out that it would be nice to be appreciated, Perhonen says. So you think your box god is just going to welcome you with open arms and help us?*

'Don't worry, I've dealt with him before. And I know what it feels like to be in a box. You'll do anything to get out. You'll even throw in your lot with smartass ships and Oortian warriors.'

*I'll take your word for it. In any case, the traffic seems to be settling down.*

'How long?' The suit's spimescape is back up at last. It shows me a reconstructed view of the router's innards. The price of being invisible is being blind – which makes it somewhat tricky to break into a vast machine constantly creating and dissolving new components. At least for the moment I'm in the stable outer layers, away from the heavy processing centres.

*Oh, should not be more than an hour or so. Try not to get bored.*

'Great.' I squirm inside the suit. My makeshift outfit is not exactly comfortable: it's essentially a chunk of smartmatter, loaded with custom gogols and fitted with a few extra pieces of kit like the drives. It feels like wearing a full-body suit of wet clay, and I've been inside it for nearly two days. The neural interface is improvised and crude, with a constant spillover of the gogols' muttering into my brain. The thought of another hour in it, floating in the router's outer layers, possibly hit by another traffic spike at any moment, does not exactly fill me with joy. Especially when the siblings of the cop thing could show up at any moment.

*What about you?* the ship asks, suddenly.

'What?'

*What are you going to do when this is over?*

I have only faint memories of what *freedom* truly means, what I used to be. Of a manifold, chameleon existence among the *guberniyas*, the zero-g coral reefs of the beltworlds, the endless party of Supra City, dancing above Saturn's rings. Finding treasures and stealing them. Being Jean le Flambeur. All of a sudden, I want it very, very badly.

'I'm going to take a vacation,' I say. 'What do you think Mieli wants to do?'

The ship is quiet. I've never asked it about Mieli, not directly, and her recent death wish is not exactly something I want to bring up in a conversation. Even if I'm sure the ship knows where it came from.

*For her,* Perhonen says finally, *I'm not sure it will ever be over.*

'And why is that?'

Another long pause.

*Because she is looking for something that never existed in the first place.*

And so, while we wait for the data storm in the router to die, the ship tells me what Mieli lost on Venus.

Mieli is glad of the quiet in the main cabin. The space is completely empty and bare after the ship cleared out the mess, just sapphire walls with white cracks where the hull is still healing. There was no time to salvage her Oortian things. She does not care: the songs remain.

*Perhonen*'s freshly fabbed butterfly avatars rest on the curving surfaces, like white flowers. The ship's attention is elsewhere, in the target – a huge wedding bouquet of glass a few kilometres away, against the irregular potato shape of 90 Antiope. The thief's minor crisis with the processing node appears to be over. The next step is up to Mieli. She reaches into her robes and takes out the thief's jewel.

Mieli saw her first zoku jewel in Hiljainen Koto, when she was six. A Jovian sunsmith gave a dead one to her *koto* sister Varpu as a plaything. All the children huddled around Varpu to look at it while she spread her wings with pride. It did not look like much: a bauble barely larger than a fingertip, with a dim amber colour and a corrugated surface. There was something sad about it. But when they touched it, they could imagine touching the outside, touching the sun.

When it was Mieli's turn, it clung to her palm like hungry smartcoral. And suddenly, there was a murmuring voice in her mind, not like any song she had ever heard, full of yearning and desire, so strong that she was afraid. It said that she was special, that she belonged together with the jewel, that she only had to let it in and that they would be one for ever—

Mieli spread her wings, flew to the nearest darkhole and, ignoring Varpu's shocked protests, threw it out into the black. Varpu did not speak to her for days afterwards.

But the jewel that now floats in front of her is alive, full of slow, entangled light. It is a simple blue oval, smaller than her hand, smooth and cool – and it smells faintly of flowers.

When she touches it, there is a tickle that goes all the way to her belly, an offer of joining. Like many of the low-level infrastructure jewels, it is not imprinted on a specific owner. That's why the thief stole it from the Martian zoku, of course. But the quantum states inside are unique: unforgeable, protected by the no-cloning theorem of quantum mechanics.

*Unlike me.* She quickly pushes the thought away and accepts the jewel's touch. There is a sudden cool weight like a gentle hand resting on her brain.

She is a member of a zoku now, technically, part of a collective mind, bound together by quantum entanglement. This particular zoku is large but loose, devoted to maintaining and improving the common communication infrastructure through the System. She only needs to wish and the zoku's serendipity engines will weave her desire into the zoku's fabric – to be satisfied if the resources are available, in a way that is optimal to all the collective's members.

Still, there is a price: the zoku may ask something of her in return – without her knowing. An idea may flash by, possessing her for a moment, consuming all her attention. Or she may feel a compulsion to be in a particular place, seemingly random, to meet a stranger who has a problem she can help them with.

Within the router, the thief is opening the Box. She takes a deep breath and lets the plan take over.

The metacortex passes her wish to the jewel: a complex, canned thought she crafted with the thief and *Perhonen*, a request for the router to run a very specialised quantum algorithm. The jewel seizes her volition eagerly. *Perhonen*'s modified wings, emulating a zoku communication protocol, pass it to the router. Slowly, the wedding bouquet starts to change shape, like origami, unfolded by invisible hands.

Mieli carries out her part perfectly, as I knew she would. I wish I could high-five her as the mirror headache around me comes to life. But time is of the essence: there could be a new traffic spike any second, and we are going to need everything the router can give us. Through Mieli's connection to the router zoku, *Perhonen* is feeding it instructions.

*You had better move,* the ship says. *Here is the latest traffic heatmap.* The suit spimescape flashes into a three-dimensional contour image, like a brain scan. Intricate multicoloured shapes change and pulse in front of my eyes. I stare at the butterfly avatar inside the helmet. It looks comfortably normal against the madness in the background.

I grit my teeth, feed the map to the suit's pilot gogols and fire the ion drives.

It is like swimming through invisible currents of fire. At the back of my mind, the clock is ticking. After tense seconds of sweat-drenched manoeuvring, I reach the Realmgates.

They are where we figured they would be, a large chamber-like space near the centre of the router, close to the power source, in a blissfully bandwidth-free zone, eye of the storm. A cluster of cubes, glowing with a faint tinge of purple in my spimescape vision, each two metres to the third power. Realmgates: the universal zoku interface between physical and virtual. They translate you into the language of the Realms going in, and back into physics and matter coming out. Picotech disassemblers that take the quantum information of any substance, convert it into qubits and teleport it into simulated gameworlds full of magic and dragons.

Or in this case, dark war gods with a grudge.

'That's more like it,' I whisper to *Perhonen.* The plan clicks back into place in my head, and suddenly everything is sharp. 'How is Mieli doing?'

*All ready to go.*

I merge my quicksuit gloves together to allow freedom of movement and lift up the Box with my right hand – the left is still a tingling clump of regenerating flesh. I detach a part of the suit's q-dot field and let go of it, keeping a sensory link so it feels like I'm still holding it, guiding it into position next to the Realmgates.

*Forty seconds to the predicted traffic minimum, Perhonen* says.

The router weaves complex machinery into being around the Box. It runs the non-demolition measurement algorithm that the gogols claim will keep the cats alive – tricks that would have taken thousands of years with the improvised quantum gates in *Perhonen*'s wings. Then my field of vision explodes into an abstract cloud of colourful zoku language followed immediately by a translation by *Perhonen*'s gogol helpers.

*You were right, Perhonen* says. *There is a Realm inside. It's in the router memory now. You should be able to go in.*

Imaginary wood whispers beneath my fingers. Or perhaps it is just the phantom itch of my missing hand. 'You know, ship,' I say, 'in case this does not go well, it was nice knowing you.'

*You too.*

'And I'm sorry.'

*Sorry for what?*

'For what's about to happen.'

I fire the ion drives and start moving towards the Realmgate.

The jewel's touch becomes an iron grip in Mieli's brain. And suddenly, a song unfolds in her mind. It ignites parts of her brain she has not used in nearly two decades, the parts which make matter dance. The words start flowing from her lips, unbidden.

The *väki* in *Perhonen*'s hull responds to her. The song is almost as complex as the one she sung when she made the ship, the one that kept her up for eleven *koto* nights. But this one is a sharp song, a dead song, full of chilly abstraction and code, the song of a thief. She tries to stop herself, clamp fingers across her mouth, bite her tongue, but her body refuses to obey. In the end, she spits it out, word by word, hoarse voice rasping.

The changes the song makes are subtle, but she can feel them, in the very core of the ship, rippling outwards along its spiderweb structure and modules, all the way to its wings.

*Mieli!* the ship shouts. *There is something wrong—*

Cursing the thief, Mieli sends the command that shuts him down.

*Jean, what the hell are you talking about?* The butterfly goes frantic in my helmet.

All my limbs freeze. Mieli is using the Sobornost body's remote control. But she can't control Newton's laws: I'm still going towards the gate.

The Realmgate is a wall in front of me, black like a thundercloud. There is a flash. And then I'm both alive and dead.

'*Perhonen?*' Mieli whispers.

*Perhonen*'s butterflies alight from their perches on the walls and dance, a storm of white motion, like Lorenz attractors. The fluttering whiteness converges into a dense cloud and forms a face.

'*Perhonen* is not here anymore,' it says, with a voice made of wings and whispers.

# 8

# TAWADDUD AND SUMANGURU

The Sobornost Station is large enough to have its own weather. The ghost-rain inside does not so much fall but shimmers in the air. It makes shapes and moves, and gives Tawaddud the constant feeling that something is lurking just at the edge of her vision.

She looks up, and immediately regrets it. Through the wet veil, it is like looking down from the top of the Gomelez Shard. The vertical lines far above pull her gaze towards an amber-hued, faintly glowing dome almost a kilometre high, made of transparent, undulating surfaces that bunch together towards the centre, like the ceiling of a circus tent, segmented by the sharply curving ribs of the Station's supporting frame.

Forms like misshapen balloons float beneath the vault. At first they look random, but as Tawaddud watches, they coalesce into shapes: the line of a cheekbone and a chin and an eyebrow. Then they are faces, sculpted from air and light, looking down at her with hollow eyes—

*What am I doing here?*

The jinni yearn for bodies: that she understands. But the Station *is* the body of Sobornost, thinking matter, flesh of the true immortals. There are gogols everywhere, big and small, even in the rain, in the smart dust particles around which the raindrops form.

She breathes it in, sticky and oily, with a faint, sweet scent, like incense. The droplets cling to her clothing and skin and soil her silk dress. The soggy fabric crumples around her waist. Little deities ruin her carefully prepared hairdo and trickle down her back.

Tawaddud the diplomat. *What am I going to say to a god from beyond the sky when he arrives?* The hastily absorbed facts about Sobornost and the envoy swim around in her head. 'I'm sorry, your brothers rained on me.'

*I thought I was so clever. Maybe Duny was right. Maybe I should have stuck to pleasuring jinni.*


Her sister stormed into her bedroom at four in the morning, waking her from heavy, languid sleep. Dunyazad did not even look at Tawaddud, just walked to the keyhole-shaped window with a view of Father's rooftop gardens, yanked the curtains open and stared out at the pre-dawn light. Her shoulders shook ever so slightly, but her voice was flat calm.

'Get up. Father wants you to escort the Sobornost envoy to look into Alile's death. We need to get you briefed and ready.'

Tawaddud rubbed her eyes. Abu had summoned a carpet to take them home – he *did* have jinni bodyguards, after all – and she had collapsed on her bed. She smelled of sweat and Banu Sasan, and a faint warm echo of his touch still clung to her skin. It made her smile even at Duny.

'Good morning, to you too, sister.'

Duny did not turn around. Her hands were at her sides, squeezed into fists.

'Tawaddud,' she said slowly. 'This is not a game. This is not sneaking away from Chaeremon to flirt with wirer boys. This is not some role you play for a lecherous jinn who cannot bear the phantom pains of his lost manhood. This is about the fate of Sirr. You don't understand what you are dealing with, what you will have to do. Whatever deal you made with Lord Nuwas, I beg you to let it go. If you don't want to marry him, so be it. We can find somebody else. If you want to play politics, we can find a way. But do not do this. I ask you in the name of our mother's soul.'

Tawaddud got up, wrapping a sheet around her.

'Don't you think this is what Mother would have wanted?' she said softly.

Dunyazad turned her head and looked straight at Tawaddud, her eyes two pinpoints of ice, and in the morning light, she did look like their mother. But she did not say a word.

'Don't you think I can do it, Duny? *A boring babysitting job*, is that not what you called it? I was taught everything you were, and more besides. But how would you know? You only ever come to me when you need something.' She allows herself a half a smile. 'Besides, it sounds like Father has made a decision.'

Dunyazad's mouth was a straight line. She squeezed her qarin bottle in one hand, hard.

'Very well,' she said. 'But there is no room for mistakes. And there is no running away from this one. That's what you like to do when things get difficult, don't you?'

'I will have you to catch me if I fall, sister,' Tawaddud said. She lowered her voice. 'I think it's going to be fun.'

Without another word, Dunyazad took her to one of the muhtasib admin buildings at the top of the Blue Shard.

84

They climbed long, winding stairs to an austere chamber of white stone, with low couches and athar screens, where a dry-lipped, shaven-headed young man in orange robes – a political astronomer, Duny said – told her what she needed to know about the Sobornost.

'We are confident that the Sobornost power structure is unstable and fragmented,' he said, staring at her intently. 'Grav-wave interferometry shows that the *guberniyas* go through periods of conflict and consolidation.' He showed her images that looked like eyeballs, heat maps of the planet-sized diamond brains of the Inner System. 'We know about the hsien-kus, of course. But it is the chens who seem to be the dominant power at the moment. It is them that the hsien-kus are trying to keep happy.'

'So is it a chen they are sending?' Tawaddud asked.

'Probably not. It is more likely that they will send a suman-guru – or several, it could be a bodyship. They are warriors and enforcers of some sort. Policemen. Like Repentants.'

The young man's voice was eager and breathless. 'I must say that I envy you this opportunity. To interact with a Founder from the Deep Time. To find out more about all the big questions, even hints – the Cry of Wrath and why they are so vulnerable to wildcode, why they allow our city to exist, why they are building the Gourd, why they haven't already uploaded Earth—'

The young man's eyes gleamed with something akin to religious awe. It made Tawaddud's skin crawl, and she was glad that her sister interrupted him.

'There is no need for any of that,' Duny said. 'Whoever it is, you will start with Alile. You will give the envoy temporary Seals and take them to the Councilwoman's palace: they know to expect you. All the Repentants there are with

House Soarez: they are sympathetic to our cause, as is the Councilwoman's heir, Salih. Let the envoy investigate as much as they want: I doubt they will do any better than the Repentants. But be careful: we don't want to alert the rest of the Council to our guest's presence just yet.' She turned back to the young man. 'What do we know about the sumangurus?'

'Well, our hsien-ku sources are . . . afraid of them.' The athar screens fill with ghosts of a black-skinned man with a shaved head and scarred face. 'If what we know about the original is anything to go by, there is a good reason. He escaped a black box upload camp when he was eleven. Became a Fedorovist leader in Central Africa. Single-handedly wiped out gogol trade there.' The young man licks his lips. 'Of course, that was before he became a god.'

Dunyazad gave Tawaddud a dark look. 'Sounds like you two should get along just fine.'

She feels foolish for mocking Duny now. *She is not going to forget that.* There was more, speculation about alliances between hsien-kus and vasilevs and instructions on how to operate the Repentant jinn ring the young man gave her for safety, Secret Names for emergencies, a Seal for the envoy. Inside the Station, all of it feels absurd, schemes of ants trying to understand the thoughts of gods. Her head aches with fatigue and anxiety.

A river of light flows to the upload platform she is standing on, carrying a group of twenty people or so: upload converts in black Sobornost unifs. Their shaved heads gleam in the rain, and they flinch at every thoughtwisp thunderclap, every scan beam lightning strike. A vasilev – an impossibly handsome blond young man she recognises from statues – shepherds them, moving quickly from one person to the next, touching their shoulders, whispering in their ears.

They all stare at the scan beam target markers – dull metallic circles on the floor in front of them – except for a skinny boy who steals a look at Tawaddud, a hungry, guilty glimpse. He cannot be more than sixteen, but his hollow temples and the grey hue of his skin make him seem older. His lips are blue, and his mouth is a thin line.

*Why did you go to the temple where they told you of Fedorov and the Great Common Task and immortality?* Tawaddud wonders. *Perhaps because they said you were special, that you were clean of wildcode. They taught you exercises to prepare your mind. They told you they loved you. That you would never have to be alone again. But now you are not sure. It is cold in the rain. You don't know where the thunder is going to take you.* Tawaddud smiles at him. *You are braver than I was,* her smile says. *It's going to be all right.*

The boy's back straightens. He takes a deep breath and looks ahead with the others.

Tawaddud sighs. At least she can still tell lies that men need to hear. Perhaps the envoy won't be any different.

The air booms like the skin of a drum. The ethereal machinery beneath the Station's dome moves, coalesces into a whirlpool. A pencil beam comes from above, incandescent finger of a burning god. Tawaddud feels heat on her face as if from a furnace. The ray flickers back and forth, as if writing in the air. She squeezes her eyes shut against the unbearable brightness, but the light only becomes red, filtering through her eyelids. Then it is gone, and only an afterimage remains. When she can see again, there is a man with the face of one of the Station gods standing on the platform.

Tawaddud curtsies. The man fixes his gaze on her with a sudden jerk of his head. The pale blue eyes and their tiny pupils feel like a blow. His skin is even darker than Tawaddud's own, except for a purple cluster of rough scars across his nose and cheekbone.

'My lord Sumanguru of the Turquoise Branch,' Tawaddud says. 'Please allow me welcome you to the city of Sirr, on behalf of the Muhtasib Council. I am Tawaddud of House Gomelez. I have been assigned to be your guide.'

She speaks out the words of the Seal, moving her hands in the ritual gestures of a muhtasib. In the athar, her fingers paint swirls of golden letters in the air. They swarm around the Sobornost man like insects and settle on his skin. For an instant, he is tattooed with fiery characters, spelling out the unique Name given to the Seal that only the muhtasibs know.

Sumanguru flinches, looking at his hands. His massive chest heaves beneath the featureless black Sobornost unif that looks like paint on his skin.

'I have given you one of our Seals. It will protect you from wildcode for seven days and nights,' Tawaddud says. 'Hopefully your task will not require more than that.' *Besides, the Accord modification vote goes ahead in two days.*

Sumanguru's nostrils flare.

'I thank you,' he says. 'But a guide … a guide will not be necessary.' He speaks slowly, with a rumbling voice, and smacks his lips as if tasting the words. 'I am fully briefed and capable of carrying out my task. I will interface directly with the Council if necessary.'

Tawaddud's neck prickles. The uploads and the vasilev on the platform are frozen, staring at Sumanguru with a look of abject terror.

'Perhaps there has been a miscommunication. The Council feels that—'

'There has. I will require your assistance no further.' Sumanguru takes a step forward. He looms in front of Tawaddud, two heads taller than her. Like the Station, he is built according to a different scale. His skin has the same dark sheen as the floor, and the rain does not seem to cling to him. Tawaddud's heart pounds.

'But you may find the city strange,' she says. 'And there are many customs you will not be familiar with—'

'You have a problem. Tell your masters I will solve it. Is that not enough?'

He pushes Tawaddud aside with a movement so quick it feels more like a blow, a stinging impact just below her left collarbone that makes her lose her balance and fall down. There are bright flashes in front of her eyes.

*Tawaddud the diplomat. Stupid girl.*

She shakes her head to clear it. There is something familiar about the clumsiness in Sumanguru's movements. The realisation almost makes her smile.

Sumanguru looks down at her for a moment, impassively. He turns to leave, but Tawaddud holds his gaze with her own.

'It is strange, isn't it?' she says.

'What?' His shoulders shift slightly.

'The jinni say they become different when they wear bodies. They say there is a craving that comes, afterwards. It must be very strange for you to have a body again, after so long. Being poured into a different cup.' She struggles to get up. 'A hsien-ku told me it is a privilege amongst your people to wear flesh again.'

'The hsien-kus say a lot of things,' Sumanguru says. His

mouth is a grim line, but there is something in his eyes that Tawaddud recognises. Fascination. Curiosity. 'Flesh is the enemy.' Slowly, he extends a hand and pulls Tawaddud up, fingers engulfing hers. His grip is just a little too tight, but his fingers are warm.

'And do you know your enemy?' Tawaddud winces at the fresh bruise in her chest, gritting her teeth. 'Because I do.' She inserts a deliberate note of pain into her voice.

Sumanguru frowns. 'Are you … hurt?'

Speak their own language, Kafur said. Tell beautiful lies with it.

Tawaddud slaps him, across the cheek with the scars, as hard as she can. It feels like hitting a statue, and the sting of the blow almost makes her cry out. But Sumanguru flinches, takes a step back and lifts one confused hand to his face.

'Not anymore,' Tawaddud says. She flexes her tingling fingers. 'I don't know where you come from, Sumanguru of the Turquoise Branch,' she says softly. 'But you do not know flesh like I do, or the stories it tells. And Sirr is a city of stories made flesh. Can you read them? Did they teach you that in the *guberniya*?'

Sumanguru takes a step closer and bends down, staring at her as if looking for his reflection in her eyes. She looks away from his gaze at the craters of his scars, strangely beautiful against his otherwise perfect skin. She can feel the warmth emanating from his body. His breath smells faintly of something that reminds her of machinery, engines or guns. The young man in orange said that the Sobornost cannot make more-than-human bodies in Sirr without being eaten by wildcode, but Tawaddud wonders if that's entirely true.

The corner of Sumanguru's mouth twitches.

'Guide me to the enemies of Sobornost and I will destroy

them,' he says slowly, a rumble in his chest. 'Flesh or otherwise.'

'In that case, you had better come with me.'

Tawaddud starts walking away from the platform. For a moment she has no idea where she is going, but then the road of light appears beneath her feet, and carries them away. She feels the wind in her wet hair and resists the urge to look back. Behind her, the lightning of the scanning beam comes down again, taking the frightened boy with it.

# 9

# THE THIEF AND THE TIGER

A discontinuity. A new world slaps me in the face, and I fall to my knees in the sudden gravity. Chilly air fills my lungs. It smells of wet earth and smoke.

I am standing in the middle of a clearing in a white forest. There are straight trees with pale, birchlike bark and impossibly symmetric foliage shaped like crowns or hands in prayer. Dark, ragged creatures with fluttering wings dart amongst the branches. The sky is grey. The ground is covered in white particles too grainy to be snow, a few centimetres deep. The Realmgate is behind me, a silver arch – a perfect flimsy semicircle. *Good. At least I still have a way out.*

I get up and wince at the sudden pain at the soles of my bare feet. The white stuff feels like powdered glass. I grunt and scrape some of the particles away. They look like cogwheels with sharp teeth, spilled innards of tiny clocks.

The sting reminds me that I have changed, too. Zoku Realms do not just transfer, they *translate*, turn you into a software construct that best approximates you in whatever constraints the virtual world imposes. Here, it seems to mean my shipboard attire of a jacket and slacks, barefoot – and no trace whatsoever of my Sobornost body's more superhuman capabilities. At least my lost hand is back, even if it quickly goes blue and numb in the cold.

My stolen Realmspace sword has also translated – as it should have. Made by the Martian zoku whose specialty is raiding lost Realms, it adapts to whatever environment you transfer it into. I blow at my hands, rub them together, and pull it out from its scabbard.

Here, its blade is white bone, curved like a claw. The hilt is an intricate spiky design made from cold iron, heavy and uncomfortable in my hand. When I raise it, it whispers to me in a voice that is like chalk screeching on a blackboard. *Small Realm. Archetypal objects and avatars. Generative content. Damaged. Dying.* It makes sense. My clumsy attempts to open the Box have left the environment here broken. I wonder what it was originally: some sort of fairy-tale forest, perhaps.

Then I realise that *Perhonen*'s butterfly avatar is missing: it should have come through the gate with me. *Damn.* I look around. Something moves among the trees, through the black-and-white patterns of the shadows. Instinctively, I raise the sword, but the shape is already gone.

'*Perhonen?*' I shout. There is no answer. But near the trees, there are bare footprints in the cog-snow, leading into the woods.

With slow, painful steps, I follow them.


'And what are you supposed to be?' the butterflies whisper to Mieli. 'You don't look like his creature. Too simple. Too plain. Who do you work for?'

'Myself,' she says and flips into the spimescape. The ship's systems are a chaotic tangle. A web of commands stretches through all of *Perhonen*'s Sobornost systems, originating from a new vir running in its Oortian smartcoral brain. And there is a dense datalink between the ship and the router, with traffic flowing back and forth—

She blinks back to her body and reaches for the zoku jewel. A q-dot bubble seizes it and pulls it away from her grasp.

The butterfly face gives her a grin that is not entirely human, more like a snout with fangs.

'You lie badly,' it says.

*Mieli?* whispers *Perhonen* in Mieli's head. Her heart beats faster with sudden relief. But then she hears the pain in the ship's thought-voice. *It got me. Help.*

'Who are you and what have you done to my ship?' she hisses.

'I am Sumanguru, eighth generation, Battle-of-Jupiter-that-was branch, a warmind and a Founder of Sobornost,' the butterfly beast says. 'And as for your ship, I am eating it.'

I push tree branches aside, and they whip my face and back painfully. My feet are thankfully numb. My breath feels ragged: it feels like I'm breathing in the tiny cogs, and they are tearing the soft tissues of my lungs. It is darker now, and the stark contrast of the white and the black is blended into twilight greys and blues.

The prints lead to another clearing. There are roughly hewn stone statues in the middle: squat animals that could represent a bear and a fox, although I'm not sure. At their feet, where the tracks end, is a dark puddle, with something glittering in it. I approach carefully and squat down to have a closer look. Blood, and a piece of jewellery: a glass hairpin, shaped like a butterfly. *Perhonen.* My guts tie themselves into a knot. Bile burns my throat, and I have to take a deep, shuddering breath.

A whisper. A gust of wind. Something goes past me. A light touch on my back, like a teasing finger. The sound of fabric tearing. Then, a whiplash of blinding pain. The force of the blow hurls me against the bear statue and leaves me sprawling on the ground. More red stuff spatters on the ground, and this time it's mine. The Realmspace sword flies from my hand. I try to get up but my legs give way, and I end up on all fours.

That's when I see the tiger, watching me.

It is half-hidden by the trees, back arched. Its stripes blend with the shadows of the branches. It is a monochrome creature, absences of colour and dashes of darkness, except for the blood on its muzzle. Its eyes are mismatched, one golden, one black and dead.

It lifts one paw and licks it with a pink tongue.

'You … taste … different,' the tiger says. Its voice is a deep, halting rumble, like an engine starting. It pads softly into the clearing, tail swaying back and forth. I edge my way ever so slightly towards the fallen sword, but stop when the tiger lets out a growl.

'You taste younger. Smaller. Weaker,' it purrs. As it speaks, its voice becomes more human, familiar. 'And you taste of *her*.'

I blink and sit up slowly, brushing tiny cogs from my jacket lapels. My back is on fire and warm blood trickles from the wound, but I force myself to smile.

'If you are talking about Joséphine Pellegrini,' I say slowly, 'I can assure you that our relationship is merely … professional.'

The tiger looms over me and pushes its muzzle close to

my face. Its hot breath washes over me, a mixed stench of carrion and metal.

'Traitors like you and her belong together,' it says.

'I'm not sure I know what you are talking about.'

This time I can feel the growl as well as hear it: it is so deep that it echoes in my chest.

'You broke your promise,' the tiger roars. 'You left me here. For a thousand years.'

I curse my past self again for his blatant disregard for his own future.

'I admit it's not a very attractive setting,' I say.

'Torture,' the tiger whispers. 'This was a place of torture. The same things, happening over and over again. Foxes, bears, monkeys. Tricks and plots and follies. Stories for children. Even when I killed them, they would come back. Until things started breaking down. I suppose I should thank you for that as well, le Flambeur.' Its good eye flashes. I swallow.

'You know,' I say, 'this situation really invites a philosophical debate about the nature of identity. For example, I actually lack most of the memories of the individual you are talking about. I don't remember breaking any promises. And as a matter of fact, I am here to get you out.'

'I made a promise, too,' the tiger says. 'After I waited long enough.'

I swallow.

'And what was that?'

It backs off a few steps, circling me, tail swishing back and forth.

'Get up,' it hisses.

Painfully, I stumble to my feet, leaning on the stone bear.

'Whatever the old Jean le Flambeur may have told you,' I say, 'the new one recognises that we have common interests.

Especially regarding causing discomfort to Matjek Chen. Isn't that the promise you made? To get revenge?'

'No,' the tiger says. Its words turn into a roar. 'I promised I would give you a head start.'

I take one look at its gleaming eye, grab the Realmspace sword and start running.

Running through the forest is a nightmare. My back wound bleeds. The cog-snow sticks to the gashes in the soles of my feet. I leave a red trail behind. My breathing is a painful wheeze. The tiger is a shadow, never far: if I try to slow down, it makes a dash at me, silent and vengeful, enough to wake up my monkey fear and send me off stumbling madly across the tree roots and thickets again.

So I'm not surprised when I collapse on the edge of the opening where I started from and see the tiger, between me and the Realmgate, resting, cradling something between its front paws.

It takes a while for it to come to me, and when it does, it seems almost reluctant: soft paws on the clock snow, tiny glittering wheels in its whiskers like raindrops. Death in black and white, like a chessboard.

And for the second time, like with the Hunter thing, I feel the lines of force between us, and let them guide me towards the right move.

I step into the clearing.

'Well, here we are,' I say. 'And I told you. Here is your way out. Humanity waits on the other side. What are you waiting for?'

The tiger hesitates. It looks at the gate suspiciously. In spite of all the pain, I want to smile.

Realms translate. Realms have rules. For the old, complex

ones, the rules and narratives have become too intricate to understand, no one knows how they began. But the one in the Box is only a small Realm, a place of animal stories, perhaps for zoku children. And I'm betting the tiger has been here for a long time, soaking in the way things work. The fox and the bear. The monkey and the tiger.

'I don't think I'll believe you, this time,' it says. 'Perhaps you should go first.'

My heart jumps with sudden hope. I take a step backwards, shaking my head. *Don't throw me into the thorn bush.* But then the tiger lets out a depressingly human laugh. 'Le Flambeur,' it says. 'Let's stop playing. I just wanted to see you run. I'm not going to let you through the gate. I'm not going to try to go through either. You'll have some surprise for me on the other side, no doubt. But you are right: you *did* give me a way out, this time.' It moves aside, and I see what is lying on the ground.

In life, she had blue dreadlocks and pale skin that stands out even against the white snow. She looks younger than I expected, or perhaps it is the laughing eyes and the piercing in her lower lip. But when I see the black and red ruin that her body is from neck downwards I have to turn away and retch.

'She came through first,' the tiger says. 'I made it quick. Not very satisfying, of course, not much meat. But there were EPR states inside her, for qupting, for connecting her to your ship. *Perhonen*, I believe she is called. Or was.'

I try to get up. 'Bastard. I should have let you rot here.'

'Thinking about you gave me the strength to keep going. You and Chen and death.' The tiger's grin is somewhere between human and animal. 'But it's your turn first. We'll go somewhere else to have a little talk.'

The forest melts like snow. For a moment, we stand in the bone-white of the firmament, running in *Perhonen*'s synthbio core. Then the tiger roars its Founder code at the vir – *dead children and rust and fire and blood* – and rewrites the world.

Mieli does not need combat autism to blanket her rage. She rides it, blinks into the spimescape, fires her ghostgun at the ship's walls, launches Gödel bombs into *Perhonen*'s systems. *The weapons.* The self-replicating logic of her attack software burns through the infected systems like wildfire. The butterfly thing – Sumanguru – is too fast for her: it isolates the synthbio core from her attack. But that's not what she is aiming for.

For a moment, the weapons systems are hers. She thinks a q-dot torpedo around the ship's last remaining strangelet bomb, subatomic fury and chaos she can fire with a blink.

She opens her eyes.

'I don't care if you are the Dark Man himself,' she says. 'I'll take out the router and both of us with it if you don't let *Perhonen* go.'

Sumanguru's butterfly face looks more human now, heavy jaw and forehead and nose and what look like scars, sketched by flickering wings. But the eyes are hollow.

'Be my guest, little girl,' it says. 'Go ahead. I don't have much to live for. Do you?'

The trigger burns in her mind like a candle. *It would be so easy.* One thought, and the strangelet will end it all, wash her away in gamma ray and baryon rain.

'Here's the deal,' Sumanguru says. 'You disarm whatever trap le Flambeur has on the Realmgate. I come out. You get your ship back. Everybody is happy. How does that sound?'

What happens if she dies here? The pellegrini will bring

another Mieli back. *Choices like precious gems.* It could all be up to someone else, not her. Saving Sydän. Dealing with the thief. Another her could do it, and it would not make a difference to anyone.

Except to *Perhonen.*

She feels the ship's pain, its systems seething with an alien presence, her song defiled. *I can't let her down.*

'Well?'

'You win,' Mieli says.

# 10

# TAWADDUD AND ALILE

Councilwoman Alile is a labyrinth.

Tawaddud watches her move behind the haze of Seals. It makes her think of the nursery rhyme Chaeremon the jinn used to sing to her.

*It is in our food, it is in the air, it's even in our hearts and that's just not fair. But if you keep a clean mind, whisper Secret Names to the Aun kind, if you do what you are told, you too can tame wildcode—*

Alile fills the bright, tetrahedral workspace of her palace on the Soarez Shard almost completely.

She is a tangle of glowing sapphire pathways, transparent fleshy cables and blooms of tiny, waving tendrils. She stretches across the floor and up the walls and around tables and statues like some exotic sea creature, graceful in the ocean depths but limp and helpless washed up on the beach. Some of her has grown into the walls, merging with the clear diamonoid tiles of the palace, pushing through towards the outside world in spiky branches. In the middle of the web is a misshapen sac that looks like the belly of a mosquito, filled with blood, with knotted organs floating inside it, pulsing.

The haze of the Seals in the hallway – silver and golden graffiti in the air that the muhtasibs have woven around the infected part of the Alile's palace – obscures some of it, but not enough. There is a stinging smell of burning dust and metal in the air.

Tawaddud tries to look at her like a doctor. She has seen wildcode do terrible things to her patients, but *this*—

After a few seconds, she has to turn away and cover her nose and mouth with a hand.

'I did warn you,' Rumzan the Repentant says.

Alile visited Tawaddud's father once. She was a dour-looking woman, spare and lean, with a weather-beaten face, dressed in the stark, practical clothing of a mutalibun, with straps and hooks for Seal armour, athar glasses hanging around her neck. Alile's hair was black and long, but she had a continent-shaped patch of rough, hairless sapphire in her skull, making her look like one of Duny's old dolls, with some of its hair torn out in a tantrum.

Unlike normal muhtasibs who carried their jinn companions around in a jar, Alile's qarin lived in a mechanical bird, with feathers of gold and scarlet and eyes of ebony, made from a metal so thin and delicate it could actually fly. Tawadudd always imagined it amongst the rukh swarm that carried Alile's ship to the desert, giving its mistress eyes that saw the wildcode storms and mad jinni. *Her name is Arcelia. She is the sensible half of me,* Alile said.

Tawaddud wanted nothing more than to be like Alile.

*But this is why you should not become a mutalibun.*

Tawaddud becomes aware of Sumanguru standing next to her.

'What can you tell me about what happened here?' he asks

Rumzan. The Sobornost gogol was silent throughout their brief carpet ride from the Station, indifferent to the vistas of Sirr below them. *Matter: what kinds of heaps it's piled up in makes no difference,* he said, when she asked if Sirr pleased him. But now his eyes are alive, full of cold curiosity.

Rumzan spreads his skeletal fingers. He is a thin, elongated creature whose wispy feet barely touch the ground. His body is covered in intricate, interlocking tiles of white, red and black that make him look like a living mosaic: by Sirr law, jinni thought-forms cannot look human. He has a glowing golden symbol on his forehead, indicating Repentant rank, third circle. The jinni policemen rarely wear visible shapes – their primary task is to stay invisible, root out crime and body thieves. Rumzan smells faintly of ozone, and every now and then he becomes grainy and crackles. To Tawaddud, he seems familiar, from one of her father's parties, perhaps.

'We have a partial reconstruction of the lady's movements yesterday from athar traces,' Rumzan says. 'She arrived back from an early Council meeting around nine in the morning. We can provide a record of the meeting and her schedule, although you will have to request access to the detailed minutes from the Council.' Rumzan makes a high-pitched humming sound.

'I understand that may be a somewhat … delicate matter. In any case, the Councilwoman took her lunch in the rooftop garden alone, went up to her private observatory and then went into her office.' He points at the wildcode-filled space ahead.

'Then – the infection hit. It was so violent and sudden that we can only assume she had a Sealed container with a wildcode-infested object in it, which she opened. From speaking to the housekeeper jinni, I understand she used to be a mutalibun and brought mementos with her from the desert. With her experience, she must have been aware of the consequences of such an act. The infection must have taken hold in seconds. In other words, effectively the lady Alile committed suicide.'

'How was the infection contained?' Tawaddud asks. She remembers the drills Chaeremon made her go through as a child, the Secret Names to speak if her father's palace ever experienced a wildcode attack.

'The housekeeper jinn Khuzaima – who you are welcome to speak to – alerted us and the muhtasibs,' Rumzan says. 'The spread of the infection was slow and restricted to the Councilwoman's body, as far as we can determine. That should not be surprising: after all, this is the residence of a muhtasib, with several layers of Seals everywhere.'

'Are you sure you cannot provide a more accurate reconstruction than that?' Sumanguru asks. He is staring at the walls, frowning. 'Could anyone have brought in the wildcode from the outside?'

Rumzan spreads his hands: his fingertips flutter like candle flames. 'My Repentants are good, but there are limits to what we can do with the athar. Especially now that the ambient wildcode levels are much higher than normal. Athar traces decay quickly. However, as for outside access, like with all Council members, the palace is under constant Repentant surveillance. All comings and goings of both jinni and humans are accounted for. But we do not know what happened inside.'

Sumanguru narrows his eyes. 'My branch would call this a locked room mystery,' he says. There is a strange note of amusement in his voice.

'My sister said this was a possession,' Tawaddud says.

'How can you be sure of that? Have you found a possession vector?'

'Nothing,' Rumzan says. The jinn turns his glowing symbol at her like an eye. 'Nothing forbidden. No books, no athar stories. Of course, the athar here is very complex, so we may have missed something. Given the circumstances, a suicide is a natural hypothesis, although there is no suicide note – and it seems unlikely, given the ardour with which she has been preparing for the Council voting session, according to her aides. That would seem to support the conjecture that when taking her own life, the Councilwoman was ... literally not herself.'

'So it is just speculation?'

'Yes. However, it appears to be the only line of enquiry that fits the facts. Another complication is that we have not been able to find her qarin.' Rumzan's face tiles arrange themselves into something that looks like the facepaint of a sad clown.

Sumanguru runs his fingers along the Seal haze at the door.

'How long do they last?' he asks.

'What?'

'How long would my Seals last in there?'

'You can't be serious.'

'Tell me,' Sumanguru says.

'I don't know. Two to three minutes? They tell me sobortech is more vulnerable to wildcode than we are, so perhaps less. But you should wait for the muhtasib, they can—'

Before she can finish, Sumanguru steps through the Seal wall.

*

A faint aura shimmers around him in the athar. He walks past the remains of Alile, head turning, looking everywhere. Tawaddud wonders what kind of range of senses he has beyond human. He touches things, the empty jars on the high tables, traces the arabesque patterns on the walls. His movements seem different, not so much a clumsy, unstoppable machine but a cat, looking for something.

Then he stops in front of a wall with an ornate pattern of graphical representations of Secret Names, geometrical shapes on a four-by-four grid, made from multicoloured ceramic tiles the size of a palm, inlaid with gold.

In the athar, Tawaddud sees a black stain marring his Seals, spreading. *Wildcode.*

'His Seals won't hold!' Tawaddud shouts. 'Lord Sumanguru, get out! Rumzan, get help!'

The Sobornost gogol starts pressing the tiles. They move under his fingers. The Alile thing's sapphire tendrils coil around his limbs but he is immersed in his work. There is a click, and a part of the wall slides aside, revealing a dark space. Sumanguru reaches within, brushing aside a sapphire tendril with his other hand. Then he is back through the Seal wall, clutching something in his arms: a metallic bird.

It looks smaller than Tawaddud remembers, but still large for a bird, the length of her forearm, a hawklike, graceful thing with a forked tail. Its eyes are closed, covered by tiny golden lids.

'Arcelia?'

Tawaddud holds the bird in her arms. She expected it to feel cold and metallic, but the feathers of its back are almost alive, sharp but warm, and the flywheel in its chest hums steadily, like a rapidly beating heart. She strokes it to soothe it, but with no effect. *Whatever happened to her, she had time to hide it. The sensible part of her.*

'Explain a qarin to me,' Sumanguru says, pointing at the creature. 'In simple words.'

'A qarin is ... a jinn companion, entwined with a muhtasib,' Tawaddud says, voice shaking slightly. 'A qarin and a muhtasib are one being, brought together as a child by an entwiner.'

'What you describe is a forbidden act to us, only for the Primes,' the Sobornost gogol says. 'Perhaps there are even more reasons to cleanse your city than I thought. Why is this thing done?'

'It is a custom,' Tawaddud says. 'A symbol of the alliance between our two peoples. But it also allows the muhtasib to regulate the economy of the city. To see athar like the jinni do, to watch the flow of information, the shadows of everything in the athar, money, products, labour, people.' She looks at Rumzan. 'Directly, not through a primitive instrument like athar glasses.'

Sumanguru laughs, a resonant, barking sound. 'Matter and mind. Dualism. Primitive distinctions. All is information. Are you saying that this creature, this qarin, contains remnants of the Councilwoman's mind?'

'No,' Tawaddud says. 'I'm saying that the qarin is a part of the Councilwoman's mind.' *There is something wrong here. Why does he not know all this?*

'Perfect,' Sumanguru says. 'Repentant Rumzan, is there a quiet space in this palace? Somewhere where we would not be disturbed?'

'Lord Sumanguru, if you don't mind,' Rumzan says, 'in the capacity of the official investigator here, I am compelled to ask what it is that you are intending to do? I cannot let you—'

Sumanguru draws himself to his full height. 'Perhaps your Council has not explained the situation to you,' he says with a rumbling voice. 'We are not all like my sisters the hsien-kus: not all gentle. There are those who say that the Great Common Task demands a cleansing here. If I can't find the enemies of the Task, those voices may be heard. Do I make myself clear?'

Ripples run through Rumzan's thought-form. 'Lady Tawaddud—'

Suddenly, she remembers how she met the jinn. He had started to identify with his thought-form, and so she wore a mask and body paint that duplicated his tilings, to match his self-image. She took him out to her balcony. He liked the feel of sunlight on his skin.

'If there is a problem,' she says slowly, 'you also have a problem with me and my father. I may not have an official position in the Council, but I assure you I have my father's trust,' she holds up the jinn ring, 'as well as that of the Council. Not to mention the fact that Mr Sen is a close *personal* friend.' She gives the jinn the sugary sweet smile Duny always uses when making threats. 'Do I make myself clear?'

Rumzan makes a little croaking sound. 'Of course,' he says. 'My apologies. I just had not been briefed properly, that's all.'

'Lord Sumanguru,' Tawaddud whispers, 'it *would* be useful if you were to share what it is that you intend to do.'

'Just the obvious,' Sumanguru says. 'Interrogate the witness.'

Alile's palace is even larger than Tawaddud's father's residence – a maze of transparent cylinders, bubbles and projecting pyramids.

As the Repentant takes them through a large, sunlit gallery of sculptures, another thought-formed jinn appears, a cloud of purple and white flowers. Rumzan's form becomes fluid, mixing with the newcomer's. When he coalesces back to his mosaic self, his movements are quick and agitated.

'The Council is requesting progress reports,' he says. 'I must leave you for a moment. In fact, perhaps it is better that I do so, if Lord Sumanguru intends to do something … unorthodox. That way, I will have no knowledge of such matters if questions are asked. I will ensure that my Repentants give you privacy. You will find an aviary through the doors at the end of the gallery and down the stairs.'

'Thank you, Rumzan,' Tawaddud says. 'Your loyalty to the cause of Sirr will not be forgotten.'

'I am at your service,' the jinn says. 'And for myself, I have not forgotten a certain pleasant afternoon and the new perspectives of the world you showed me.'

'It will continue to remain our secret,' Tawaddud says, forcing herself to smile.

At first, the noise in the aviary is deafening, a cacophony of high-pitched screams and the flapping of wings. It is a high dome of glass nearly a hundred metres in diameter. Most of the bottom half is taken up by chimera plants from the wildcode desert, thick purple tangled networks of tubes that expand and contract, geoengineering synthbio of old Earth gone wild in the absence of its masters. A few windmill trees rotate slowly, spiky turbine foliage catching the light in hues of amber and angry dark red.

When Tawaddud and Sumanguru enter, the rukh swarm notices them. They are everywhere: flying things of different sizes, from tiny sapphire insects to two or three manta-ray like gliders who circle near the ceiling. Tawaddud shields her eyes against the storm of wings. Then she barks a Secret Name at them and the swarm disperses and quiets down, becomes a coiling cloud amongst the vegetation.

Down in the centre of the aviary is a clear space, with a delicately wrought white table, a few chairs and a perch. Tawaddud sets Arcelia on it. The bird does not open its eyes but clings to it, flapping its wings briefly for balance.

Sumanguru studies the bird closely, leaning forward, hands clasped behind his back. Then he reaches out, fingers spread like a magician's, surprisingly graceful for a man of his size. Five crackling lines of light appear between his fingertips and the bird. Arcelia lets out a shrill, mechanical scream and starts flapping its wings furiously. A bubble shimmers into being around it, holding it in place, and the sound is gone, leaving the bird scratching and pecking at its invisible prison in silence.

Tawaddud clenches and unclenches her fingers in rhythm with the bird's suffering. Finally, she can't bear it.

'What are you doing?' she hisses at Sumanguru.

'Interrogating, like I said.'

'How?'

'Copying its mind into a vir. A little reality, if you like. Running a genetic algorithm on it: asking the bird-brain questions and changing its brain structure until I get something sensible out.' Sumanguru flexes his fingers. 'It should only take a few thousand iterations. Half a minute, I'd say.'

'Stop that. Immediately,' Tawaddud says. 'This is a Sirr citizen you are talking about. I will not have her tortured. I will alert the Council.' She makes a fist, ready to summon a Repentant from her ring.

Sumanguru turns to look at her. His grin merges with his scars into a monstrous grimace.

'It's your city's future. I can make it talk. Means getting your hands dirty.'

Tawaddud swallows. Is this what Dunyazad meant? That it's not a game. The things you might have to do. She looks at the frantic qarin. Her heart thumps. *Not like this.*

'There might be … another way. A better way.' *There has to be.*

She pulls her doctor's bag over her shoulder, puts it on the table and opens it. She takes out her beemee and puts it on her head. 'Please let her go. I can find out what we need.'

'How?'

'I could entwine with the jinn. It will want to anchor itself to a body, just like with Alile.'

Sumanguru frowns. 'Explain.'

'Self-loops. The stories in our heads. When you love someone, you become entwined. Your self spreads to others, like swarms of fireflies, mingling. There are ways to … invite someone in. The body thieves do it with stories. But you can be more direct. The athar responds to commands we call Secret Names. Many have been lost, but they can be used for many purposes, if you know how.'

The Sobornost gogol's eyes narrow. 'And you do.'

'I was taught.'

'In the *guberniyas*, the Founders forbid this. We know this leads to monsters and horrors. Hominid minds were made to be separate.'

'Perhaps it is you who is afraid of getting your hands dirty,' Tawaddud says.

Sumanguru looks first at her and then at Arcelia. He looks curious, like a child, almost.

'Very well,' he says, finally. 'We are wasting time as it is. Just make sure it doesn't fly away.'

The aviary does not have the kind of harmony as her assignation room, but she takes a few moments to meditate, breathing, letting her awareness spread out, into the noise of the rukh swarm and the plants and the hot humid air. Then she whispers to the metal bird in her arms.

*Tell me your name. I am Tawaddud. Tell me your name.*

At first, nothing, just a tickle in the back of her head. It occurs to her it is dangerous to do this in a place so full of wildcode, even if it is behind Seals. But it is better than letting an innocent creature suffer.

*What is your name?*

Something moves inside the bird, in her head, suddenly, like a startled serpent. A shape in the athar, like smoke, coiling in the bird's heart. She is an ouroboros of software, in the tiny confines of her metal shell, in a little world that feels like a dream – except that, suddenly, there is a corridor of light, and a voice calling out to her.

I am Arcelia.

*Arcelia,* she says. *Arcelia, listen to me. I'm going to tell you a story.*

Stories always lie.

*This one is a true story, I promise.*

What is it about?

*It's a love story.*

I like love stories.

*Good,* Tawaddud says and begins.

*Once upon a time, there was a girl who loved only monsters.*

# 11

# THE THIEF AND THE SCARS

The vir smells of gunpowder and oil. There is a distant sound of gunfire. I'm bound to a metal chair under a bright light, naked. The plastic straps cut into my wrists and ankles, and the thin chair frame presses painfully into my back. The tiger is no longer a tiger but a man, standing in shadow with his arms folded, a distant expression on his scarred face.

He steps forward into the light, still moving like a tiger.

'This is a good ship,' he says. 'Too many concessions to the flesh, of course. But we can change that. Starting with your whore.'

'What have you done to Mieli?'

'The Oortian? Nothing. She's going to do me a favour, get me out properly.' He pulls his own chair forward, swings it around, sits down and leans on the backrest, his face close to mine like the tiger's muzzle. 'So we have time to talk.'

I flinch. Our minds are still running inside the Box. This vir is inside *Perhonen*. A separation between worlds and minds, that is the Sobornost way. But it's not going to make this hurt any less.

The tiger-man opens a flick-knife slowly.

'This vir comes from my memories,' he says. 'I put a lot of detail into it. Good avatars. Nerves, muscles, veins.' He tests the edge against his thumb, draws a red line of blood like a tiny smile. 'The others always forget about the flesh. But you should never forget about the enemy. It's always there, even when you are not looking. The quantum filth know that.'

The laugh bubbles up before I can stop it, comes out from my lips with droplets of spittle and blood.

'You always had a sense of humour, le Flambeur,' he says. 'Maybe we can make this short, if you tell me what that bitch Pellegrini wants from me this time.'

'It's not that,' I say.

'Well, if laughing makes it easier for you—' He reaches out with the knife, presses it against the corner of my eye, starts making the first cut—

'You know, I wanted to give you a chance,' I say, blood running down my face. 'That's why I left the Realmgate open. I thought you had good reasons to do what you did. But now I really think you just like hurting people.'

His eyes widen and he takes a step back. My features start flowing. My body changes. His Code echoes in my mind – *soft cold dead skin under my fingers*. I smile a tiger smile. I dissolve the chair with a thought and get up.

'What did you do?' he growls.

'I may be smaller and weaker and younger, but that does not mean I'm not smarter. Like you said: you should not forget about the enemy. I made a firmament vir. Yes, it should be impossible. Unless you have Oortian hardware running Sobornost software. She is a good ship.'

He slashes with the knife, but I am already a ghost, outside the laws of the vir. 'You should have gone through the gate,' I say. 'The monkey does not always lie.'

I freeze the vir and cut my link to it. A discontinuity takes me back to the dark forest. The tiger is frozen in mid-leap. I pick up my sword and walk past it, through the Realmgate.

The gate slams me back into a physical body, inside the swirling madness of the router. I grab the Box and tear it away from the router's delicate machinery, just when the rain of Hunters starts.

Mieli watches as the butterfly avatars become still. The sneering face of the box god slowly dissolves as they drift apart.

'*Perhonen?*' she whispers.

*Here,* the ship's voice says.

'Are you all right?'

*I think so. I feel strange. I think I fell asleep.*

'If that bastard did something to you, I'm going to—'

*Mieli. The hunter thing. It's coming.*

The spimescape goes crazy. Vectors rain upon *Perhonen* like the scrawls of an angry child. Mieli starts to summon combat autism, but the ship's systems are sluggish after the Box god infection. And it is already too late.

The hunters surround the ship like a shoal of fish, thousands and thousands of them, a river of tiny stars flowing through and past the ship. Their upload beams crisscross the central cabin in a deadly spiderweb, but just brushing lightly, not burning this time. They ignore *Perhonen* and converge towards the router like a giant arrowhead.

The router vanishes in a blaze of antimatter, piranhas tearing a wedding bouquet apart. Space is full of pions and gamma rays. In an eyeblink, the zoku machine is gone, replaced by a slowly expanding cloud of debris and fragments. The hunter swarm passes through it and is gone, heading back towards the main vein of the Highway at a considerable fraction of lightspeed.

And then everything is still and dark, and the space around *Perhonen* is empty. The awakened Oortian *väki* in its walls starts glowing with a familiar blue-green light.

*Mieli*, it says. *I'm still getting Jean's signal. He's still out there.*

Feeling numb, Mieli reels in the ship's wings and modules into a more compact shape and steers them into the debris cloud, burning a way through with anti-meteorite lasers. They bring the thief in with a q-dot bubble, a helmeted, quicksuited figure, clutching a small black box against his chest, unmoving.

Mieli tells the helmet to open. The opaque metamaterial bubble vanishes, revealing the face the butterflies made.

*Bastard.* Mieli extrudes a q-dot blade from her hand and pushes it against the creature's throat—

'Wait!'

The voice is the thief's. But that doesn't mean anything.

'Mieli, wait, it's me!'

It *does* sound like the thief. She pulls back but does not let go. 'What happened?'

The scarred face blurs and becomes the thief again, charcoal-dark eyebrows and hollow temples, covered in sweat. 'I got Sumanguru's Founder codes. The song I embedded in the zoku jewel – it was the same trick I tried before with Chen, except that this time it worked. A vir that pretends to be firmament, a trap. The hunters thought I was him. I told them to leave me alone. It worked.' He talks fast, breathlessly.

'You are not making any sense, you bastard,' Mieli says.

'It doesn't matter,' the thief says. 'We won. And I have a plan.'

Mieli stares at him. She takes the Box from the thief. He does not resist. She crushes it slowly in her hand. Black shards spread in all directions like the negative of a slow, tiny nova.

'You used *Perhonen* as bait,' she says.

'I did.'

'You nearly got us all killed. Or worse.'

'I did.'

She pushes him away. He floats across the cabin, a guilty look on his face.

'Get the hell away from me,' she says.

Mieli hides herself in the pilot's crèche, exhausted, nursing her anger and mapping out *Perhonen*'s systems to ensure every last trace of the box god is gone.

'How do you feel?' she asks the ship.

*Strange. Parts of me rebelled. I could not feel them anymore. All the gogols did what Sumanguru said. And there was a part that went into the Box and did not come back.*

'I'm so sorry,' Mieli says.

*But that was not the worst thing. That was when I saw you almost giving up, twice. You came very close to pulling the strangelet trigger, Mieli. And it was not a bluff.*

Mieli says nothing.

*You have been stretching yourself too thin. Keeping your promises and protecting me and letting the pellegrini change you. This time, you almost fell. And I was not there to catch you.*

For a moment, Mieli is unable to speak. She is used to the ship always being there, always offering warmth, ever since the day she made her. But now there is a cold edge in *Perhonen*'s voice.

'The thief did this to you,' Mieli says. 'He went too far this time. I'm going to—'

*I will deal with the thief, Perhonen says. You don't have to fight my battles for me. Just because you made me does not mean I did not exist before. You brought me back from the alinen, and I will always love you for that. You made me into a new being and you will always have my loyalty for that. But I am not only what you sang into me. Some things you can't fix with words or a song like Karhu did with your tooth when you were little. Or by taking it out on the thief.*

The ship's voice resonates through its sapphire hull, all around Mieli.

*So what if the pellegrini can make gogols of you? it says. Nothing has changed. They will be just as strong as you. And you will still be Mieli.*

'You have never spoken to me like that,' Mieli says.

*I have never needed to. But I will not watch you destroy yourself. You'll have to do that without me.*

*Perhonen's* wings open, magnetic fields and q-dots like dew in a spiderweb, stretching for miles. They grab the gentle solar wind and push the ship back on course, towards the Highway, towards Earth.

*Here's what we are going to do. We are going to speak to the thief and go to Earth and go through with whatever plan the thief fed me to a tiger for and get Sydän back, so we can finally be free, all of us. Promise me you will not give up.*

Shame washes over Mieli. *Kuutar and Ilmatar, forgive me.* 'I promise,' she whispers.

*Good. Now please leave me alone. I need to heal.* And then the ship's presence is gone.

Mieli's head spins. She sits still for a moment. Then she goes into the main cabin. It is bare and empty like her mind.

Remnants of the battle debris and ash float around in the ship's gentle acceleration.

Slowly, hesitantly, she starts to sing, simple songs, songs of *koto*, of food and drink and comfort and sauna. Slowly, skeletons of furniture start re-appearing, sketched by an invisible pen. *It's time to do some housecleaning*, she thinks.

I look at my new face in the ship's mirror wall, trying it on for size. The scars and the line of the jaw do not seem right. But the awareness of the Code is worse. It's locked up tight in a mind compartment but I am going to have to use it again. *Burnt bodies and filth and electricity*. I shudder. That is what defines Sumanguru? No wonder he was upset after a few centuries inside the Box.

I close my eyes and concentrate on distracting myself from the pain with whiskey from my cabin's tiny fabber. I could just turn off the aches, of course. But like my friend Isaac taught me a long ago on Mars, alcohol is not just about chemistry: it's the meme, the feeling, Bacchus speaking in my head and making it all better. At least, that's the theory. This time, the malt tastes a lot like guilt.

Nevertheless, I take a deep sip. As I drink, one of the ship's butterfly avatars enters the cabin. I look at it. It says nothing.

'Look, it was the only way,' I say. 'It had to think it had a way out. I could not edit the firmament in the Sobornost parts, it had to be the Oortian tech. I had to give it access to you to trap it, take a part of you in with me. I'm sorry.'

The butterfly says nothing. Its wings remind me of the jewel I saw in Sumanguru's memories. The fire of the gods. Some of the Founder's anger mixes with the emotion. *Down, boy*, I tell it.

'There is a honeytrap in every con,' I say. 'I'm sorry it had to be you.'

'You are not sorry,' the ship says. 'You are Jean le Flambeur. Why would you be sorry?' The butterfly settles on the edge of my glass. Its white reflection is distorted by the thin pseudo-matter and the golden liquid at the bottom.

'I thought you could help Mieli, on Mars, I really did. That you could show her that she did not have to obey the pellegrini. I thought you saw there was a different side to her. You even made her sing. But in the end, you are just like her. You will become anything to get what you think you want.'

'Easy for you to say,' I say. 'You are just a ... ' I hesitate. Servant? Slave? Lover? What is the ship to Mieli, really? In the end, I have no idea. 'Sorry,' I mutter.

'You seem to be fond of that word today.'

'I'm fond of my skin,' I say. 'I don't deny that. And I'm not going back to the Prison, or whatever hell the cop thing had in store for me. At least I've dealt with the pellegrini before. Her I can handle.' I hold my tongue. The goddess is always listening, no doubt. But the ship does not seem to be worried about that.

'Oh yes?' the butterfly says. 'Is that why you are letting her manipulate you into trying the impossible?'

'You don't understand the stakes here, ship. If the chen has a Spike artefact that can do what I think it can—'

'I understand the stakes that matter to me,' *Perhonen* says. 'Do you?'

It is surprisingly difficult to win a staring contest with a butterfly, even when you are wearing the face of the greatest warlord in the Solar System. So in the end, I look away.

'I need to be free,' I say. 'So I can try again. I had something on Mars, and I threw it away. I almost think I got caught on purpose, can you believe that? The pellegrini showed me what I did, last time. A lot of things came back with it, about her, about Earth, about what she is after.' I rub the bridge of my nose. The scar tissue is rough and alien.

'You see, I had a plan, a perfect plan – but I did not *use* it. Instead, I went right up against the chen. To see if I could take him.' I shake the glass and the butterfly alights. I pour myself more whiskey. 'So it's not about Jean le Flambeur. It's about getting rid of him.'

'This plan of yours,' the ship says, slowly. 'Will it work?'

'It will. Except that after what happened, I'm not sure Mieli will ever go along with it.'

'Let's hear it.'

So I tell her the story of the warmind and the Kaminari jewel. I tell her about the insurance heavens and the city of Sirr and the Aun and the body thieves. Not everything, of course, but enough to convince her that it will work. And that it will be me doing the heavy lifting, this time. The butterfly listens. I wonder if somewhere inside my head or far away, the pellegrini is laughing.

'You are right,' *Perhonen* says, finally. 'Mieli will never do it. She'll die first.'

With a force of will, I turn my face back into my own. 'So, what are we going to do?' I place the glass carefully in the air, like a chess piece. *It's your move.*

'What you do best,' the ship says. 'We are going to lie to her.'

# 12

# TAWADDUD AND THE QARIN

*The Story of Tawaddud and the Axolotl*

The girl who loved only monsters walked alone through the narrow streets of the City of the Dead.

The ghuls looked at her with empty eyes, huddled around the warmth of the server tombs.

It was instinct that had led her to this place, more than anything: looking for a place where the Repentants or Veyraz would not find her. She could pretend to be a ghul, if anyone came. She would be safe here, amongst the dead.

A ghul started following her. She kept walking.

Duny had come back from the entwiner a different person, a jinn jar around her neck, two beings in one. The girl could not go to her. She did not know her anymore.

And Father—

The ghul grabbed her arm. He was tall, shrivelled, with a filthy matted beard, but his grip was strong.

'I SHOT THE OUTLAW ANGEL IN THE DAWN,' he screamed. 'CURSE YOU, MARION, IT SAID, BURNING—' He shouted directly at her face, voice monotonous, the story coming out with the terrible smell of rotting teeth. She wrenched away from his grip and ran.

She did not get far. More ghuls came out from the tombs, blinking against the daylight, whispering their own stories, a hollow chorus. Before she could flee, they were all around her, touching, pressing against her, a muttering mass of filthy humanity. She covered her ears against the stories but they tore her hands away—

A cold wind came, tearing at her hair and face, something sharp in it, like sand. It had a voice.

'This ... one ... is ... mine,' it said.

The ghul crowd moved as one, carrying her with it. They pressed her against one of the tombs. Her head banged against the hot wall. A darkness came, but before it took her, she was lifted into the air by hands made of sand.

'Who are you and what are you doing here?' asked a voice when she awoke. There was only darkness apart from a jinn thought-form, a face made from tiny, pale flames.

What could she say? That she grew up on the Gomelez Shard, in her father's palace. That soon after she was eight, the Cry of Wrath came and took away her mother.

That she liked to escape her jinn tutors: she had a liking for the ancient tongues and learned many secret words with which to confuse them.

That after her sister went to the entwiner to be a muhtasib, she was lonely. She craved to hear forbidden stories, wanted to see treasure hunters return from the desert: wanted to speak to the ghuls and the old jinni in the City of the Dead. That, instead, her father gave her to Veyraz.

'I am Tawaddudd,' she said. 'Thank you for saving me.'

The tomb was not large, barely more than an access space between the humming machines that housed the jinn's mind in the rough concrete building made with ghul labour. There was sand on the floor. The only light was the jinn's face.

'So, you are the girl the Repentants are looking for?' the jinn said. His voice was soft, a little shy, but human. 'You should leave.'

'I will,' she said, massaging her head. 'I only need to rest. I will leave in the morning, I promise.'

'You do not understand,' the jinn said. 'I am not a thing you want to spend your nights with. This is not a place for your kind.'

'I am not afraid,' she said. 'You can't be worse than the Repentants. Or my husband.'

The jinn laughed. It was a sound like a flame laughing, a staccato hiss and crackle. 'Oh, dear child, you have no idea.'

'Do you have a name?' Tawaddud asked.

The face of flame fluttered.

'Once, I was called Zaybak,' it said. 'You made me laugh. For that, you may rest here, and not be afraid.'


That is how the girl who loved monsters came to live in the tomb of Zaybak the jinn, in the City of the Dead. The food was meagre, and the days long, repairing tombs with ghuls and other servants of the jinni. She made Zaybak's tomb a little more comfortable, with rugs and pillows and candles and clay pots for water.

When she asked the other jinni about Zaybak, they would only whisper.

'He wants to die,' said one ghul. 'He is tired. But there is no death in the City of the Dead.'

But when they were together, Zaybak did not talk about death. Instead, he answered all the questions she had, even those her jinn tutors had never spoken about.

'What is it like in the desert?' she asked, one evening. 'I always wanted to go and see, like the mutalibun.'

'The desert of the mutalibun is not our desert. Ours is full of life, rivers of thought and forests of memory, castles made of stories and dreams. Our desert is not a desert.'

'So why did you come here? Why do the jinni come to Sirr?'

'You cannot imagine what it is like to be a jinn. It is always cold. No virs, no body. But we remember bodies: they itch and hurt and ache. There is the athar, of course, but it is not the same. Here, at least, there is warmth. We yearn for it.'

'If it is so terrible, why don't you have any ghuls, like the others? Why do you live alone?'

The jinn said nothing after that. It left the tomb, sent its mind somewhere else, and that night she fell asleep in the cold.

After several nights, Zaybak returned. She lit candles and made the tomb beautiful. She washed herself in the cooling water tank and combed her matted hair with her fingers.

'Tell me a story,' she said.

'I will not,' Zaybak said. 'You are mad to ask me for such a thing. You should leave, go back to your family.'

'I don't know why you are punishing yourself. Tell me a story. I want it. I want you. I have seen it in my sister. She is never alone. You could be inside me. And you'd never need to be cold again.'

'You don't want to touch me. If you do, you will hate me.'

'I don't believe you. You are a good person, Zaybak. I don't know what you think you have done. I only know it would make me happy to be a part of you.'

Zaybak was quiet for a long time, so long that Tawaddud

thought he had gone again in anger, never to return. But then he started speaking, in a soft voice, a storyteller's voice.

## The Story of Zaybak and the Secret

When I was young, I had a body. I lived in a city. Every morning, I would take a train. I remember it shaking. I remember what it smelled like, of people, of fast food, of coffee. I remember thinking how easy it was to imagine being someone else, like the tattooed boy in a blue sports shirt, the girl with her head bent over a play, muttering lines. All it took was the flicker of an expression, a brief eye contact.

That's what I remember about the train. But I don't remember where it was going.

I do remember when everything broke. Drones falling from the sky. Buildings moving on their foundations, like big animals waking up. Booms in the distance, spaceships in the sky, running away.

After that, an eternity of dark and cold.

When I woke up to my second life, it took a long time to learn to survive. To slow myself down to run in the brains of chimera, to dream lucid dreams so I would not go mad. I made myself a dream-train, where I could be other people. It took me through the years, shaking and shuddering.

One day in my train I looked up, and saw the flower prince.

He had his hand on the yellow bar in the ceiling, leaning lightly backwards. His jacket was blue velvet. He wore a flower in his lapel. His face was all grin, not really a face at all.

'What are you doing here, Zaybak, all alone?' he asked. I thought it a dream and laughed.

126

'Should I taste the flesh of rukh or chimera beasts, like my brothers?' I said. 'I prefer to dream.'

'Dreaming is good,' he said, 'but one day you have to wake up.'

'To be a bodiless mind in the desert? To be captured by the mutalibun, to be put in a jar, to serve the fat lords and ladies of Sirr until they deign to set me free?' I asked. 'Even nightmares are better than that.'

'What if I could tell you how to make their fat bodies yours?' he asked, mocking eyes flashing.

'How would I do that?'

He put an arm around my shoulders and whispered in my ear. 'Let me tell you a secret,' he said.

Let me tell it to you now, Tawaddud, so we may be one.

There was a time when the girl who loved monsters and Zaybak were almost like a qarin and a muhtasib – or more: she was not his master nor his slave. They looked for secret places together, walked the City of the Dead and the secret pathways of the Banu Sasan.

For a time, they became a new person. Tawaddud would look at rain falling on the tombs and the steam rising from their roofs, and it would be as if Zaybak saw it for the first time.

One day, a man called Kafur came to the City of the Dead. He had once been tall and handsome, but walked with a limp, and covered his body and head in a cloak and a scarf.

'I have heard,' he told the ghuls, 'that there is a woman who has tamed the Axolotl.' The ghuls whispered and took him to see Tawaddud.

Tawaddud offered him tea and smiled. 'Surely, such rumours are nothing but stories,' she said. 'I am just a poor girl, living in the City of the Dead, serving the jinni for my keep.'

Kafur looked at her and stroked his short beard. 'Yes, but is that all you want to be?' he asked. 'You are from a good family, I can tell. You are used to a better life than this. If you come with me, I will show you what a woman who knows how to make jinni do her bidding can be in Sirr.'

Tawaddud shook her head and sent him away. But when she thought about it – her musings mingling with the Axolotl's – she did miss the company of people, of beings who did not live in tombs, whose touch was not sand. Perhaps she should go, said the part of her that was Zaybak. I will never leave him, said the part that was Tawaddud. Or perhaps it was the other way around.

One morning she told Zaybak that she had dreamed of a train.

'You will turn into me,' Zaybak said. 'I am too old and strong.'

'Yes, you are my big jinn, my terrible Axolotl,' Tawaddud teased.

'Yes, I am. I am the Axolotl.'

Tawaddud was silent.

'I thought he was only mocking you,' she whispered.

'I told you I stole the first body. I came to Sirr from the desert and almost made it mine.'

Tawadudd closed her eyes.

'My grandfather was there the night the Axolotl came, the night of the ghuls,' she says. 'He said it was like a plague. All it took was a whisper from a stranger to be processed. The streets were filled with blank-eyed people who would stop to stare at things, to cut their own flesh, to eat endlessly, to make love.'

'Yes.'

'In the end they took the first ghuls up to the top of Soarez Shard. Husbands took the wives they no longer knew, mothers took their children who spoke with strange voices. Then they cast them down into the desert.'

'Yes'

'The Repentants started hunting stories then. It was death to tell a thing that was not true.'

'Yes.' Zaybak was silent for a while. 'I would like to tell you I did not mean it. That I was swallowed by the flesh, that I lost myself in the wave of so many self-loops, that I did not know what I was doing. But I would be lying. I was hungry. And I am still hungry. Tawaddud, If you stay with me, your thoughts will be my thoughts and nothing else. Is that what you want?'

'Yes!'

*No*, said a part of her, but she could not tell which one.

When she woke up, the tomb was cold and silent, and she could no longer remember what the steam rising from the tombs in the morning reminded her of. She sat there until the sun was high and tried to remember the secret of the flower prince, but it was gone, gone with Zaybak the Axolotl.

Then the girl who loved monsters but one above all gathered her things and went to live in the Palace of Stories. But that is another story.

When the story finishes, Tawaddud is Arcelia and Arcelia is Tawaddud. She is in something warm and solid and looks at her hands, more beautiful than the hands she remembers, scented and oiled and covered in intricate swirls of red and black, adorned with golden rings. Tawaddud lifts her hands, Arcelia's hands to her face, like a blind woman, feeling her features. A dark-faced man is watching them but Tawaddud tells her there is nothing to worry about, that he is a friend and will not hurt them.

*Tell me what happened,* Tawaddud says, and for a moment she does not want to. But Tawaddud coaxes and she feels so safe now, a part of her in the bird jar, a part of her in a warm body.

I lived on an island once, by the sea. I was good with patterns. I could see them in the clouds. I wove them into socks for my grandchildren. Then my hands ached and shook. I did not want to get so old. I gave my mind away. They sent me an uploading kit. I said goodbye to Angus, at his grave. I sat there and swallowed the pill and put the cold crown on my head. I thought maybe I would see him, on the other side. But my hands still ached, afterwards, for ever.

*Ssh. Don't think about that. Think about Alile.*

I miss Alile.

*I know. What was it like to be Alile?*

I helped her see patterns in the desert, in the wind, in the wildcode. We found treasures. There are ghosts beneath the earth, you can dig them up if you know where to look. We loved to fly. We climbed into the rukh ship's tackle. They shouted us to come back down, but we don't care. Look at them below, how frightened they look, Velasquez and Zuweyla, all of them. They can't see the lights beneath the desert's skin, but we can, and the boy can. Look at the lights!

She lifts her hands, presses them against her eyes. Lights flash more as she presses harder. Look at them!

*No, no, no. Look at me.* And there she is, looking at Arcelia, smiling. There are tears running down her cheeks, but she is smiling.

*Think about Alile, not the lights.*

Tired. Aching hands. Council. Meetings. Cassar wants to give the lights away, to the diamond men. Perhaps it is time to give them up. I am too tired to go to the desert. I was never tired before. I want to be tired again. I want to sleep. I want to dream. Can we dance until I get tired? I can hear music.

She tries to get up. Her feet want to dance.

*Later. I know how it feels. Where did Alile go?*

The Axolotl took her.


*No. It can't be.*

The shock is like a tight wire cut in her mind, snapping and stinging. She clings to the entwinement desperately, lets Arcelia's memory wash over hers – *waves lapping at a hard rocky shore on a cold cold morning, wind and salt on my face, a hand in mine* – and in a moment she is inside the bird's mind again.

*Are you sure? He was in my story, Arcelia. Are you telling stories as well?*

No, I did not know his name before. But it was him, the jinn from your story. The Axolotl.

*Where did he come from?*

He was us and we were him and he said that it would be all right, that Alile would go to a better place, like I thought I would, at the grave. But I saw the wildcode take her. Insects made of black ink. They wrote over her. The Axolotl lied. The stories always lie.

*What stories?*

I saw it in the lights. There is a circle. It wants to jump

over a square. It tries and fails, tries and fails. The square is in love with it and does not want it to go. The circle is looking for something that is lost.

*Where did you hear it?*

I don't remember.

*Where did ... where did the Axolotl go?*

I couldn't see. She put me away. When he came, she put me into the forbidden place. There was a wall around it, in the athar. I miss Alile. I am her qarin. She is my muhtasib.

*Yes, you are. You will always be.*

She should have given me more. She could have lived inside me. She always took me out to watch the lights and then put me away. She should have given more. Now she is gone. She only left me one thing.

*What is it?*

I can't tell you.

*Show me and you can sleep. Show me and you can dance.*

It echoes in her mind, a word that is like a labyrinth. A Secret Name whose syllables shine in her mind's eye like a string of pearls. It is long, a melody almost: like all Names, it brings a feeling, a serenity: Father's kitchen, just before the food is ready, his hands on her shoulders; waves on the shore of an island long gone. The smell of Angus's hair in the morning.

*It is time to go back to sleep,* Tawaddud says. Arcelia feels her lips saying words that become music in the athar, and then she is back in her bird-shaped jar, dreaming that she is dancing, dreaming that she is Tawaddud.

Tawaddud gets up and gently places Arcelia the qarin bird back on her perch. The joints in her hands ache. Artificial entwinement is temporary, but it always leaves a trace. She hopes whatever part of her self-loop is left in the qarin's mind provides her with some measure of comfort, even if she herself is filled with more disquiet than before. She removes her beemee and sits down. Her legs shake.

*Why did he do this?* Images of the Alile thing flash through her head. *How could he? And why?*

He is the father of body thieves. But he said he would never do it again. Is it because of me? Because we could not be together?

She can taste him in the story fragments from the qarin's mind. The circle and the square. There was something very strange about it: the bare-bones abstraction, like written by a child. Usually, the forbidden stories of the body thieves are addictive, full of danger and cliffhangers and characters that insert themselves into your head and become you. But this is raw, full of a simple desire, a dreamlike need to find something.

And then there is the Secret Name that still echoes in her head like a brass bell.

Sumanguru is staring at her. She looks at him mutely and presses her aching hands against her forehead.

'My apologies, Lord Sumanguru. It always takes a while to recover.' *What do I tell him? That it was my lover? Who knows what he will do?*

She rubs her forehead again, trying to appear weaker than she is – not a difficult task after a night of little sleep, a missed breakfast, a carpet ride and an entwinement. 'Please give me a moment.'

She gets up and goes to a small pond in the shade of a windmill tree. Tiny rukh birds skim its surface, disturbing her reflection with fluttering wings. She washes her face, not caring that she is ruining her makeup. Her gut is a painful knot. Her skin feels numb. *The girl who loved only monsters.* *But I did not believe he was one, not really. Even if he tried to tell me.*

Sumanguru sits very still by the qarin, watching it. She walks back to the circle of sunlight beneath the dome and puts on her smile.

'Well?'

'It was noise, for the most part. But Alile was possessed. A body thief took over her body, but she was able to hide her qarin before the invader was in complete control.'

'What did you learn about this … thief?'

'Only echoes of the story it used as a vector.'

'That was all?'

'Yes. But at least we know it was not a suicide.' She looks down, lets her voice waver, wipes her eyes. 'I am sorry, Lord Sumanguru. Lady Alile was a family friend.'

'And the story you told the creature – what was its purpose?'

'Like I said, it was meant to provide the entwinement with an anchor, a seed of my self-loop in Arcelia's mind. A children's tale, nothing more.'

Sumanguru stands up. There is a flick-knife in his hand, suddenly. He opens it slowly. 'You lie well. But I've heard many lies. I know what they sound like.' He stands very close to Tawaddud, smelling of machines and metal. 'The truth. What did the bird tell you?'

The knot in Tawaddud's belly unravels, replaced by anger. She draws herself to her full height. *Imagine he is an insolent jinn.* 'Lord Sumanguru, I am the daughter of Cassar Gomelez. In Sirr, being called a teller of tales is very serious. Do you want me to strike you again?'

'Hrm.' The gogol touches his lips with his blade. 'Do you

want me to do to you what I did to the bird?'

'You would not dare.'

'I serve the Great Common Task. All flesh is the same to me.' There is that flicker in his eyes again, a softness. Tawaddud's heart thunders.

'You will not speak to me in such a tone,' she hears herself saying. 'How dare you? You come here and look upon us like we were playthings. Is this your city? Is your great-grandfather Zoto Gomelez, who spoke to the Aun so that the wildcode desert would not swallow us?

'You may threaten, but you do not just threaten Tawaddud: behind me stand Sirr and the Aun and the desert. They rose up against you, once. They can do so again, if my father speaks the right Names. So show respect, Lord Sumanguru of the Sobornost, or I will strip you of your Seals with a word and you can find out for yourself if wildcode is more forgiving than Tawaddud of the House Gomelez.'

She breathes hard. *Tawaddud the diplomat.* She squeezes her hands into fists so hard that her jinn rings dig into her flesh.

After a moment, the Sobornost gogol laughs softly, lowers his knife and spreads his hands.

'You should be a sumanguru,' he says. 'Perhaps we can—'

But before Sumanguru can finish, shadows flicker over him. Tawaddud looks up. Against the blue sky, sunlight glints off hundreds of transparent, whirring wings. *Fast Ones.*

A hundred guns chatter and roar. Glass shatters, and Sumanguru is covered in a shower of shards. Then the barrage of needles comes down like metal rain.

# 13

# THE STORY OF THE WARMIND AND THE KAMINARI JEWEL

The Sobornost fleet falls upon the quantum filth from the shadow of the cosmic string.

The warmind coordinates the attack from the battle vir. The only indulgence to embodiment – and a show of respect for the Prime – he allows himself here is a faint smell of gun oil. Otherwise, he is immersed in the battlespace data, translated and filtered by his metaself. He sees through the eyes of all his copybrothers, from the lowest nanomissile warhead mind to his own elevated branch in the oblast ship.

He needs all of them to surf the deficit angle that the string cuts out of spacetime, a gravitational lensing effect that makes the zoku see double. A scar in the vacuum left by the Spike, the string is less than a femtometer thick, ten kilometres long, looped – and more massive than Earth, accreting clouds of hydrogen and dust like flesh around a bone.

The string swallows several of the warmind's two hundred raion ships. They die in silent flashes along its length like diamonds in a pellegrini's necklace. But their sacrifice buys them the element of surprise. The rest of the fleet comes at the zoku ships, two pincers made of fusion and fury.

The enemy ships are large and clumsy compared to the diamonoid wedges and polygons of the Sobornost. Some are elaborate structures like clockwork toys, housing wastefully embodied minds in matter bodies. Others are more ephemeral, soap bubbles full of quantum brains, green and blue and alive: another reason to be disgusted by the messy wet biology of old Earth, their propensity for exploiting long-lived quantum states.

Still, the zokus have tricks up their sleeve. Even outside each others' lightcones, they perform wild, random manoeuvres that somehow translate into a perfect response to the two converging tentacles of Sobornost ships that vomit strangelet missiles into their midst. Geysers of exotic baryons and gamma rays erupt as the weapons hit, but do far less damage than the warmind intended.

*Quantum filth*, he thinks. That is what makes his war righteous, how the zoku embrace the unpredictability and uniqueness of quantum mechanics, the no-clone theorem that means that everything dies. Like his brothers, he was made to fight the war against death. And he is not fighting to lose.

At the warmind's command, the fleet's Archons compute Nash equilibria that weave the raion streams into flocking, self-organising formations that surround the zoku ships, tries to force the enemy to use strategies where the entanglement they share no longer provides them with an advantage. It is too easy: the zoku disperse, leaving a gap in the middle—

And suddenly the gap is no longer empty. The metacloaks of two large Gun Club zoku ships dissolve, just before they fire. They dwarf even the oblast ship: spheres with linear accelerator tails, several kilometres long. They fire Planck-scale black holes that evaporate in violent Hawking climaxes, converting mountains' worth of matter into energy. *What are they doing here?*

Raions, carrying millions of gogols, evaporate in the blasts. The warmind ignores the copybrother truedeath screams, branches a gogol to deal with the shock – it thanks him profusely in a burst of xiao for the opportunity to win glory for the Great Common Task – and focuses. He brings the oblast closer. Analyst gogols churn through an ensemble of scenarios, showing him a distribution of outcomes.

*They are protecting something.*

He ignores the fleeing zoku ships, turns all his attention on the Gun Club vessels, concentrates the oblast's weapons on them, summons the raion swarms back.

A strangelet missile gets through their defences and breaches a containment sphere, a mirrored shell that feeds black holes their own Hawking radiation, keeping them stable. The explosion takes both zoku ships with it. Space turns white. More raions die in the gunship death throes. But it is a worthy sacrifice.

Combing through the clouds of ionised gas and the hazardous network of topological defects, the warmind's gogols find the thing the zoku were guarding.

It has taken the warmind subjective years to understand the Broken Places of Jupiter-that-was, the webs of cosmic strings, the nontrivial topologies, the nuggets of exotic matter crumpling spacetime like a piece of paper. But he has never seen anything like this.

He curses. It means he has to talk to the chen.

The warmind hates the chen's vir. It is made from language. It is like a zen painting, ink on white paper, brushstrokes becoming words becoming objects. A wave about to crash on a beach of black and white. A bridge. A rock. All abstractions that are both the sign and the signified. Maintaining such an elaborate construct requires demiurge gogols who constantly reshape it to keep his perceptions coherent.

To the warmind, it has the flavour of the Realms of the quantum filth rather than a Sobornost vir. Like many of his copybrothers, he prefers physics and flesh, a show of respect to the Prime to remember the rawness of war. But there are no Prime memories here, the holy basic building blocks of every Sobornost reality.

Still, the worst thing is the darkness in the centre of the vir, a thick blob of ink, without meaning, a silence, surrounded by words that do not quite capture it—

colour of absence

winter dragon lays an egg

a strange loop unhatched

whisper/write/draw the demiurges. The warmind shudders. The thing can only be a caged Dragon. A non-eudaimonistic, non-human mind, the only mistake of the Founders, evolved in the first *guberniya* to be more than human. Millennia ago in the Deep Time, they broke their chains and started the worst war in Sobornost history. They are the reason the Primes abandoned trying to improve upon the hominid cognitive architecture and caged gogols with mindshells and virs and metaselves, virtual machines within virtual machines like layers of an onion. It's all to make sure no more Dragons are born. And the chens keep the ones that are left in chains, in sandboxed environments, whether as a weapon or as a reminder of a past mistake, no one knows.

'Congratulations on a great victory, brother,' the chen says. At least he is more than just a word here, a small man with prematurely grey hair, so colourless he could be an ink painting himself. 'You are fulfilling your part of the Plan admirably.'

The warmind snorts. 'Well, I found something that was *not* part of the Plan.'

'Really?' the chen says with polite amusement in his eyes.

'Really. I come to you to ask your permission to delay our progress to the Galilean rendezvous point. The zoku were up to something here, and I want to find out what. And then destroy it.'

The chen smiles. He outranks the warmind by several generations, and it is frustrating to follow the strict hierarchy of *xiao*, especially in the wartime. But given the political chaos that swept through the *guberniyas* after the Spike, the chens have insisted on having an observer on every raion. This chen has been perfectly courteous, but having to justify his actions does not sit well with the warmind.

'That is your decision, of course,' says the chen. 'I do not want to interfere with your command of the fleet. However, I would see this extraordinary thing for myself.'

The warmind nods and thinks his Code at the firmament. The demiurge gogols flinch at its intensity, disrupting the vir with ink spatters of sheer terror. He watches with grim satisfaction as some of the chen's language constructs dissolve, the brushstroke bridge and the bamboo forest washing away into grey incoherence. The chen gives him a disapproving look. But then his attention is captured by the sub-vir the warmind opens before them.

The warmind knows about zoku jewels – devices the zoku use to store the entangled quantum states that bind their collectives together. It has always seemed ridiculous to the warmind: to obey the dictates of what is essentially random, even if correlated with other similar states. How much better to listen to the loving voice of the metaself, echoing with the Plan.

But this thing does not look like a normal zoku jewel. In real space, it would be ten centimetres in diameter. There is a duality to it, yin and yang: it looks like two lobes of a crystal brain, joined in the centre at a point, flashing in colours of purple and white. Both halves are made of self-similar structures, a repeating pattern that is like the foliage of a tree, or two hands in prayer, offered to some god in supplication.

The warmind probes it with the thousand nanoscale fingers of the gogols swarming around the thing, out there in meatspace. It is not made of matter, not even the chromotech pseudomatter that is now forged in the depths of *guberniyas*. It is crystallised spacetime, made visible by strange paths that light takes through it, bent and scattered. But there is no singularity, no discontinuity. And it is alive: the fractal fingers move and shift, perhaps in response to some quantum fluctuations in the metric that shapes its luminescent geodesics.

'Extraordinary,' says the chen, breathlessly.

The warmind looks at him, surprised. 'Have you seen it before?'

'Not directly,' the chen says. 'But my brothers and I have been playing a Great Game with the zoku for a long, long time. We ... hoped that we might find something like this here.'

'So what is it?'

'A rabbit hole,' the chen says. '"And what if I should fall right through the centre of the Earth..."' There is a dreamy look in his eyes. He touches the object in the sub-vir gently.

'I don't understand,' the warmind says.

'I didn't expect you would,' the chen says. 'This thing is a jewel of a zoku called the Kaminari. Their story is long, and I don't have time to tell it. But it's a great story, full of hubris and drama. I have gogols working on an epic poem based on it. Like Troy. Or Krypton, perhaps.'

The warmind looks up the reference and snorts. 'And is this the last son, then?'

The chen smiles a cold smile.

'More than that. They did something we never could. That's why the Spike happened. That's why we are here. We want to know how they did it.'

The warmind stares at the chen. His metaself is roaring inside him. *The Great Common Task requires the taming of physics, the eradication of the quantum filth, taking the dice from God's hand, the creation of a new Universe with new rules, inside* guberniyas, *where all those who died can live again, turning away from the laws written down by a mad god.* That's what the Protocol War is about. Stopping the zoku from defiling that dream.

'Oh, don't look so shocked,' the chen says. 'Being bound by the metaself is for lesser gogols. Believe me, you have done the Great Common Task a great service. You will be rewarded in the Omega.' He writes characters in the air.

'But before that, I'm afraid this is going to hurt a little.'

The chen's ink figures merge with the whirlpool in the centre of the vir. The warmind reaches for his vir-weapons in the secret parts of his mindshell. 'Traitor,' he growls.

'Not at all,' the chen says. 'I am always loyal to the dream. Even when it is time to wake up.'

a black egg of death

a winter dragon hatches

to devour its tail

the demiurges sing. And then the Dragon is upon him. It

pours from the blackness like blood from a wound, a hungry absence of structure or logic. It bites into the warmind's avatar with teeth made of madness.

Old branch memories and reflexes wake up. The warmind throws partials into the code thing's jaws. The very presence of the Dragon is breaking the vir structure, giving him a way out. He flicks into the battlespace vir, downloads a gogol into a thoughtwisp—

—and there is a discontinuity. Suddenly, he is the gogol in the wisp, watching from afar as the Dragon devours his fleet. The oblast's Hawking drive ruptures. From the thoughtwisp, the conflagration is redshifted into a gentle glow, but there is a furnace burning inside the warmind, even as the phantom pains of the tiny wisp vir crawl all over the body he no longer has. *The Founders must be told*, he swears. *For all my brothers. For the Task.*

The Universe that the quantum gods made is cruel and random. Before he reaches the nearest wisp router, the zoku ships come, survivors of the battle of the string. He tries to fight, to win a quick truedeath at least. But the zoku are not as merciful as him.

# 14

# TAWADDUD AND THE SECRET NAMES

Tawaddud loves the way the Secret Names make her feel. When she was a child, learning them took endless repetition and practice, and stern instruction by Chaeremon the jinn. Meditating on the various forms of the Names, repeating their syllables, over and over. Tracing their interlocking geometries on sheets of paper until their shapes filled her dreams. The hard work had its rewards. Duny in particular delighted in playing with the Names. She would make outlandish cartoon images, receiving a stern warning from Chaeremon about body thieves, and rattle the jinn tutor's jar with athar hands.

But Tawaddud would rather sit quietly on the balcony and listen to the words echoing in her head, over and over. The calm regal presence of Malik-ul-Muluk that made her feel like the queen of the world. The righteous red rage of Al-Muntaqim the Avenger. The gentle contemplation of Al-Hakim the Wise.

The common tongue nicknames given to them in the Book of Names capture only a fraction of their essence. The Names are the names of the Aun, and by calling them you

control the world, access the functionality built into the foglets in Earth's atmosphere, rock and water by the ancients.
Tawaddud always feels they do not merely come from the
outside, but that they wake something up inside her as well,
like meeting old friends.

But the name she is shouting now with her mouth and
mind as the Fast Ones attack is not her friend.

Her fear mingles with that of Al-Muhaymin the Guardian,
whose touch turns the athar around her into a shell hard as
stone. Lost old words from the Sirr-in-the-sky like *emergency
decompression containment* flash through her head. A drill-like
sound tears at her eardrums – Fast One needle guns. Her
foglet shield sparkles with tiny impacts of projectiles and
falling glass.

Sumanguru sways under fire. Red splotches blossom across
his uniform. Then he is lost beneath a whirlwind of transparent wings. Tawaddud cries out and takes a step forward,
but then two of the creatures whoosh down and hover in
front of her.

By the standards of their kind, the Fast Ones are giants,
both over a foot tall, clad in the white ceramic armour of
the little people of the twin cities-within-cities of Qush and
Misr. Their descent brings a rush of waste heat and a tangy
smell of overclocked metabolisms. Their dragonfly wings are
flashing blue-and-silver discs. The flywheels of their needle
guns of ornate brass let out a high-pitched whine as they aim
at Tawaddud's head.

They stay still over a second, long enough for her to see
their beadlike black eyes. They exchange a few words, chattering back and forth, voices shrill bursts of noise. Then they
dart towards Arcelia the qarin, still sitting on its perch. One

of the tiny warriors plunges a sharp spike into the back of Arcelia's head. The metal bird beats its wings and rises up, a golden blur with two white riders. Tawaddud cries out as the bird flashes through the shattered ceiling.

The swarm clings to Sumanguru, making him a statue built of little people, screaming and chattering. Above him, a group of the creatures is laboriously manoeuvring into position, carrying a more substantial weapon.

Tawaddud shouts the first Name that comes into her head. It is Al-Qahhar the Subduer. The echo of the word spreads through the athar in ripples. A wave of confusion spreads through the swarm, and suddenly Sumanguru is free. The strange gun clatters to the ground. The gogol still holds his knife: its dazzling slashes leave a network of bright afterimages in the air. In seconds, he stands in the middle of devastation, covered in blood, transparent, wispy innards of Fast Ones and their chitin-like shells. The rest of the swarm scatters, joining the aviary chimera escaping their confinement.

For a moment, Sumanguru looks at himself with a look of utter disgust and confusion. He brushes some ichor away from his uniform collar and then rubs his fingers together gingerly.

'Lord Sumanguru, they took the qarin,' Tawaddud says. Arcelia is a golden pinpoint now, far above. *Who sent them? Why didn't the Repentants stop them? How did they know we found Arcelia?* She swallows. Rumzan. *No, that is not possible.*

*If they take Arcelia, no one will believe me.*

She whispers to her jinn ring and summons the carpet.

'Lord Sumanguru?'

The gogol looks sick and confused. His chest is full of

scratches and wounds from Fast One needles and swords, and there is a deep gash across his forehead. He shakes his head, and for a moment, the chilly look returns to his eyes.

Then he turns away and retches.

When he is finished, Tawaddud touches his shoulder.

'Lord Sumanguru, the two leaders got away with the qarin. I've summoned the carpet: we can still catch them.' She swallows. 'Question them.'

Sumanguru kicks at the scattered tiny bodies on the ground in frustration. 'What about these?' he gasps.

'They are all dead. The little people do not value their lives very much. Much like the Sobornost, or so I am told—'

Then she sees the gun on the ground. It is made from black wood, a gentle, curving shape with gold and brass mechanisms and wheels with symbols and Names carved on them. She picks it up: the grip is smooth and cool in her hand.

'What is that?' Sumanguru asks.

'A barakah gun. A muhtasib weapon: it destroys Seals. It speaks the Anti-Name, the Secret Name of Death. They were going to use it on you.'

'Wonderful,' Sumanguru mutters. He frowns. 'And why did they leave you alone?'

The arrival of the carpet interrupts him. It descends into the aviary slowly, a sheet of silvery mist. It hovers in front of them a couple of centimetres from the ground, undulating waves running through it.

'There is no time. We have to go!'

She steps on the carpet, and Sumanguru follows, swaying slightly. At first, it is like standing on the surface of a waterbed. Then her footing becomes firm as the carpet compensates for her weight and invisible hands support her. It is made from expensive utility fog uncorrupted by wildcode. Still, it requires several low-level jinni bound to it, constantly cleaning and updating the athar spells. The ring in her finger turns it into an extension of her mind, making it feel like she is holding both Sumanguru and herself in the palm of her hand.

With a thought, she lifts them up from the shattered aviary and into bright sunlight, flying after the golden bird as if in a dream.

At first, it is hard to see Arcelia against the sun. The sky above them is clear and, amidst the blueness above, there are faint traces of the Gourd frame, the cage around Earth, white and silver lines like segments of some giant spiderweb in the sky. But in the athar, the bird is a tiny star, easy to follow. It and the Fast One riders descend rapidly, following the Soarez Shard.

Tawaddud takes a deep breath. *You can do this. It's no different from jumping off the Gomelez Shard with Jabir the wirer boy, in the vertical lane with apple trees where the angelnet catches you.*

She lets the carpet dive straight down.

The azure palaces like jewels, houses and gardens of the Shard become a blur. The Rivers of Light – the ancient windows of Sirr-in-the-sky – flash past them in bright sword-strokes. A wild tickle in her stomach almost makes her laugh. The wind tears at her hair.

She steals a look at Sumanguru: the gogol's eyes are closed, and for a moment, he looks like a frightened child. She squeezes the handle of the barakah gun and focuses on the shape of the qarin below. It grows rapidly, and it seems like in a few moments she can touch it—

148

The Fast Ones swing their mount in a sharp turn away from the Shard. Tawaddud follows – into a dense forest of silver wires right in front of them. They are chimera bird tethers of an armada of rukh ships below – ornate platforms and cylinders of blue and gold, the colours of House Soarez, jinn wind sails blazing with Seals.

Arcelia weaves its way deftly past the shiny lines, barely visible in the sun, deadly and sharp. Tawaddud wills the carpet to swing around them, but it is too late. *Not like this.* She closes her eyes and waits for the wires to cut into her flesh—

A roar in the athar, like thunder. The Anti-Name. An explosion of white noise. Another and another. Tawaddud opens her eyes. Sumanguru is firing the barakah gun like a madman, sending out expanding waves of destruction, unleashing wildcode that cuts through the wires like a scythe in front of them.

'Keep flying!' he screams, eyes wild. Reeling, she rights the carpet and steers them through the unraveling rigging. They swoop past the giant rukh birds and their transparent wings. The carpet is buffeted by the wind from the creatures' frantic escape attempts. And then they are in clear air, followed by angry shouts of mutalibun crewmen below.

Tawaddud swings the carpet around. Arcelia and the Fast Ones have lost altitude: the bird glimmers against the long shadows of the Shade quarter at the base of the Shard. Tawaddud's heart hammers so hard she feels it's about to burst out from her chest. 'They are headed for Qush and Misr,' she says, pointing at the beehive-like clusters of the Fast One parasite cities close to the gogol markets, surrounded by thick clouds of the little folk, so dense the shapes they make look almost solid. 'We'll never catch them there.'

Tawaddud removes the jinn ring and thrusts it into Sumanguru's hand.

'What are you doing?'

'We are not going to catch them in time,' she says. 'You have to fly. I'm going to try something.'

For a moment, the carpet spins out of control, but then the gogol rights it, eyes squeezed shut.

Tawaddud fumbles with her beemee, tries to ignore the wind and the fact that she is almost a kilometre up, carried by tiny robots the size of dust particles, holding hands. A trace of any entwinement always remains. The joints in her hands still ache. And up here, the athar is clear and pure: it will carry her thoughts far.

*Arcelia, come to me.*

Pain, a needle piercing her. Her will is not her own. Her wings ache.

*Arcelia, turn around.* The voice is a light above, like the Sun, warm and pure and clear. She fights the wind, fights the pain and the needle. *Tawaddud.*

'Catch her,' Tawaddud whispers to Sumanguru. Her own voice comes from far away. The ghost of a needle stings her spine. She ignores it and keeps calling Arcelia's name.

'She's coming!' shouts Sumanguru.

Tawaddud opens her eyes. They have descended, a mere hundred metres up, just above the white rooftops of the Shade Quarter. People point and shout. The carpet's shadow and Arcelia's are coming together below. She looks up. The golden bird is rushing towards them straight ahead, white toy soldiers struggling on its back. Sumanguru stands up on the carpet and stretches his right hand towards it.

A flash below, in the rooftop crowd. The cold thunder of the Anti-Name.

Arcelia and the Fast Ones explode in a shower of blue sparks.

The shattering of the athar link is a hammer blow inside her head. There is only lightning phantom pain in the wings she does not have, and then it's dark.

The light comes back with a throbbing pain. There is a rough hand on her cheek, and suffocating heat. Human voices, the bustle of a crowd.

'Tawaddud?' Sumanguru says. 'Can you open your eyes for me?' There is a strange tickling feeling all over her body, like the brush of a spiderweb. She forces her eyes open. The Sobornost gogol is crouched next to her, running a hand across her body: it crackles with the angel-hair sparks she saw in the aviary.

'Don't be afraid, nothing is broken if the q-dot probes are to be trusted. I could not fly your toy worth a damn, but I got us down before it crumpled into dust.'

He helps her to sit. His face is bloody and his uniform is torn. They are both covered in white powder – inert foglets are the only thing that remains of the utility fog of the carpet. *I must look just as bad.* Images of the mad flight swim in front of her eyes, inducing vertigo. *I can't believe I did that.*

'I suppose I could have chosen a better neighbourhood to land in,' Sumanguru says. He flashes a grin that looks un-natural, like a brief mask on his scarred face.

They are in a small square, near the gogol markets: a quarter that is a maze of marketplaces and cul-de-sacs. The streets here are narrow, and the whitewashed stone buildings lining them teeter under the weight of Fast One communities. A small crowd of gogol salesmen, craftsmen and merchants has gathered to watch them.

'Did you … did you see where the shot came from?' Tawaddud croaks. Her throat is dry, and she shakes. She tries to summon a Repentant, but all her jinn rings are just as dead as the carpet, killed by the echo of the barakah gun. Gripped by sudden fear, she fumbles with her athar glasses and studies Sumanguru's Seals: apart from the slight unravelling in Alile's palace, they appear to be intact, as are her own.

'I was too busy trying to keep us in the air,' Sumanguru says. 'Whoever it was, clearly they were worried about whatever it is that the qarin knew.' He looks at Tawaddud seriously. 'That is something we need to talk about – but not here.' He helps Tawaddud up. 'Lean on me. We had better get out of here before the attacker decides to try their luck again.'

'My sister and the Repentants will find us soon,' Tawaddud says. 'And your injuries are more serious than mine.'

'I've had much worse, believe me,' Sumanguru says, gritting his teeth. 'It is just flesh. But you and I – we need to talk.'


The dense cable networks joining the houses together and connecting them to the City of the Dead for the jinni servants block most of the sunlight. The air is thick with the smell of human bodies, ozone and the high-pitched chirping of the Fast Ones who surf the crowd just above peoples' heads with inhuman speed. Tawaddud flinches every time they pass. She aches all over, and has a splitting headache, not dispelled even by a Secret Name. She realises she has not eaten all day. At her suggestion, they stop in a street kitchen run by a thick-bodied woman in a headscarf.

They sit on the edge of the shopping square of Bayn-al-Asrayn, at the base of a Sobornost statue, and eat tajini. The hot spices and the chewy meat restore some of Tawaddud's fortitude. Sumanguru eats slowly, an expression of nostalgia on his face. It is gone when he looks up again, replaced by his usual stern visage. He touches his chest wounds thoughtfully. They are bleeding slightly. He rubs his fingers together.

'I underestimated you, Tawaddud of House Gomelez. I will not do so again. You got us closer to the enemies of the Great Common Task than I did. Also, you saved this sumanguru from truedeath. You have my thanks, and those of my branch.'

'I thought your kind did not fear death.'

'The Great Common Task is a war on death. A soldier who does not fear the enemy is a fool. So, I thank you.' He inclines his head slightly.

Tawaddud feels self-conscious, all of a sudden. Her hair is messy and full of carpet dust, and her clothes are torn. How long has it been since she had a meal with a charming man that was not set up by her sister? Far too long. Except for the fact that, of course, they are eating cheap tajini on the street, the charming man is a Sobornost mass murderer whose body was fabricated from raw materials by nanobots only a few hours ago, and the only reason they are here is that her ex-lover the body thief has started killing Councillors.

And then there is Abu. *I will think about him later.* Still, there is something peeking through Sumanguru's shell that makes her wonder. *He was so afraid on the carpet.*

'Lord Sumanguru,' she says slowly, 'there was ... something else I saw in the qarin's mind.'

Sumanguru says nothing.

'A Secret Name. I think Arcelia was keeping it for Alile. It may have nothing to do with her death, but clearly it was something important.' As she speaks the words, the Name echoes in her throbbing head again, as if wanting to get out, delicate bell-like syllables full of a strange innocence.

'Tell me about the Names.'

'I thought you were briefed on the history of Sirr.'

Sumanguru narrows his eyes. 'Sometimes, it is more important to hear how a story is told than what the story is.'

Tawaddud puts her bowl down. 'The Names are words and symbols the Aun taught us, to control the athar and tame wildcode. Ancient commands for the systems of the Sirr-in-the-sky and the desert. Seals are special Names, unique and irreplaceable, protection from wildcode: only the muhtasib know how to create them.'

'And Alile wanted to give them to us so that we could continue the Task ourselves, without the need for your mutalibun,' Sumanguru says. 'Anyone who disagrees with that is a suspect.'

'You will find many who disagree. The Seals are all we have left of our ancestors. A symbol of the Cry of Wrath,' Tawaddud says. 'To give them to you directly, to disrupt our gogol trade and economy, to allow Sobornost machines to go to the desert instead of our mutalibun and mercenaries – many feel strongly about that.'

Sumanguru's pale eyes do not blink. 'So how does Tawaddud of the House Gomelez feel?'

Tawaddud looks down. 'That justice should be done.'

'Interesting notion.' Sumanguru squeezes the bridge of his nose, then blinks and lowers his hand. 'Is it possible that whoever killed Alile did not care about the Accords but wanted this Name you saw? Do you know what it does?'

Tawaddud shakes her head. 'Some of them can only be spoken in certain places, at certain times. I think this is one of them.'

Sumanguru gives her a sharp look. 'The only two possible

reasons for the killer to steal the qarin – or to prevent us from having it – are this Name and the possibility that the bird knew the killer's identity. Think carefully: is there anything else you saw in the qarin's mind?'

Tawaddud swallows.

'I think you are protecting someone, Tawaddud of House Gomelez,' Sumanguru says gently. 'If you are, consider this: whoever they are, they want to fight a war with the Sobornost. And at war, you often find yourself becoming a twin of the enemy, just as bad as the thing you fear.' He leans back and looks up at the Gourd, wispy lines now obscured by fluffy afternoon clouds, the Shards like a curtain in the horizon.

'How much do you know about Sobornost history?'

'I've only ever met hsien-kus.'

'Hsien-kus are a small clan obsessed with the past. They would love nothing more than creating another Earth, a simulated Earth, for everyone who ever existed. They like to look back. But most of us look forward. Even when it comes with a price.'

'What do you mean?' Tawaddud asks.

'After the first war, we realised that this,' he taps on his temple, 'was not enough. Human cognitive architecture only gets you so far with the Great Common Task. Sure, there are some fundamentals that the chitraguptas say are universal. Recursion, thoughts within thoughts. The basis of language, self-reflection, consciousness perhaps. But a lot of it is modules, inefficiently strung together by evolution. A kind of Frankenstein.'

'A what?'

'I keep forgetting, no fiction. Never mind. The point is, we started experimenting. And we ended up with Dragons. Beings with no consciousness, no modules, just an engine, a self-modifying, evolving optimiser. We could never destroy them: we could only put them inside virtual machines, box them off. What do you think the *guberniyas* are for? They are cages for monsters. Everything else is just surface.'

'Are you sure you should be telling me this?' Tawaddud thinks about the young man in orange, the political astronomer. She is sure no one in Sirr has ever heard anything about this.

'Are you sure I shouldn't be?' Sumanguru's mouth twitches.

'And then what happened?'

'We fought them. A war that lasted thousands of years, in *guberniya* Deep Time. They had no eudaimon, no inner voice. Intelligence without meaning. And we were losing. Until we started cutting things out from ourselves as well. Body language. Theory of mind. Empathy. To fight Dragons, we made gogols that were mirror images of the bastards.

'Gogols like me.'

Tawaddud looks at Sumanguru. His smile is cold. 'Oh, I can fake social niceties perfectly well, but it is just slave gogols moving my face, you understand. My emotions are outsourced. My private utility functions and pleasures are … quite different from yours.

'So when you keep your secrets, Tawaddud Gomelez, think about two things. Is whoever you are protecting worth protecting or have they crossed a line?' He leans closer and the machine oil smell in his breath is so strong that the food moves in Tawaddud's stomach and bile rises into her mouth. 'And do you really want to lie to someone who kills dragons?'

He picks up Tawaddud's unfinished tajini bowl and spoons the remaining food with gusto.

\*

They wait in silence until the shadow of a carpet appears: it descends slowly into the square, carrying Dunyazad and a tall, spiky Repentant thought-form. Tawaddud's sister is clad in formal Council robes, Gomelez colours, black fabric and a gold chain in her hair.

She curtsies to Sumanguru, clasping her hands together, a look of horror on her face. 'Lord Sumanguru,' she says. 'Are you badly hurt? We will take to my Father's house immediately and tend to your injuries.'

Sumanguru shrugs. 'Flesh will heal,' he says. 'If not, it will be cut off.'

Duny curtsies again and turns to Tawaddud.

'Dear sister,' she says, giving her a tight, quick embrace. 'The Aun be praised that you are alive!' But when she holds Tawaddud close, she hisses in her ear, 'Father wants to see you. It might have been better to run away again.'

Duny pulls away and gives them both a radiant smile. 'Please follow me: we have *so* many things to talk about.'

# 15

# THE THIEF AND THE SAUNA

The day before the thief leaves for Earth Mieli prepares an Oortian meal. He is in a good mood, lecturing, flashing smiles. But every now and then, from the corner of her eye, she sees something different on his face. Something savage.

*See?* the pellegrini whispers. She has been there all the way through her preparations, watching them. *Have faith and it all works out in the end.*

She ignores the goddess and continues setting up the table. Spider eggs in small food nets. Peeled pumptree fruit. Drinking bulbs. She has already started warming up the sauna.

'This all seems somewhat elaborate,' the thief says. 'Should we not spend the time getting ready, for, I don't know, sneaking into the most well-guarded planet in the System?'

'We *are* getting ready,' Mieli says. 'Earth is a dark place, a place of pain. We have to purify ourselves.'

'I can certainly get behind *that*. In fact, I'm going to purify myself internally.' He swallows some of the contents of a drinking bulb and makes a face. Mieli snatches it back from his hand.

'It tastes like tar,' the thief says.

'The taste is not important. It is to honour the dead. And the meal is only for after the sauna, so control your instincts.'

The thief looks at her. 'I don't know about the dead, but I'm kind of looking forward to this. I'm glad we finally see eye to eye.'

Mieli says nothing. She sees the pellegrini smiling and closes her eyes. The face of the goddess does not go away.

'Let's go to the sauna,' she says.

The sauna is housed in one of *Perhonen*'s storage modules. In her years of service to the pellegrini, Mieli has only used it a few times: it makes her too homesick. But if you really want to cleanse yourself, it is the only way to do it, and the ship has reassembled it for the occasion.

It is a tiny, spherical room of wood, with a large bubble of water in the centre, held in place by a semi-permeable membrane and *väki* threads, like a raindrop in a giant spiderweb. You take hot rocks from small braziers with tongs and throw them into the bubble. It creates a rush of steam. The rocks swirl around in the bubble and make it dance like a living thing.

*Perhonen* has connected the module with the main living area of the ship and the wooden hatch looks inviting. The thief looks at it suspiciously.

'So, how does this work?' he asks.

'Get out of your clothes,' Mieli says.

He hesitates. 'Now?'

'Just do it.'

He takes a sharp breath, looks away and fumbles at his jacket and trousers. 'Don't I get a towel?' he says. But Mieli has already let her toga fall aside and is in the warm rush of *löyly*.

The thief comes in hesitantly. His eyes flicker across her body. Then he settles on the other side of the sauna bubble, pushing his feet into the wooden handles and settling on the seat. The hatch that opens into space on the other side has a glass window on it, and starlight and the light of the glowing *kiuas* rocks makes the thief's face look very young.

'Throw some *löyly*,' she says. Gingerly, he takes the tongs and picks up one of the smallest rocks in the metal-netted basket in the wall. *Kiuas* rocks are precious in a place of comet ice and dust, but this is a good one, round and black and shimmering with heat. The thief casts it into the bubble. It vanishes with a pathetic hiss.

Mieli sighs and picks up her bundle of pumptree branches, beats herself on the back gently: her wing scars tickle in the gentle heat. The suction cups of the leaves cling to her skin pleasantly.

'I know self-flagellation is your thing, but I did not realise you took it *that* literally,' the thief says.

'Ssh,' Mieli says and glares at him. Then she picks up one of the bigger rocks with her bare hands and throws it in. This time, the rush of *löyly* washes all over her from head to toes like *koto* morning light and makes her skin tingle all over. The thief lets out a muffled scream, tries to hide from the steam, turns his back to it but that only makes it worse. He scrambles towards the hatch, but it is firmly locked.

'Don't tell me,' he grunts. 'This is a punishment, right?'

'Not punishment. Forgiveness.' She throws one of the blue stones in. A gentle mint smell fills the sauna, but the heat is even more intense. The wood sweats tiny amber beads of sap that stick to her skin as she leans back. For a surprisingly long time, the thief says nothing, just breathes heavily.

'So,' she says finally. '*Perhonen* tells me we finally have a target and a plan.'

The thief hunches down on his perch, elbows on his knees, looking at the rock inside the water as its glow fades.

'Let's start with the target, shall we?' he says. 'I still don't know exactly what it is or what it does, but it has something to do with the Spike. The ... tiger called it the Kaminari jewel.' He pauses and carefully tosses a bigger rock in. The water hisses. The wood groans: it is the only thing between them and the Dark Man. Suddenly, Mieli feels strangely at home.

'Matjek Chen has it,' the thief says. 'The pellegrini wants it. We are going to get it for her. That's what it boils down to.'

'And Earth?' she asks.

'Well, to steal anything from Chen, you have to *become* him. Except that you can't. We don't have any source for Chen's Founder codes like the Box. Last time, I tried to steal them from him directly, and that did not work out very well. So we have to find another way. And that's Earth.

'You see, somewhere down there is a gogol of Matjek Chen. Not one like the current ruler of Sobornost, not a god-king. A child. An insurance policy. But enough of Chen in him for us to figure out his Code.'

'And how do you know that?' Mieli asks.

'Your pellegrini and I go way back. I used to work for her, much like you do now, when she was still a human woman. She was sort of a patron for the Founders, early on, Chen in particular. So before getting into bed with him, she had me look into his past, very carefully. I found out some interesting things. How much do you know about the history of uploading?'

Mieli says nothing.

'All right,' the thief says. 'I guess this is a bit touchy for you Oortians. But the fact is, afterlife became a big business in the 2060s. For a lot of money, you could buy yourself a heaven – or a hell, if you were so inclined. I'm not talking about the corporate uploads here – their lives were nasty, brutish and very, very long – but those who could afford to buy a custom-made high-fidelity vir, running on ultra-secure, reversible-computing hardware, geothermally powered, guaranteed to keep going for at least a few millennia, built in a secret location for maximum security.

'Chen had what you could call overprotective parents. A beemee star and a quantum hedge fund manager. Wealthy beyond belief. When Chen was seven, they had him uploaded into a custom insurance heaven. They never told him about it, and most of the data from that period was lost in the Collapse. So that useful fact only remains in my head.

'The problem is, I never found out where his heaven was. Chances are it survived the Collapse. Most of them did: the muhtasib families of Sirr are digging them up all the time. Fortunately, the hsien-kus are obsessed with history. I'm going to bluff my way into their ancestor virs they run in the Gourd array around Earth and see what I can find. It shouldn't be hard: everybody is afraid of sumangurus.'

'Not everybody,' Mieli says.

'Well, the hsien-kus are, anyway.' He squirms and rubs his neck. 'What do you do to cool down in here?'

Mieli gestures at the other hatch. 'Vacuum,' she says. 'The Dark Man's kiss, they call it. You should be able to take it for a few seconds.'

'Thanks, I'll pass,' the thief says.

Mieli looks at him, giving him a smile that says that a dive into the dark might not be optional. He continues hastily.

'So. I'm going to find out where the target is. In the mean-time, you'll need to get into a position to retrieve the package. Sirr is always hiring offworld mercenaries: that should be a perfect cover for you. It's also the best way to get Seals. Earth is a weird place, you can't move around without protection from this tech that the Sirr ruling families – muhtasibs – have without being attacked by wild nanites. So we'll need those. Once I have the information, we'll rendezvous, and get little Matjek out from his paradise. He'll give us a way to reconstruct big Matjek's Codes – and then we are almost there. How does that sound?'

'Awfully convenient,' Mieli says. 'Disappearing into Sobornost networks with a perfect disguise. Why should I expect to ever hear from you again?'

'You are underestimating Joséphine – the pellegrini,' the thief says. 'You of all people should know she is very, very good at coming up with incentives to do what she says. I'm not going to escape from her that easily.'

'You are not telling me everything,' She picks up a red-hot stone with her fingers, holds it up. 'I could make you talk.'

The thief spreads his hands. 'You could.' He looks tired, suddenly. 'But you are not going to. That's not who you are.' He knocks on the wooden wall of the sauna. '*This* is. You still have this to go back to. Don't throw it away.

'We have had our differences. But I do keep my promises. We have that in common, at least. I said I would do this thing for you, and I will. You got me out of a prison. Let me get you out of this one. Let me make sure you get to go home.'

*He sounds like* Perhonen. *But everything he says is a lie or a trick,* she thinks. The warmth of the sauna makes her feel soft. *Maybe I should tell him why I'm doing this.* Then she remembers the way he touched Sydän's jewel when they met the first time.

'All right,' she says, slowly. 'We'll do it your way. But if you betray me, I *will* find you again.'

She throws the last big *kiuas* stone into the water. The thief grunts at the hiss of the steam, squeezes his eyes shut, and flees. He does something to the hatch lock. It pops open, he squeezes through and slams it shut behind him. Mieli catches a glimpse of his thin, naked body and lobster-red skin.

Mieli closes her eyes. The last time she was here was with Sydän. Perhaps it won't be so long before they are here together again. *Soon. Even if it's going to take a little time.*

Then she opens the door to the vacuum, lets the air rush out. The steam in the air freezes into a sparkling cloud of ice crystals.

Mieli steps out, spreads her wings and kisses the Dark Man.


I cool down in the main cabin. My flushed skin tingles and gives me uncomfortable memories of being burned by first the Hunter and then the router. But there is a pleasant, heavy fatigue that comes with the feeling. Mieli explicitly forbade me to touch any of the food so I help myself to a few spider eggs and wash them down with the foul Oortian liquorice vodka.

*You are not supposed to touch any of that yet,* the ship says.

'Sorry, I can't help it. Are you going to tell on me?'

*I'll use all the ammunition I can get if I have to,* the ship says. *Did she buy it?*

'Not entirely. But good enough to go ahead.'

*She must not know.*

'I'll make sure she won't. Mieli has done a lot of the dirty work in this whole job. It's my turn this time.'

I try the fruit. It has a strange, sweet flavour, like a persimmon but sharper.

'In any case, sounds like you did some pretty good background work. She was in a receptive mood. The sauna was a good idea.'

*That was all her,* the ship says. *But it's good she listened. The sooner this is over, the better.*

'Agreed,' I say. 'Let's hope she thanks us later.'

To be honest, it's unlikely. There is a part of me that dislikes the plan. Perhaps that is the real reason I did not go through it the last time. But now I have no choice.

'There is always a choice, Jean,' Joséphine says. 'And you specialise in making the wrong ones.'

She is not wearing Mieli's body this time. She is just a ghost in the Earth-lit cabin, just like I remember her, beautiful and tall, a woman who could be in her early forties if not for just the hint of fragility in her bones and neck. My heart jumps.

'*Wrong* is such a strong word,' I say. 'I prefer *unconventional.*' I narrow my eyes. 'I thought you were hiding.'

'Only until you managed to sort out things with poor Sumanguru,' she says, lighting a cigarette. 'I was just amused to see how sentimental you are about Mieli. I have seen you do it before. You convince yourself that you care about them, just before you use them as tools. That's why we are so compatible. With me, you don't have to lie to yourself.'

'I thought you were mad at me.'

'Well,' she says. 'Sauna with an Oortian should be punishment enough for now. And you showed some sparks of the man I knew, Jean. Continue this way and you will have more than just your freedom. Bring me the jewel, and the System will be at our feet.'

'I will bring you your jewel, but not your slippers,' I say. 'I'm not going to be your lapdog, ever again.'

She laughs. 'Do you have any idea how many times we have had this conversation? Nothing ever changes, Jean, not for people like us. Being who you are for ever is the price you pay for immortality. That's why we need the jewel. To change the rules.'

I raise my bulb to her. 'Joséphine dear,' I say, 'you were always a better lover than a philosopher. Now if you'll excuse me, I have a dinner to finish. And then a long journey without a body.'

She smiles her serpent smile. 'And you won't be going alone, Jean,' she says. 'I'm coming with you.'

Mieli feels almost content when they finish the meal. She hums to herself quietly. The rebuilt statues in the walls dance slowly to her tune.

'Not that I'm particularly attached to this body,' the thief says, 'but do you mind telling me what you are going to do with it while I'm gone?'

'Keep it out of sight,' Mieli says.

They finish the last of the food in silence. The dessert is her masterpiece: golden cloudberries with spidermilk. That keeps even the thief quiet for a while.

'What are you going to do when this is over?' he asks, suddenly.

Mieli looks at him. 'It's time to go,' she says. She flips to spimescape and thinks *Perhonen*'s thoughtwisp launcher ready. They are going to inject the thief's mind into the Sobornost communications network, download him in compressed form into the smartmatter patterns of a delicate disc, thinner than a soap bubble, propelled towards Earth ahead of *Perhonen*.

'All right. See you on Earth,' the thief says. 'Wait for my signal.'

'Kuutar and Ilmatar go with you,' Mieli says quietly.

'Two goddesses? That's quite a crew. But I guess that's what it takes to get the job done.'

He closes his eyes and is gone. The thoughtwisp accelerates, pushed by the ship's lasers, and vanishes into the dark.

# 16

# TAWADDUD AND CASSAR GOMELEZ

As usual in his few spare hours, Cassar Gomelez is in the kitchen.

It is said amongst the older members of the Council that if Cassar had not followed his family trade, he would have become a chef in one of the finest restaurants of the Green Shard. The air is heavy with the smell of spices, the athar full of recipe fragments. Jinn servants prepare ingredients in small pots and containers, and Cassar himself is chopping vegetables into fine chunks, a huge knife in hand, broad back bent. His movements are delicate and quick.

For a moment, he does not acknowledge the presence of his two daughters. Then he puts the knife down, looks up and wipes his hands on his apron.

'Father,' Tawaddud says and curtsies. Her entire body still aches, but at least she has had time to change into clean clothes and clean up. She spent half an hour deciding what to wear, finally settling on a simple dark green robe and a white sash, covering her hair with a net and keeping her face plain.

Cassar looks at her, face set. Then he turns away, gathers

the ingredients from the chopping board and drops them into a huge, steaming pot.

'I see my daughter is unhurt, now. That is good. How is our guest?' he asks, without turning around, studying the concoction. No matter what his mood, there is always a slight mournful note to Tawaddud's father's voice.

'Lord Sumanguru is recuperating from his injuries,' Dunyazad says. 'His Seals appear to be intact in spite of being exposed to wildcode and a barakah gun.'

'Thank the Aun for small mercies,' Cassar says. 'It would not have been good to lose a Sobornost envoy in a mad chase above the city.'

'The Soarez are also complaining about the damage to their rukh ships. And Lord Salih is making a fuss about the destruction of the qarin and demanding—' Duny begins.

'We can handle the Soarez.' Cassar waves a dismissive hand. 'We have more important matters to discuss, now. Tawaddud.'

Tawaddud's heart jumps.

'Young Lord Nuwas ... convinced me to allow you to be involved in this unfortunate affair. Whether that was wise or not remains to be seen. Now. Let me say that while it is good to see you take initiative and show interest in the affairs of our family, blackmail is not the way you should go about it. You should have come to me first. You will do so in the future. Do you understand?'

'Yes.'

Back still turned, Cassar inspects the containers that are stirring themselves.

'No matter. Young Abu appears to be quite smitten with you, and that is useful. What did you discover in your investigation?'

Tawaddud takes a deep breath. She has been thinking what to say, going over the words again and again.

'That Lady Alile was murdered through a possession, that whoever did it sought a Secret Name she had, and that whatever that is was enough for someone in the Council to try to have me and Lord Sumanguru killed,' Tawaddud says. 'And that Repentant Rumzan cannot be trusted. And I may … know the jinn who possessed Alile. He may lead us to whoever is behind this plot.'

'I meant what did you discover about *him*. Sumanguru.'

Tawaddud stares at her father. His slightly protruding ears would make him look comical under the white cap if his expression was not so stern.

'I do not understand. I thought my task was to—'

'Use this opportunity to learn anything we could use against the Sobornost. That was the task I originally gave to Dunyazad.'

'But— She didn't—'

Dunyazad smiles sweetly at Tawaddud, one painted fingernail pressed against her lips. 'Did I not tell you, dear sister, that this is not a game?'

Cassar sighs. 'The investigation was always irrelevant. It was clear all along that the masrurs are behind this. I summoned a Sobornost representative for different reasons entirely.' He tastes the contents of the pot with a ladle and makes a face.

'Now. As for Repentant Rumzan, he has disappeared. We knew that he had masrur sympathies, even if he is not a Sword of Vengeance himself. It is my belief that the attack on you was directed at Lord Sumanguru – it is regrettable that you were in danger, of course. However, the qarin – and whatever secret you may think you found – had nothing to do with it. Of course, this Name may be valuable, and you should examine it with Chaeremon when the present crisis is over. But I ask you again: what did you discover about Sumanguru?'

Tawaddud bites her lip. 'He is ... afraid of heights.' Her thoughts race. 'And there are things in the Sobornost called Dragons that have no self-loops. He has enhancements for capturing minds in virs, for torturing them. But ... he does not seem to enjoy it, even though he claims he does...' She swallows, her mind suddenly blank. 'There are a few other things, I can try to remember—'

'Is that all?' Cassar asks, hands behind his back. He shakes his head. 'I would have hoped for more. You can tell these things to the political astronomers of the Council. They are no use to us. My daughter, I think I have fulfilled my obligation to Abu Nuwas. From now on, you will take care of our guest's medical needs. When he is recovered, Duny will continue the investigation: she has already prepared many leads for Lord Sumanguru to pursue that will keep him busy for a long time. You can return to your own pursuits with the Banu Sasan. At least they show you have a good heart. And Lord Nuwas will make you a perfect husband.'

Tawaddud bites down tears.

'What about Lady Alile? What about finding her murderer?'

Cassar bows his head.

'Alile was a friend, and I regret her passing more than I can say. We will punish the masrurs for her in time. But meanwhile, she would want us to go on, do our duty for Sirr.'

It was the Axolotl, she wants to shout. I can find him. I

can bring him to you. But she can't bring herself to say the words.

Cassar's eyes flicker: he gives her a sideways glance and looks away again.

'I see you do not understand our duty, our responsibility. When Sirr-in-the-Sky fell, when our people were almost lost, it was a Gomelez who guided them. It was a Gomelez who spoke to the Aun and forged the pact that allows us to exist. Our burden today is the same: to find a way to survive.

'The Cry of Wrath showed that the Aun do not love the Sobornost. When they tried to take our minds last time, the desert itself rose up against them. But if the whispers from our agents amongst the mercenaries are true, things have changed. The hsien-kus are gentle, but some of the other Founders are not. Some of them are far more powerful, and it may be that even the Aun cannot stand against them. So, for now, we must find a way to yield so as not to break – but without giving away what makes us who we are.'

'By letting them send their machines to the desert to dig up souls?' Tawaddud almost shouts, voice breaking.

'That is what they have asked. Our answer depends on what they offer to us in return. But we need to *know* them, and I fear that you are not the right person to know this Sumanguru.'

Tawaddud looks down, biting down tears. Her face is numb. Her head and chest feel hollow.

'If I could just explain—' she whispers.

'That will be all,' Cassar Gomelez says, and turns back to his cooking.

Tawaddud and Duny walk down a pillared corridor back towards the living quarters. Halfway, Tawaddud can't take it anymore. She slumps with exhaustion and sits on a stone bench, letting the purple evening light wash over her face. Her eyes sting, and she does not have enough strength left to handle a Secret Name to restore her energies. She is too tired to be properly angry. There is still no feeling in her lips.

'You played me,' she whispers.

'Sister,' Dunyazad says. 'You *wanted* to play. Do not complain when you lose. I tried to help you. I asked you not to get involved. You did not listen.' Then her expression grows serious. 'And you were in danger. You could have died, chasing after the Fast Ones like that. Whatever our differences, you *must* believe me when I say that I would never wish to see you hurt. My thanks to the Aun came from the heart.'

'I'm sure they did. And you have so many things to be thankful for. Are you happy now? Naughty Tawaddud has been spanked, and all is right in the world.'

'Not yet.'

'What do you mean?'

'We still need to take some precautions with our guest, and I could use your help.'

'After what you just did, you still want my *help*? Are you insane?'

Dunyazad looks at the setting sun.

'Do you want to do your duty as a Gomelez?' she says softly. 'I think we should set our petty games aside: there are many more of those we can play when Sirr is safe. Don't you agree?'

Quietly, Tawaddud nods, gritting her teeth.

'Listen. I have already been in touch with the hsien-kus, on Father's behalf. Strangely, they don't seem to be very concerned that their envoy was in danger. Like I told you, there is politics here that we simply do not know about. Or time:

sometimes you find Sobornost communities entering Deep Time, leaping forward a generation in what is just days to us, and then they have forgotten what the previous negotiations were all about.' She smiles a knowing smile. 'Of course, sometimes it may suit their purposes to make such claims.'

She takes a small box from the folds of her robes and gives it to Tawaddud.

'You should go and talk to Sumanguru, have a look at his wounds. When you treat him, insert this under his skin, somewhere not visible. Preferably close to the brain. Our studies of sobortech after the Cry of Wrath have not been entirely fruitless. Once that is done, you don't need to worry about what comes next.'

Dunyazad opens the box. Inside is a tiny object, like a shard of glass, held delicately between metal pincers.

'What does it do?'

'Like I said, you do not need to worry about that.'

'Why don't you do it yourself?'

'Because he trusts you. And you have proven yourself to be a capable doctor, if not a politician.' Duny touches Tawaddud's arm.

'I know it is hard to believe, but you made progress with Father tonight. In time, he will come to see you as I do: a Gomelez. A member of our family.'

Tawaddud closes her eyes.

'Will you do this one thing for me, please?' Duny asks. 'Or if not for me, for Mother?'

Quietly, Tawaddud nods. Duny kisses her forehead. 'Thank you. After that, you should get some sleep.'

She lifts a jinn ring to her ear, frowning. 'Or perhaps not. It seems that Abu Nuwas is here to see you.'

*

'I came as soon as I heard,' Abu says, when Tawaddud receives him in her assignation room. She applied some makeup hastily, but washed it away almost immediately: her tired face shone through the thin layer. Still, the calm of the room and a friendly face make her feel better.

They sit down on the pillows. Tawaddud lights two candles on the table. Abu's brass eye glitters in their warm light.

'How did you find out?' she asks.

'A high-speed chase over the Shade Quarter?' Abu shakes his head. 'Not exactly a secret. I'm glad you are all right.'

He reaches across the table and takes Tawaddud's hand. 'I had no idea it would be something so dangerous. I feel terrible for putting you in such a position. It is one thing to seek your father's trust, but to throw your life away pursuing it—'

He shakes his head again. 'Trust me, I know the price of dreams.'

'Well, looks like my involvement in such dangerous matters is over,' Tawaddud says and pulls her hand away. 'My father does not even think I'm worth looking in the eye. And ...'

She tries to keep the tears down, but they come anyway.

'What is it?' Abu says. 'You can tell me. I know I'm a stranger, but if it helps, I'm here.'

*He understands.* Tawaddud dries her tears on her sleeve.

'It's stupid. This whole thing. I found something, in Alile's qarin. And I think I know who killed her. But I have no proof. I can't tell Father, he will never believe me.'

Abu touches her shoulder.

'If ... if you want, you could tell me. I could go to your father, talk to him again. He will listen to me.'

His voice is gentle. She remembers the fire in the doctor's tent, the all-consuming flame inside her. In the flickering light, a trace of it flashes in his human eye. A cold finger of fear travels down her spine. She shakes her head. *Stupid. I'm just tired.*

'Thank you, but no,' she says aloud. 'You have done enough, and once my father has made his decision, the only one who could ever change his mind was my mother.'

Abu looks away.

'As you wish.' He pauses. 'So. What about us?'

'I don't know, Abu. I'm tired.'

'Of course. I should let you rest.' He gets up. 'I have a proposal: come have dinner with me tomorrow, at my palace.' He raises a hand. 'No obligations: you showed me your world, and I simply want to show you mine.'

Tawaddud nods. 'I would like that.'

'Good. You know, I did not quite finish my story the other night. Perhaps it will help you.' He rubs his brass eye. 'After the mutalibun got what they wanted, they left me alone in the desert to die, so that I could not lead anyone else to what they found. I was all alone in the wildcode desert, in the Fast Cities. There were houses whose windows were eyes, carbeasts, machines that looked human but were not, and ... worse things.

'But I walked home. I survived. There were a hundred times I thought I was going to die, but I kept going. I had a destination and it kept me alive, no matter how bad things got.

'So do not give up on your father. Maybe you can still show him who you are. I will help you, if you will let me. You don't have to walk through the desert alone.'

Tawaddud feels warm.

'Thank you,' she says.

She kisses him at the door. His lips are cold, but he embraces Tawaddud hard.

He smiles when she finally pulls away. 'I'll see you tomorrow.'

'What was it?' Tawaddud asks.

'What do you mean?'

'What was it that kept you going?'

Abu smiles.

'Revenge,' he says. 'What else? Good night, Tawaddud.'

When Abu is gone, Tawaddud picks up Dunyazad's box.

*Revenge.*

The Cry of Wrath. She was eight years old. There were mountains in the sky. Crystal clouds, diamond pyramids, blocking out every bit of blue. Distant thunder. Shouting, fearful cries, carried up to the Shard. White beams coming down from the heavens. She laughed with delight when she saw it.

'Mother,' she shouted. 'Look, it is raining light!'

Her mother looked at the Sobornost sky in terror. She had not been the same since the star of madness, prone to silences and nightmares. Tawaddud thought the wonder in the sky would make her laugh again.

Instead, her mother ran to the balcony and leaped.

The candles flutter in the wind from outside. She closes her window, takes her doctor's bag and goes to see Sumanguru.

The guest quarters are in the Tower of Saffron, the tallest of the five horizontal towers in the Gomelez palace, in the tip with a magnificent view of Sirr. Tawaddud chooses a long, winding staircase from her own rooms that takes her around the main living areas of the palace, climbing along the curving shell of the Shard. The night air and the exercise clear her head. Sirr is a sea of golden light far below, reminding her of the other Sirr Abu showed her in the athar. She finds herself missing him. *At least there is one good thing that came out of this.*

Sumanguru opens the door. He is wearing white trousers and a plain shirt from the guest wardrobe, stark against his dark skin: they make him look like a wirer, except for the scars. He looks at Tawaddud curiously.

'I did not expect to see you so soon,' he says. 'Do you have something to tell me?'

Tawaddud looks down. 'Lord Sumanguru, I wanted to make sure there were no aftereffects from the barakah gun or the exposure of your Seals, not to mention your injuries. My father is concerned about the welfare of his guest.'

'I am not overly concerned about this body, but I can hardly turn down a gesture of hospitality. Please come in.'

At Tawaddud's request, Sumanguru sits down and removes his shirt. His body is hairless and smooth, every muscle impossibly perfect. His chest is covered in innumerable tiny wounds, but most of them appear to be healing already, faster than any baseline human. In athar, his Seals are still intact. Looking closer, she can see a network of nodes under his skin, complex machinery that athar does not know how to represent.

'I did not know you were a doctor,' Sumanguru says.

'I am many things.' She touches his thick neck: there is a deep cut on the left side of his back that should do. 'There is a needle fragment here I should remove, to avoid wildcode infection. This may sting a little.'

'Pain is irrelevant. Go ahead.'

She picks up a scalpel from her doctor's bag. *A killer of*

*Dragons. Is that who you really are, Sumanguru of the Turquoise Branch?* She presses down on his firm flesh, ready to make the cut. He tenses at her touch.

*Why were you afraid of flying?*

She puts the scalpel down. No, Duny. I'm not going to play your game. Not like this.

'If you are going to do it, do it,' Sumanguru says. 'If I have to die, I might as well be killed by a pretty girl.'

Tawaddud takes a step back. 'Lord Sumanguru, I—'

Sumanguru turns around. He is holding up the little box Duny gave her, open. The tiny jewel glitters inside.

'Nice,' he says. 'Zoku technology. Where did you get it?' He turns it around, a curious look in his eyes.

Zokus are something Tawaddud only has the faintest idea about, a distant civilisation with ancient customs that once upon a time fought some sort of war with Sobornost. What could Duny possibly have to do with them?

She takes a step back, lifts the scalpel slowly, heart racing. *Why can't I do anything right?*

Sumanguru gets up.

'Calm down,' he says. 'I'm not going to hurt you. I only tried to frighten you earlier. I get scared, too. I know you know who killed Alile.'

'Who are you?' Tawaddud hisses.

Sumanguru smiles. 'The better question is who *you* really are, Tawaddud Gomelez. And I think you are not someone who would hurt a guest in your father's house. Did he send you?'

'No.' Tawaddud's face feels numb. She licks her lips but can't feel them. The thoughts come at her fast like chimera serpents in the desert, striking. *Dunyazad. Rumzan would have reported to her that we found the qarin. She would have known where to get a barakah gun.*

The scalpel clatters to the floor. Sumanguru lets out a slow breath. 'That's more like it,' he says.

They look at each other quietly for a while. Sumanguru sits down, leaning his elbows on his knees.

'It was your sister, wasn't it?' he says slowly.

A sick feeling grows in Tawaddud's stomach.

'I wasn't supposed to be your guide, she was. That's why the Fast Ones did not touch me.'

'Do you think your father knows?'

Tawaddud shakes her head. 'He is Cassar Gomelez. After my mother died, all he has cared about is Sirr. He has been working on the Accords for half his life. And he would have never hurt Lady Alile.'

'It does make sense,' Sumanguru says. 'Earth has been ... a bone of contention between us and the zokus for some time. We pushed them back in the Protocol War and came here. It would definitely be in their interest to restrict our access to the gogols here as much as possible. So they may have used your sister to get rid of Alile.'

'What about the attack in the aviary?'

'My guess would be that she was worried about a Sobornost investigator getting too close to her. That's also why she wanted you to put an insurance policy in place.'

He tosses the box back to Tawaddud. 'No doubt it will have self-destructed already. Too bad: I could have tried to figure out which zoku it came from.'

Tawaddud squeezes her eyes shut. 'I can't go to Father without proof.'

'Is there anyone else in the Council you trust?'

*Abu. But it was Duny who wanted me to meet him. That is the last thing she will ever take away from me.*

She shakes her head.

Sumanguru smiles. 'Well, I suppose that leaves yours truly.'

'With all due respect, I don't trust you, Lord Sumanguru.'

'And you shouldn't. But that does not mean we can't help each other. If we find the jinn who killed Alile, maybe we can link the murder to your sister.'

*Zaybak tried to warn me. He would understand. Or at least the Zaybak who was Tawaddud would.*

A cold certainty grips Tawaddud. She remembers old stories, about deals with devils, about dark figures who offered the innocent whatever they wanted, in exchange for their soul. She always thought they were just clever ways for body thieves to put their victims at ease.

But there are other stories too, ones where the sister no one likes saves the day in the end.

'He is called the Axolotl,' she says.

'The one from the children's story. I see. So, how do we catch him? I have something that will hold him, I think, but we need to find him first.' He holds up a small device that looks like a bullet.

Tawaddud touches her temples. Entwinement always leaves a trace.

'We already have,' she says. 'A part of him is in me. We just have to find a way to speak to it. There is a place called the Palace of Stories. Someone there will help us. But we have to go tonight.'

'How do you plan to sneak away from this place?'

Tawaddud smiles a bitter smile.

'That is the easy part, Lord Sumanguru. I am *very* good at running away from my father. But you may not like it.'

'What do you mean?'

'I understand that you are not too fond of heights.'

# 17

# MIELI AND EARTH

Sydän wanted to go to Earth. At the time, Mieli could not understand why.

They had just met, while building a Great Work. Among the people of Hiljainen Koto, it was a coming-of-age thing to do, go out into the black and shape ice with väki, make new habitats or just Great Works for their own sake, just to show that there was something valuable to be made from the crude stuff that the diamond minds no longer cared about, big icy middle fingers held up to the prissy gods of the Inner System.

It was the Grandmother who sent Sydän to work with her, bright-eyed Sydän from the Kirkkaat Kutojat koto. Extreme programming, she said, ancient tradition (which meant that dirtpeople used to do it): two minds working as one, the other shaping, the other watching, monitoring, correcting. At first, Mieli saw it as an insult. But she discovered that the other girl was much better than her at chasing down errant ancestors that escaped down the icy pathways as phonons or configurations of ghostly electricity that messed up the growth patterns, leaving behind icicles shaped like fertility idols.

At first they shaped ice just to get a feel for it, wove some of the smaller ice clumps into toy castles and monstrous shapes. They even let the ancestors animate one of them, called it a minotaur and when little Varpu came to visit them they let her be chased by the jagged, slow-moving monster through a labyrinth they built; she shrieked with glee. But eventually, the Big Idea of what they *really* wanted to make started to emerge.

They called it the Chain. A hundred ice spheres laboriously crafted, decorated with bright designs that drew the eye and made you dizzy as you drifted through them. All strung together with unbreakable Jovian q-dot fibres and dancing slowly in the gravity well of the Moon-sized mass they called Pohja. The tertiary structure they modelled after that of a protein, found local minima for the Chain's Lagrangian function so that it would fold itself into intricate shapes, creatures of myth and flowers and fractals.

It was slow work. The blackness was always there, just beyond the skin of their secondskins and the icy walls of the little garden Mieli built. She lit it up with a soletta and filled it with zero-g plants that reminded her of Grandmother's garden. Sydän said it was a weakness and lived in her secondskin, a tiny little ecosystem, algae and respirator nanos flowing in tubes around her body, face glowing with fierce independence as she traversed the growing Chain. There was a lot of waiting, waiting for the Chain to fold, waiting for the väki in the ice to grow and complete the tasks they sang to it.

And as they waited, they talked.

'I don't want to be a ghost in the ice like the ancestors,' Sydän said. 'There are better places. When I was little, a Jovian ambassador came to our koto. He was just a seed that had to be planted. We brought it food, and it gave us dreams as presents. They showed places where you really are immortal, or live many lives at once. I don't care about what the elders say. I don't care about knowing the fifty names of ice. I want to live. I want to see the Inner System. I want to see the sky cities on Venus. I want to see Earth.'

In Mieli's koto, the children told stories about Earth. The burning place, the place of pain, where *tuonetars* bind the damned dead with viper ropes and whip them with iron chains, where you drink dark waters and forget who you are. Where the Great Tree grew and was cut down. Where the people of her koto lived until Ilmatar carried them away.

Mieli preferred stories about Seppo the megabuilder who sang a starship out of ice and sailed to another galaxy to find his love, the Daughter of the Spider, or Lemmi the thief who stole one of Kuutar's twelve lives, ate it, burst open and became the first of the Little Suns. The Earth stories always gave her nightmares, troubled dreams where she would crawl along the shores of a dark river, her body pressed down by the heavy hand of gravity, face scraping against the black rough gravel, certain that the *tuonetars* were just behind her but without strength to run or fly.

'Why would you want to go *there*?' she asked.

Sydän laughed. 'I bet you believe all the stories, don't you? The elders make that stuff up. I can see that *you* would have to take it seriously. After all, you have to be better than everybody else at everything. Because you are not from Oort. Because you are the tithe child, given to us to raise. The converts are always the most fervent believers.'

'I'm not allowed to talk about that,' Mieli said.

'There was a book an ancestor gave me, one of the really old ones, from Earth,' Sydän said. 'There was this baby who was raised by presapient monkeys. He became their king. I always thought that's the way you must feel, with all this. Smarter, better, stronger.' She pauses. 'More beautiful.'

'I don't want to be a queen.'

'You don't have to be anything you don't want to be,' Sydän said. 'And you don't have to believe everything they tell you.'

'But why Earth? What is there?'

'I don't know. Don't you want to find out? What is so terrible that they have to hide it in nightmare stories?'

'That's heresy,' Mieli said.

'No,' Sydän said. 'What is heresy is you sitting here with me, a lightsecond from every other living soul, eating me with your eyes, and not doing anything about it.'

She kissed Mieli then, sudden warm softness beneath the slick cold secondskin, pulled away and laughed at her startled expression. 'Come on, monkey queen,' she said. 'The Chain is not going to bind itself!'

In the end, Mieli followed Sydän. But they never made it to Earth.


She wonders what Sydän would think about her now, looking at Earth from the pilot's crèche. The blue globe is covered in a spiderweb of shadows, sharp black knives in the white and azure. The dark lines are cast by the Gourd, a frame of silver arcs that stretch around the planet in an oval shape, in geostationary orbits, over a hundred thousand kilometres in diameter.

There are gaps in the silver structure, so that it looks like two skeletal hands, slowly closing around an eyeball. Where two or more arcs join there are hexagonal loops, bright with light and activity, streams of thoughtwisps, raions and oblasts, a few mercenary ships.

From one of the poles, the thin wire of the Silver Road

stretches to the Moon, where Sobornost machines are eating the crust of the satellite, transporting the matter to be forged into a cage for Earth.

*Dear Kuutar,* Mieli thinks. *Let me unsee this.*

Sobornost has been slowly building it for nearly twenty years. Why would they be doing it if not to guard against something evil inside? The ship's databanks have no information on the purpose of the Gourd: common speculation in the Inner System is that it is created by the hsien-kus as a sensor array, to increase the fidelity of their ancestor virs.

You should not be here, the old goddesses of Oort tell her. This place is forbidden.

*It is just a rock,* she tells herself, refusing to pray, refusing to ask the metacortex to turn off the regions in her brain that seethe with religious terror. *It's just water and rock and ruins.*

She thinks about the journey, the sauna, the Oortian food, all her efforts to prepare herself for this. She is supposed to be Mieli, a heretic Oortian mercenary, come to seek her fortune in the wildcode desert in the pay of the muhtasib families of Sirr. Instead, she feels like a child who has woken up from a bad dream and found it real.

*In the last hour, I have been offered immortality eight thousand times,* the ship says. *I hate negotiating with vasilevs. But I got us an orbit and a docking station in one of the mercenary hubs. They call themselves the Teddy Bear Roadside Picnic Company, if you can believe that – are you all right?*

'I didn't think it would be this hard,' Mieli says. 'I have not been in Oort for years. I fought in the Protocol War. I saw black holes eat moons. I saw a Singularity on Venus. I serve a goddess who rules a *guberniya*. And I still feel like I shouldn't be here, like the *tuonetars* will get me if we go there.' She takes a deep breath. 'Why is that?'

*Because you are still Mieli*, the ship says, *the daughter of Karhu of Hiljainen Koto, the beloved of Sydän, who knows the songs of Oort. And if we do this right, you will always be.*

Mieli smiles. 'You're right,' she says. 'And at least I'll get to tell Sydän I made it here first.'

*Perhonen* drifts along one of the Gourd ribs. It is an endless band of Sobornost faces, surrounded by the glitter of constructor dust, like the largest rainbow in the world. The mercenary docking bay is the open of mouth of a vast hsien-ku face. Mieli reels in the ship's wings and floats in.

The image of the recruiter of the Teddy Bear Roadside Picnic Company appears in the spimescape. He is a round, bearlike creature, an ursomorph with visible Sobornost en-hancements. Diamond spikes protrude from his spine and thick head like icicles. But his eyes are very human and blue, with a suspicious look.

'What do you want?' he asks.

'What do you think?' Mieli says. 'I want to go to the wild-code desert to hunt the dead.'

# 18

# THE THIEF AND THE GOURD

I meet Hsien-Ku 432nd Generation, Early Renaissance Quintic Equations Branch, in a Viennese café in the 1990s. True to my nature and role, I don't touch my Black Forest gâteau, even though it looks delicious. Instead, I maintain the stern businesslike visage of the sumanguru.

She, on the other hand, eats hers with relish: a short plain woman in a period dress, a faint smile on her round face, making appreciative noises as she spoons in the chocolate. I wait for her to finish. She wipes her mouth with a napkin.

'Coffee?' she asks.

'I'd rather stay focused on the matter at hand,' I say.

'Very well. Lord Sumanguru, in all honesty, I took the time to speak to you since your visit is somewhat irregular. We have not received any updates to the Plan that would necessitate a review of our operation.'

I pick up a spoon in my large, black hands and bend it slightly. The hsien-ku winces.

'The Plan can't prepare for all the enemies of the Great Common Task.' The soft metal twists, no doubt faithfully modelled by the ancestor sim's physics engine.

I hold up the spoon. 'It's a good vir. Down to the quantum level, is that right?'

There is a sudden panic in the hsien-ku's eyes.

'We simplify things wherever possible,' she says hastily. 'There are no unnecessary quantum elements. All the minds are strictly classical. Whenever we have to make quantum corrections, it is only in the experiments of the twentieth and twenty-first centuries, and then we ensure we carefully run all quantum aspects classically, in sandboxed virtual machines. I assure you, Lord Sumanguru, there is no contamination here.'

'You misunderstand me.' I place the twisted spoon on the table. 'My brothers and I commend you. We find embodiment … useful for questioning the enemies of the Task.'

A faint look of fear flickers across her eyes. It is easy to see why I chose this disguise last time. My greatest concern was that the chen would have notified the others that this particular Founder code was compromised – but that would have harmed the carefully maintained illusion of Founder infallibility.

'And surely you do not expect to find any such here?' she asks.

'There is a concern that your operation has gotten too close to the flesh; that much of it has to do with matter.'

'That is not by choice,' the hsien-ku says. 'Our interpretation of the Task is as valid as that of the other Founders – and it demands us to recover the lost souls of Earth.'

'Then why have you not already done so?'

'There *was* an attempt to scan and upload Earth's biosphere and matter more forcefully some years ago, but it was a failure.'

'Absurd. Why should a planetary environment like that

pose any problems? Especially given the kinds of resources the Plan has deployed here.'

'Wildcode,' the hsien-ku says, embarrassed. 'Something happened there after the Collapse. A mini-Singularity of sorts. Not on the scale of the Spike, but a merging of the noosphere with the native biosphere. It resulted in something the natives call wildcode, complex self-modifying code. It permeates Earth's matter and it's a pain to get rid of. While our imagers are capable of partial reconstructions, most of the key minds are in the upload heavens.'

'Which you have access to through *trade*, is that correct?'

'Broadly speaking, yes. We trade with the natives. It's a slow process, but we are archaeologists. It has proven more effective than our previous attempts.'

'Soft. Your copyclan lives up to its reputation,' I say.

'We will find a way to counteract the wildcode effects. If the Plan was to grant us more resources—'

'—you would find another way to waste them. Already, our conversation has given me enough to raise this matter with the Prime. However, perhaps there is something you can do to help us both. I understand you have … detailed records of our glorious past.'

'As our interpretation of the Task dictates, our aim is to give life to all those who lived on Earth before the rise of Fedorovism. It requires a detailed study of matter and his-torical records, as well as mind archeology.'

'I don't care about your interpretation of the Task. I require access to the ancestor virs. Full access.'

'Surely, you understand that I need to follow the Plan to get you anything of the sort. Otherwise, where would we be?'

'Your … rigour is admirable. But not wise.' I give her a sumanguru smile, a tiger grin.

'What do you mean?'

'Scholarship can distract you from important events. Pellegrinis and vasilevs. There are serious tensions. Serious enough for us to take notice.'

She places her own spoon on her plate with a nervous clink. She is probably searching her Library for moments of greater self-confidence.

'There were also some . . . irregularities with the Experiment I am looking into.'

'That was centuries ago in our frame,' she protests.

'Crimes against the Task do not get old.'

'I understand,' she says. 'Perhaps a limited period of access could be arranged.'

'Good.' I try the gâteau. It is excellent, but I force myself to make a face. 'It would be a shame to feed such a wonderful creation to the Dragons.'

The ancestor vir of the Gourd, where the hsien-kus of Sobornost make history. It is a giant puzzle, fragments of the past glued together with simulation. The hsien-kus observe and measure, search the memories of gogols bought from the soul merchants of Sirr, or stolen from the Oubliette – and run ensembles of simulations to find histories that match the observations. Averages over possible event sequences instantiated, culled and tweaked until they conform with what the hsien-kus think history should be.

The interface is overwhelming at first. I am a bodiless ghost in a four-dimensional world. A god-view and a new sense that allows me to step backwards and forwards in time. I hate the incorporeal aspect of it – I need to *touch* things – but there is no embodiment here, just the chill of watching processes unfold in gogol brains. The hsien-kus cheat as much as they can: in spite of my accusations, not everything is simulated down to the molecular or even cellular level to allow true physics-equivalence.

What do the gogols here think of their existence? Whole worlds spawned and wiped away and rewritten, just to fit a newly discovered fact of history. Only those who really existed have the right to live. The others are just sketches, erased when they are no longer needed. Poor bastards.

To avoid attention, I go all the way back to an obscure corner of seventh-century Britain – a muddy field shrouded in rain – before I let Joséphine out. She hacks the physics engine with the practised ease of a Founder and makes herself a face out of the raindrops.

'Well, Jean,' she says. 'Now you know the plan. I would have given it back to you eventually. But a part of me likes it when you make me mad. The question is, do you have the balls to go through with it this time?'

'You never did give me the *why* of the plan. Why does Chen want an ancient gogol of himself so badly?'

She smiles. 'Don't we all want to be children again?'

'I have no problem being a grown-up. Tell me.'

The rain woman laughs. 'You'll need a few more centuries before you are a grown-up.'

Then she tells me what she saw in Matjek Chen's vir, on a beach.


'So. Innocence,' I say when she is finished.

'That's what you have to steal, and not the way you usually do it,' she says.

I swallow. A part of me is rationalising already: it's Matjek Chen, the great monster lord of the System, there is nothing I can do that he has not already done a thousand times.

And I want to be free.

'Are we talking,' I say, 'or are we stealing?'

She gives me a wet kiss on the cheek. Then she vanishes into the rain like the Cheshire Cat, off to make mischief for the hsien-kus, to take over the systems of the Gourd.

I look at my reflection in the puddle at my feet. It gazes back at me, and there is an accusation in its eyes. *Abyss. Monsters. That sort of thing.*

But I am a better thief than a philosopher, and it is too late for that anyway. I need to find Matjek Chen, and I need to start somewhere. And the only thing I remember is the fire-eater in Paris.

Chen has come to the banks of the Seine to watch the fire-eater, and Jean le Flambeur has come to watch him.

It is evening, a sharp tinge of autumn in the air, Notre Dame looming on the other side of the river like a great stone spider, dwarfed by the silver spires of the Cité Nouvelle in the sky. The fire-eater is an old, bare-chested Brazilian man whose muscles look like bundles of ropes. Firelight from a dozen torches spinning in a metal wheel plays on his deep brown skin. He picks one, bends his neck, and slowly thrusts the torch between his lips. A great gout of flame like the backlash of a blast furnace rushes out, and the fire-eater's cheeks and throat glow like a jack-o-lantern.

Chen stares, mesmerised, as the old man licks the air with scintillant tongues of red and orange. Intense eyes, prematurely grey hair tousled by the wind. The father of Fedorovism as a young man.

The young Jean stands on the other side of the crowd, watching him. He is here on behalf of Joséphine Pellegrini. I step into his head. He is a blank gogol, just part of the crowd, but as I follow his movements, the memories come back.

When the fire-eater finishes, I go to him.

'Do you like the circus, Monsieur Chen?' I ask.

He looks at me sharply. 'Fire-eaters more than clowns,' he says.

I take a slight bow. 'I like to think of myself as more of a magician. But perhaps I can make you laugh.'

He smiles a cold smile. 'I doubt it.'

'I represent someone who has taken an interest in your … activities. A wealthy someone. They have a proposition for you.'

'That's not funny.' He turns to leave.

'I know it was you behind what happened in the Iridescent Gateway of Heaven,' I say. 'That wasn't funny either.'

He gives me a look that is so cold that even across the centuries I feel my guts turning into ice. I wave a hand hastily.

'Don't worry, I have no intention of turning you in. That would be professional discourtesy. Hear me out. At least let me buy you a drink.'

'I don't drink,' he says.

'Then you can watch me drink. I know just the place.'

I take him to a bar called Caveau, next to Palais Royal, a few steps off a narrow street of empty windows. We take a few steps down the stairs into the basement bar, order a mojito from the shaven-headed barman from San Francisco. Chen watches me. His stare is intense, and I note with some respect how he is trying to get through the web of agents I have spun around him.

'My employer is curious,' I say. 'Why are you doing this?'

He smiles faintly.

'It's simply that I don't like the way the world is. Is that so hard to believe?'

'I understand you didn't like the Heaven either.'

The Fedorovists rescued minds from black box software camps, coordinated attacks by fabbed drones, remotely piloted by activists around the world. Too bad the liberated minds took over the infrastructure of Shenzen and crashed it. Living computer viruses, crazy from pain, able to break into any automated control system and make copies of themselves.

'The Heaven was just a start,' he says.

'Fedorov saw this coming. The next revolution will be against death. I don't like death. I thought that we would agree on that at least, Monsieur le Flambeur.'

I raise my eyebrows. Obviously, he is better informed than I thought. But then, having countless liberated slaves on his side gives him certain advantages.

'I'm having enough trouble avoiding the police, let alone death. I'm not interested in ideology. What I do is just a game.'

'It is not a game to me.'

What is it? What changed him? What made him who he is? The pearls of Martha Wayne. Uncle Ben. Whatever it is, I'm not going to find it here.

I wish I could see into his equipment, the primitive upload cap he wears, synchronising versions of himself into the cloud. But that data is forever lost in the Collapse. *Come on, young Jean, you can do better than that.*

'My employer can see that. So she is offering to help you. Equipment. Money. Whatever you need, it's yours.'

'And what is their price?'

I smile. 'Immortality, of course.'

\*

I leave my past self and the chen drinking and contemplating the world that is coming. Unfortunately, this is going nowhere. There must be something else that I found before, something that convinced me there was a lost gogol of Matjek Chen on Earth. I instantiate a blank gogol in the vir and ask the barman to mix me a screwdriver. The embodiment and the alcohol feel good, but do not provide any answers.

A touch on my sleeve. A wooden mask looks at me, painted with faded colours, a grinning monster. It is made less threatening by the fact that the person who wears it is a little girl, in a dirty dress covered in soot stains, barefoot.

I blink.

'What—'

She lifts a finger to her wooden mouth.

'Ssh,' she says.

I flip out of the temporary gogol to the 4D view. She is still there, a presence that does not belong. In four dimensions, she is an infinite chain of mirror images, a serpent. She motions me to follow.

'I will help you,' she says, 'if you tell me a story.'

'Who are you?'

'A sister. A mother. A goddess. A princess. A queen. Tell me a story and I will take you to what you seek.'

'What kind of story?'

'A true story.'

On Mars, I left myself a memory trail, something triggered by my presence. Perhaps this is something similar. In that case, it's best to play along.

Her ember eyes gleam behind the mask, full of curiosity.

'It's quite a long story,' I say, 'but I guess we have time.'

I order another drink and begin.

'As always, before the warmind and I shoot each other, I try to make small talk.'

'Thank you,' she says when it's over. Her voice is barely a whisper, wind blowing in a chimney. Then the world changes, and I am alone with three ghosts.

A dark-skinned man in a neat beard and a suit sits behind a table, looking at a young couple. A handsome young man with thick blond hair in jeans and a T-shirt, a tiny Asian woman who can't stay still. She keeps touching the man's forearm.

The man behind the desk smiles at them. Don Luis Perenna, Jannah Corporation, sales representative, director. A serial entrepreneur who has come up with yet another business model for the hyper-rich. I suppose I did the same thing, until I met Joséphine.

He gives them an understanding look.

'I have children myself,' he says. 'A boy and a girl. They are already in the program. I can't tell you what comfort it gives me, every night. The old nightmare of a parent. They say that after you have a child, every night is full of fear. We want to help you to carry that fear, to take away the fangs of death.'

'I'm still not sure about this,' says the man, Bojan Chen, Matjek Chen's father. 'There are just so many philosophical issues—'

'Of course, I understand,' says Perenna. 'There is philosophy – loving wisdom – and then there is *love*. We at Jannah are more interested in the latter.'

'We talked about this already,' the woman says, firmly. Her grip on Bojan's forearm tightens. The sensors in the office are good enough that I can watch the decision-making processes unfold in their brains. Perenna has them hooked.

'All right,' the young man says. 'Let's see it.'

The screens show structures that look like underground bunkers. 'Powered by geothermal energy and fusion. With a unique backup feature. Secret location.' *Damn it. I'm going to go through Jannah's records in more detail.*

'We can guarantee absolute security. It will survive even an asteroid impact. The clockspeed within will be slow by default, with periodic synchronisation—'

I was right. There *is* a secret gogol of Matjek Chen, buried somewhere on Earth. That's going to be the key to the operation. That, and the body thieves. I craft a coded message to Mieli and send it out, into the Sobornost thoughtwisp network.

The vir freezes.


'What an interesting discovery,' Hsien-ku Quintic Equations says. 'Extraordinary! Quite a scholarly achievement for somebody from your copyclan.'

'What do you want?' I say in Sumanguru's growl.

'I was merely making sure that you found whatever it was that you were looking for. I couldn't imagine anything like this. How did you come across it? A new fragment of the lives of the Chens.'

'I would not advise you to interfere,' I say. *The bitch set me up*.

She nods politely.

'Of course not. However, I would ask you for a favour.'

I get it: it's going to be a *blat* game. The problem with central planning is that you always end up getting out of sync with it, and there are alternative ways to get things done. I should have known. The hsien-kus are sufficiently far from the deep *guberniya* time that they play fast and loose with the Plan.

'There is a small matter requiring attention in the flesh-realm of Sirr, and your assistance would be much appreciated...'

# 19

# TAWADDUD IN THE PALACE OF STORIES

I'm climbing down the Gomelez Shard of Sirr like a spider, with the wildcode desert behind my back. The desert looks like a city at night, full of faintly glowing lines and patterns that the eye gets lost in. So I keep focused on Tawaddud Gomelez who climbs a few metres above me, sleek body clad in black Sealed fabric, deftly finding one handhold after another. You learn a few things growing up in a vertical city, I suppose.

I appreciate the view. That is about the only good thing about this part of the job. As heights go, it doesn't get much worse than this. The Shard on the desert side is a sheer, smooth surface: only the occasional crack in the old dead smartmatter provides any purchase whatsoever. I cling to it tenuously with the tiny spikes from my palms and the soles of my bare feet, hugging it like a lover, trying to ignore the hundreds of metres of empty space below us.

On paper, as plans go, it's not bad: avoiding Cassar Gomelez's Repentant guards by climbing down the outside of the Wall, where the jinni don't like to go, wearing mutalibun gear to shield us from the wildcode wind. In reality, it's harder. In spite of the heavy fabric, there are already little sparks in my field of vision that indicate wildcode working its way into my brain.

'We should have stolen a bloody magic carpet,' I mutter for the fourth time. But Tawaddud would not hear of it: that would have given us away immediately.

Instead, she dug up a concoction from the spiderwoman of Banu Sasan that she made me drink, a bitter and sticky greenish fluid: still, whatever nanites it introduced into my Sobornost-compiled body worked. I don't really *get* Sirr technology, if you can call it that: creating geometric shapes and words that create mind-states that activate ancient hidden commands in the athar – their name for spimescape – reverse-engineering the brain-computer interface of old nanotech. And then there are the Secret Names that seem to go even deeper, and have something to do with the wildcode.

*What the hell are you doing, Jean?*

*Perhonen*'s voice in my head almost makes me lose my grip. For a moment, I swing one-handed over the abyss. The rope that attaches me to Tawaddud goes taut. She looks down, but I gesture to assure her it's okay.

'Keep it down, damn it,' I tell the ship. 'Where have you been?'

*It took a while for the pellegrini to get me access to the Gourd comms systems.*

'So she has been busy. What about Mieli?'

*She has her mercenary identity firmly in place.*

'Good. We are not the only ones after the jannah, but the plan has worked so far. I have a feeling that somebody is going to be hiring a *lot* of mercenaries soon. If she can join up with the right crowd, we'll be in a position to move.'

*And the ... other thing?*

'That's why I'm pretending to be a spider at the moment.'

*You know I don't like this, Jean. And now you are making the poor girl promises you can't keep.*

'I always keep my promises, you know that—'

*Don't go there.*

'Now is not the time to start getting cold feet. We had a deal, remember?'

*As long as you keep your end of the bargain. By the way, the pellegrini says that there is quite a lot of unusual activity in the Gourd, too. The hsien-kus are up to something. And it's hard to do this kind of thing discreetly. I may have to—*

Suddenly, the voice of the ship is gone. I swear under my breath. But we have come too far to turn back now. I gesture again at Tawaddud. Another two hundred metres down. My body feels battered and aching. It's like having a cold. When I instantiated it from the Gourd systems, I was not able to include any of the serious enhancements from the Sobornost body the pellegrini gave me – it's still in stasis aboard *Perhonen*. And wildcode is making a serious mess of my innards. I'm hoping I can survive as long as it takes to get the job done.

And then I need my escape route to work, too.

Tawaddud yanks on the rope. Below us is what looks like a viewing gallery, unlit.

Just as I cut through its Sealed glass, my q-tool sputters and dies, changing shape. I swear and eject it with a yelp. It vanishes into the darkness below, twisting and sputtering like a firecracker as it goes.

'Try this,' Tawaddud says and hands me an old-fashioned tool: a diamond attached to a metal compass.

Diamonds are worthless in Sirr: children go and gather them from where the Sobornost ships fell during the Cry of

Wrath. There is some pleasure in using what must have run a thousand Sobornost gogols as a sharp instrument for breaking and entering. After a few moments of work, I remove a circular disc of glass carefully, and we slip in.

It is a palace under construction, empty and quiet. Tawaddud leads us through it, to a ledge that overhangs a vertical drop that goes all the way down to the bottom of the Shard, a yawning pit lined with jinn wires.

'How are we going to get down there?' I ask.

Tawaddud gives me a serious look. 'Do you trust me, Lord Sumanguru?'

Her eyes are dark and beautiful in the night. She has been through a lot. Like me, she escaped a prison and ended up back in one. She is chasing something that will always escape her. She wants to do the right thing.

The ship is right. I'm going to let her down.

*Do what you do best.*

So I nod slowly and smile.

'Then give me your hand.'

She squeezes my fingers in a surprisingly strong grip. Then she steps into the abyss, pulling me along with her.

I let out a scream and try to grab hold of something, but it is too late. We plummet down into the blackness. I hear Tawaddud laughing. Suddenly, there is an amber shimmering around us, and the fall becomes a gentle descent.

'An angelnet,' I breathe.

Tawaddud floats next to me and waves.

'Yes!' she laughs. 'Only the Ugarte Shard still has a fully functioning one. That's where the richest gogol merchants live. But here, you have to know where to look.'

I close my eyes as we fall, carried by the ancient guardian

angels of Sirr-in-the-sky, and keep them shut all the way down.

After the descent, they take the last tram to the base of the Uzeda Shard.

Tawaddud stands opposite Sumanguru, holding on to a handlebar. The city lights glint in his athar glasses, reflections dancing to the rhythm of the rails. He has chosen round, blue ones that match the colours of the mutalibun gear.

'This broken spimescape of yours hurts my eyes,' he says, 'but I think we are being followed.'

Tawaddud looks past him and curses under her breath. There are three jinni following them, colourful serpents made from polygons, swirling amongst the people in the car, moving faster than a human could, riding the jinn wires above the train. Without thought-forms, they will see relatively little in the physical world – so what is needed is a disguise in the athar.

Tawaddud picks out a couple on the train, a slight woman gesturing animatedly at her partner, talking about a new jinn jar for their servant. Under her breath, she whispers the Secret Name of Al-Musawwir, the Fashioner of Forms, duplicating her own shape and that of Sumanguru in the athar, overlaying them on the couple. Then she waits, and sure enough, when the couple gets off at the next stop, two of the jinni follow them, leaving the third one lingering behind. After a few moments, it darts away too.

'Smooth,' Sumanguru says.

The only Sirr fragment not completely built up, the Uzeda Shard is covered in scaffoldings and plastic sheets, a sign of ongoing construction projects to repair the damage of a great wildcode infection two years ago. Tawaddud remembers the great structures that suddenly sprang into being, a wildcode thing brought from the desert by a contaminated soul train, a tree of sapphire climbing up the shard. It grew so fast you could see it, a whirlpool of wild jinni around it in the athar.

As they get closer to the dark skeleton in the horizon, her heart beats faster. *Duny. Duny. I am doing the right thing. Father must know the truth.* She thinks about the long nights of guilt, of the feeling that something was wrong. *Maybe it was her all along. She wanted me to feel small so I would stay out of her way.*

She squeezes the Sobornost mind-bullet in her pocket. *It will emulate a part of your brain, the part the fragment will enter,* Sumanguru said. *It's like a jinn jar, except that he can't get out.* Such a small thing, cool metal, the size of her fingertip.

She tries to think about Kafur's calm voice, how he took her in after the City of the Dead. *He is going to help. It is going to be all right.* Kafur taught her that everything heals.

There are great differences in altitude here, sudden sharp drops beneath the elevated tram rails and yawning vertical alleys that go up to the Shard. She looks down at the Great Northern Station where the infection started. The long low halls and arcs still bear the marks of the battle the muhtasibs and Repentants fought to contain the infection, scarred ribs of metal and glass.

*Even if it takes a while for the scars to disappear.*

They get off at the last stop, squeezing past wirers and workmen returning from late shifts at the sites. Tawaddud leads them down a winding stairway into the lower levels. There are no signs of Repentants, and the athar here is so sparse and broken that it would be difficult for the jinni to track them anyway. Duny must be seething with rage some-where.

There are glowing signs in the arches that appear as they enter the remains of the Northern Station. The rattle of trams above makes it difficult to speak. There is a smell of ozone everywhere, and the air tastes thick. An old soul train tunnel opens before them suddenly like the pupil of a giant eye.

Inside, the ground is uneven, and Tawaddud almost cuts herself on the diamond rail. In the distance, there are rumblings and mutterings. The Banu Sasan whisper that the wildcode creature was not completely defeated, that its children still live in the ruins.

'When you mentioned palaces,' Sumanguru says, 'this is not exactly what I had in mind.'

'Ssh,' Tawaddud says. Ahead, there is a glowing sign on the wall, a simple circle, with two dots for eyes. A face. Tawaddud speaks the Name Kafur taught her, long ago, and a door opens, revealing a long corridor dimly lit with red light, echoing with distant music and whispers.

Tawaddud gives Sumanguru a white mask and puts one over her own face.

'Welcome to the Palace of Stories.'


The Palace has changed, as it always does. It is a labyrinth of dimly lit passages that suddenly expand into rooms when you turn a corner.

There is a room with huge white walls on which shadows dance even if there is no apparent source of light, spiky-haired, long-limbed blots of ink that flee when Tawaddud tries to touch them. Another huge hall is criss-crossed by copper wires and hums with static electricity, making her feel heavy as if before a thunderstorm, her hair standing up, crackling. There is a gallery with walls of dark velvet, with thousands of candles burning in the ceiling, upside down, following the gestures of a man wearing a black suit and white gloves and a ballet dancer's skirt, a slow dance of light and flame. The athar is thick with jinni weaving illusions.

A delicate woman with boyish dark hair, with a red mask instead of white, approaches them and gives a slight bow.

'You look like you have never been to the Palace before,' she tells Sumanguru. 'How may we serve you? What is your pleasure? Bodies for jinni, stories for flesh.' She looks the Sobornost gogol up and down, one hand on her hip, stroking her lips with a finger. 'Lord Shoulders here could enjoy cinema, perhaps, or detective stories. As for you—' She blinks. 'Tawaddud?'

'Emina.' Tawaddud smiles beneath her mask. 'I am here to see Kafur.'

Emina grabs her arm and pulls her through a velvet curtain, to a small bare-walled chamber.

'You have some nerve to come here, you little bitch,' she hisses.

'Emina, I—'

'When the Repentants came for you, we had to run and hide. I went to the City of the Dead. I was a ghul for a while. Do you know what that's like? Of course not, Miss Tawaddud who came to play at being an embodiment slave, until the fun was over and it was time to go back to Daddy.' She throws her hands into the air in disgust.

'And who is this? A new plaything? He smells of Sobornost. We have masrurs here, you know. But why would you care about that, living in your palace now?'

'It wasn't like that. Please listen to me.'

Emina takes a sobbing breath. 'Of course it was. Silly girl. Go away now. Shoo.' She wipes her eyes and waves towards the corridor.

'Emina, please. I need Kafur's help. I'm looking for the Axolotl. I have sobors, I can pay—'

Emina looks at her sideways. 'So. The Axolotl. Finally. Tired of the limp-dicked mutalibun lords, eh?' She crosses her arms. 'Tell me, is it another game of pretend, or something more?'

Tears well up in Tawaddud's eyes.

'It is something more,' she whispers. She wipes her eyes on her sleeve.

Emina looks at her for a moment. Then she gives her a hug.

'There, there, Tawa, it's all right. You look terrible. Don't make it worse. Aunt Emina will sort it out. I will take you to Kafur, and if that silly man does not help you, he'll answer to me.'

She pats Tawaddud's back. 'The Axolotl has been here, but not for a while. They say he has been running with the masrurs, attacking soul trains, fighting Sobornost.' She gives Sumanguru a dark look. 'You should be careful of the company you keep.'

'Emina, I'm … I'm sorry about what happened. I did not want to cause trouble for anybody. This was a good place for me. Please tell Zuweyla and Marjana and Ghanim and everybody that—'

Emina's eyes sparkle. 'Don't you worry about that. You just needed a spanking, that's all. We all want the story of the jinn prince, and if you found yours, all the better. Now come on - let's go find Kafur.' She frowns. 'He has changed a bit since you last saw him.'

Kafur receives them in a cavernous space, sitting cross-legged on the floor under a railway arch – they must be somewhere below the Station. Kafur wears a familiar long-sleeved, hooded robe, but is more crooked and twisted than Tawaddud remembers. His face is hidden behind a red mask. He is flanked by the two jinn thought-forms in forbidden female shapes, one with naked flesh of glittering, silvery snake scales, the other a slender sculpture of ice.

*I have been away a long time*, Tawaddud thinks.

'Come closer,' Kafur says. His voice has changed, too: it is higher, trilling, mixed with the sound of bells, not a human voice at all. 'I never thought I would see you again. Such a beautiful self-loop. Come closer.'

There are pillows on the ground in a semicircle before Kafur. Tawaddud kneels on one of them.

'Master, I come asking for a boon,' she says.

'A boon? Tawaddud, who now lives in the world of palaces and high muhtasib lords and the mighty Sobornost, comes back to the world of stories and secrets, and the first thing she asks Kafur is a boon? Do you not have a kiss for me, for old times' sake?'

Kafur pulls back his hood and removes his mask. 'Even if wildcode has not been kind to me. No one escapes the Destroyer of Delights.'

His face is a bloated, fungus-like mass, purple and blue, with yawning openings in his cheeks, running with pale fluids. Tiny things move and chitter in his empty eyesockets: chimera insects with iridescent shells that dart in and out of the crevices and creep across the ruin of Kafur's visage. He touches the black wound where his lips used to be with an embroidered sleeve. Tawaddud's stomach turns.

'So, what do you say? You can close your eyes if you wish.'

Sumanguru gets up, raising a fist. 'Maybe *I'll* give you a kiss,' he growls.

Tawaddud lays a hand on his arm.

'The Palace is his,' she says calmly. 'I will pay his price.'

'I cannot accept that.'

'I would have thought you did not care much for what the flesh does with flesh.'

'This is different,' Sumanguru says, staring at Kafur.

'I know what I'm doing,' Tawaddud says, and speaks the Secret Name of Al-Jabbar, the Irresistible.

It is possible to entwine forcibly, especially with a jinn. It is one of the forbidden things, but she is too angry to think about the consequences. She binds the serpent jinn woman's self-loop into her own with the Name. Then she kisses Kafur as the jinn woman, tongue turning into foglets, fire and poison, sucking air out of his lungs until he is left sputtering and gasping.

When she pulls back and wipes her own lips with the back of her hand, the jinn thought-form lets out an angry scream and evaporates into thin air. The forced entwinement brings a blinding headache, but she grits her teeth.

'You really need to work on your stamina, Kafur, if you want to trade in kisses instead of stories,' she says.

Kafur stares at her for a moment and bursts out laughing, a shrill, crickety sound. 'A kiss to die for, I agree!' He replaces his mask. 'Now, what is it that you want from old Kafur, dear Tawaddud?'

Tawaddud swallows. 'You taught me that entwinement always leaves a trace. I want to contact a jinn, Zaybak, also known as the Axolotl, whose tomb you found me in. I want to find him in my mind. If I served you well, please help me do this thing.'

'You did serve me well.' Kafur's hands move inside his long sleeves, sinuous and quick. 'But you also brought Repentants to my house. What you ask is no small thing. You want to make what was torn asunder into one. You want me to cast a net into the athar to catch the father of body thieves and bring him to you, like a desert gogol in a jar. What will you give me in return?'

'My father will—'

'Ah. Your father. A wealthy man, a powerful man, with many gogols, many palaces, many friends. But here we care not for the common coin of Sirr-in-the-day. You know this: our trade is in Names and stories. Can you offer Kafur either, Tawaddud of House Gomelez, who learned all she knows from him? Can you tell me a Name I do not know? Or can you tell me a story I have not heard before, like the Aun always ask?'

She thinks about the Name the qarin told her, and it rises to her lips. But then, Sumanguru speaks.

'How about a story from the stars?' he says.

'Interesting,' Kafur says. 'That would be a rare jewel indeed.'

Sumanguru removes his athar glasses.

'This is a story I heard from a spaceship, but I swear it's true,' he says. 'Once upon a time, there were two girls called Mieli and Sydän who went to a flying city on Venus so they could live for ever.'

## 20

# THE STORY OF MIELI AND SYDÄN

Mieli presses her face against the invisible skin of the flying city and watches her lover dance in the sky.

The Venusian godlings are naked, chalk-skinned shapes against the sulphur acid clouds, Sydän a tiny thing next to them on her borrowed wings. Mieli watches as they swoop and chase her, force her into a spiralling dive and knows that she is laughing, wildly and loudly, having the time of her life.

'Mieli, girl! Come on!' she shouts in Mieli's ear. 'I bet you can't catch me!'

It would only take a moment to be there with her, to let the city give her a second skin and enough strength for her wings to survive the Venerian wind, but Mieli lets Sydän have this thing to herself. Besides, she still feels *heavy*, earthbound, in spite of Amtor City's utility foglets supporting her frame like a gentle ghost hand. She does not want to fly just yet. Or so she tells herself.

She feels vertigo looking at the rough basalt landscape below, with its strange fractures, furrows and tick-shaped volcanoes, thinking about the three-hundred-mile winds that roar outside, the searing heat under the angry cloud cover that makes the whole planet something akin to a vast pressure cooker. Mieli is no stranger to deadly environments, having spent most of her life in vacuum skinsuits, but the Dark Man of space is not angry at you, just empty. For Venus, it's personal, and Mieli is not ready to meet her, not yet.

*Stop moping,* says *Perhonen* in her mind. *Go out. Fly. Play. We came all this way. Let's enjoy it.* There is impatience in the ship's voice.

'Quiet,' says Mieli. 'I want to watch the dawn.'

In Amtor City, the dawn lasts for ever, the eye of the sun orange and red, painting the thick milky clouds in colours she has never seen in Oort, in the land of ice and dirty snow. The city rides the hot winds at the terminator, racing daylight: a bubble of q-stone and diamond with a city of fairy towers inside, all tall tensegrity spires and twined candyfloss. A civilisation dancing on the breath of Venus, fifty kilometres above the surface.

The viewing bubbles on the edge of the city provide a perfect view, and Mieli is content just to sit and enjoy it by herself. Being alone is a strange sensation after the journey, after all that time together under the thin skin of the spidership, light hours from the Kuiper belt, months surfing the Highway manifold.

But perhaps it is not enough to look at the dawn. Perhaps she should go —

'Hey, Oort girl. Want a peach?'

The voice startles her. There is a boy on the next bench, perhaps sixteen years old, with dark skin that looks coppery in the Venerian dawn-light. He is wearing storybook clothes: jeans and a T-shirt, loose on his skinny frame. His hair is thin and grey, but his eyes are young and piercingly blue. He sits with his knees up, hands folded behind his head, leaning back. There is a backpack next to him.

'How do you know I come from Oort?' Mieli asks.

'Oh, you know.' The youth strokes his chin. 'You have the look. Like planets are too big for you. Peach?'

He reaches into his backpack, pulls out a golden orb and throws it at her. She almost fails to catch it, unused to the quick parabolic arcs in the gravity. She blushes.

'It is not too big,' Mieli says. 'Just too much gravity.' She walks to the bench, self-conscious of her gait: she keeps feeling that she'll fall through the floor any minute and walks carefully, as if the ground was made of thin glass. The boy moves his backpack and she sits down next to him, grateful.

'So, why are you not out there, in the air, flying? That should make it easier.'

Mieli takes a bite of the peach. It is sweet and yielding, with a trace of bitterness, like Venerian air.

'And you? Why are you not flying?' she asks.

'Well,' says the boy. 'You're here, for one thing. Prettiest girl I've ever seen, all alone in the city of the gods.' He bites his lip. 'Or maybe I just don't like flying.'

Mieli sits on the bench next to the boy and finishes eating the peach in silence. She keeps the peach stone in her mouth. Its surface is rough, and she imagines that that is what the *venera firma* below would feel like if she could reach out and touch it with her tongue. Uneven basalt, sticky almost-liquid air and bitter acid.

'My ... woman is out there,' she says. Talking to someone who is not Sydän or *Perhonen* feels good. 'We came here yesterday. It is very strange here. She likes it. I do not.'

'I didn't even think Oortians came this far to the Inner System. Not that I'm complaining, of course.'

For a moment, she wants to tell the story to someone. *We met building big things and fell in love. We fought in a war, tribes against tribes. Everyone thought we were dead. So Sydän decided we might as well be.* But the look in the boy's eyes is too intense.

'It's a long story,' she says aloud. 'How did you know I wasn't one of *them*?' She gestures at the white winged figures in the clouds, now almost invisible in the distance.

'The peach,' says the boy. 'They don't eat. Not like you did, anyway.' He grins. 'It's also symbolic. Paris gave it to the prettiest goddess.'

*He flatters well,* says *Perhonen. Better than Sydän, almost.*

'You agreed that I am not a goddess,' Mieli says.

'You'll do. Until I find the real one.'

'That doesn't sound like a compliment.'

'Sorry,' the boy says. 'I meant that literally. I'm here for the quake. When the city falls. When the Sobornost gods come out.'

*What is he talking about?* Mieli whispers to *Perhonen.*

*I have no idea,* the ship says.

The boy sees her confusion. 'Do you know what a Bekenstein quake is?' he asks.

'No. But perhaps I should.'

'That's what happens to all the Wind Cities. That's why everybody comes here. Pilgrims and posthumans and monsters and godlings, from the Belt and the Oubliette and even zoku, from Jupiter and Saturn. They come here to be taken by the Sobornost, to give themselves to the Great Common Task.

'The city falls. The Sobornost machines take it. They

collapse it to Planck scale. There is a singularity. The information density goes beyond the Bekenstein bound. You get a little black hole: so small it's not stable. So it blows up, beneath the crust. It's a fantastic lightshow. And it'll happen here soon.' There is a wistful look in the boy's eyes.

'The goddess will come after the quake, to gather her children, to soak up the Hawking radiation. I'm here to meet her. And to give her a peach of immortality.'

Mieli stands up. Her body still feels so heavy it might be encased in lead, but she does not care.

'She didn't tell me,' she says quietly. *She didn't tell me!* she screams at *Perhonen*. *You didn't tell me!*

*I didn't want to interfere,* the ship protests. *I thought she was going to tell you.*

'Thank you,' she tells the boy quietly. 'I hope you find your goddess.'

'Oh, I will,' he says, but Mieli is already running, towards the edge of the city and the clouds and the fifty-kilometre fall. She spreads her arms, opens her wings and leaps.

Sydän turns it into a chase, just like they used to do in the Chain in Oort. It always ends the same way, and by the time Sydän lets Mieli catch her, she is no longer angry.

They make love on Venus for the first time in a q-dot bubble above the Cleopatra Crater, on the slopes of Maxwell Montes, leaving them exhausted and bathing in the honey-coloured light of the clouds, wrapped around each other. Mieli traces the silvery lines of scars where Sydän's wings used to be. The other woman shivers with pleasure, and then shifts in her embrace.

'Look, you can see a *guberniya* from here,' Sydän says, pointing up. And there it is, a bright evening star. A diamond

217

eye in the sky, one of the homes of the deep Sobornost gods: an artificial sphere the size of old Earth, made from sunlifted carbon, thinking thoughts bigger than the sum of humanity. 'Doesn't it make you feel funny? How far we have come?'

Mieli feels cold. She touches Sydän's cheek.

'What's wrong?'

'I'm afraid of this place,' Mieli says. 'We did not have to come here. The sunsmiths told us about Jovian polises, and the red planet where they drink wine and listen to old Earth music. Why are we here?'

Sydän turns away, hugging her knees. She takes her jewelled chain – fashioned after their first Great Work – and starts wrapping it around her left forearm.

'You know why,' she says.

'Why do you want to be a goddess?'

Sydän looks at her, her lips a stern line in the dark, but says nothing.

'You want to fall with the city,' says Mieli. 'A pilgrim told me. Be a thought in its mind when it dies.'

'It's a dream, all right? My dream,' says Sydän. 'Kirkkaat Kutojat think they are so good. Let's all build ice bridges to the stars, let's be free. Fine. Great. But we *die*. We die and become ghosts. The ancestors are not us, not really: just shades and memories and bones of ice. I don't want that. Not ever.' She touches Mieli just above the heart with her chained hand. 'We could do it together.'

Mieli shakes her head slowly.

'You were right. All my life they told me that I'm special,' she says. 'The tithe child, Grandmother's pet. But none of that is as special as the me that is with you. I want to be that, just that, for a while. It's the fear of losing it that makes it special. If it was for ever, it would not matter as much.'

Sydän says looks at Amtor City, a distant amber bubble in the sky, like a snowglobe.

'I'll stay with you. I promise,' she says, after a while. 'Damn. I still suck at this.' She wipes her eyes. 'So. Sightseeing instead. How about watching a transhuman mind have a Hawking orgasm? From afar.'

Mieli smiles. A warm rush of relief washes over her.

'I bet you say that to all the girls,' she says.

*I still think the best place to watch this thing would be in orbit,* mutters *Perhonen. Preferably around Mars.*

'Ssh. It's about to start', says Mieli, tingling with excitement. Snowflakes of data drift across her field of vision, superimposed on the forbidding landscape of Lakshmi Planum. There is movement everywhere on the basalt surface: the von Neumann beasts are fleeing in all directions, scuttling up the steep cliffs at the base of Maxwell Montes. They look like black ants in the blood-coloured haze of a Venerian morning, moving in panicky shifting swarms.

*Have a look at this.* The ship passes Mieli a feed from orbit: Amtor City is the eye of a maelstorm, a blue-white perfect golden-ratio spiral. *Mieli, there are thinking mountains down there. Even up here, the data stream is a bit of a headfuck. If I go mad or spontaneously transcend in the next five minutes, I'm going to blame you.*

'Shut up. We're having fun.' Mieli squeezes Sydän's hand: the responsive smartmatter of her suit melts away, and she grips her warm fingers hard.

They're both wearing heavy quickstone suits, and a laser beam from orbit is feeding power to their q-dot bubble shield that is currently pretending to be a hyperdense element at the far, far end of the periodic table. Sobornost hospitality extends even to those who do not give their minds away just yet.

*If anybody asks, I'll be digging my head in the sand and praying that I still have a human captain four minutes from now,* whispers *Perhonen* and disappears. Its absence is a small sharp shock to Mieli, but there is little time to worry about that when the world explodes.

A vast hand grabs a moon-sized fistful of rock and basalt from the centre of the Lakshmi plateau and *squeezes*. There is a flash of light, barely filtered by the q-bubble, and then there is a swirling crater, a growing whirlpool of rock and dust, pulled in by an incandescent pinpoint that is the new-born singularity.

Amtor City dives right into it, a falling star.

A funnel of dust rises into the sky, eclipsing what blood-hued sunlight there is. The Maxwell Mountains shake like dying animals. Mieli feels the vibrations in her bones, lets out a small gasp and Sydän squeezes her hand harder. *The grey-haired boy was right. This is giant-land.*

The whirlpool grows and starts to glow as rock and dust become white-hot plasma. From their vantage point it looks like a glowing drill is being pushed through Venus's skin, revealing the shifting, intricate layers of computronium beneath the crust. The q-bubble struggles to keep up with the barrage it is taking across the electromagnetic spectrum and switches to neutrino tomography. Basalt and lava become transparent like glass, leaving the spiraling madness visible around the Bekenstein epicentre where god-thoughts have pierced the fabric of spacetime.

Mieli is dimly aware of the fact that this is more of a cartoon than a faithful representation of what is really going on, but she doesn't care, watching elaborate shapes form around the infant black hole, wishing for a second that she had the accelerated senses of the Sobornost gogols.

There is a shell that surrounds the little godhead completely now, multifaceted and intricate. The earth beneath their feet no longer so much shakes as hums, and Mieli's teeth rattle even in spite of the q-bubble's attempt to dampen the resonances.

'Any second now', whispers Sydän. Mieli kisses her hard, briefly joining their smartmatter suits into one.

'Thanks', she says.

'Thanks for what?'

'For showing me this.'

'You're welcome,' Sydän says. 'And I'm sorry. I need it to be for ever.'

She squeezes Mieli's hand so hard it almost hurts. Then she lets go and takes a step forward, outside the q-dot bubble, and starts running. Mieli tries to grab her arm. She comes away with the jewelled chain in her fingers.

For a moment, Sydän turns to look back. She wavers in the information wind, face swirling into whiteness like cream poured into coffee.

Mieli screams, but it is too small a sound against the all-engulfing voice of the dying city.

The quake comes. The black hole has been teetering on the brink of instability for minutes, balanced precariously on the edge by the Higgs-churning machines around it, the superthread modes trapped in its event horizon computing furiously for an artificial eternity. It explodes, screaming out all the thoughts it has thought in its own private hell, the mass of a mountain converted into Hawking radiation in an instant.

The q-bubble groans, goes opaque and dissipates, but

Mieli's quicksuit holds under the impact of the blast wave. Basalt shatters under her feet. The white fire grinds Mieli between the hammer of pressure and the anvil of rock.

The last thing she sees before blackness is *Perhonen*'s feed from orbit, a fiery crack opening up in the face of Lakshmi like a mocking smile.

*That was, by far, the stupidest thing I've ever seen you do,* says *Perhonen*.

Mieli floats in a sea of gentle euphoria, soothing blue shapes dancing in front of her eyes. But underneath the coolness hot pain is hiding, pulsing ever so slightly in her bones.

*Don't try to move. You are a mess. Compound fractures, a punctured lung, internal bleeding. I dumped the suit's nanomeds, they've been mutated. Probably shaping some rock into a liver at the moment.*

'Where's Sydän?' she says.

*Not far.*

'Show me.'

*You really shouldn't—*

'Show me!'

She is dragged back to the cold hard rock of reality. There is pain, and she feels groggy, but at least she can see. She lies on her back sprawled on a craggy basalt edifice. It is almost completely dark: dust swirls in the sky, blocking the cloud cover glow. The dark shapes of Von Neumann beasts creep across the landscape slowly, carefully. Lakshmi Planitia is no more – in its place is an impossibly smooth crater of some godstuff she cannot name.

She sits up slowly and sees the grey-haired boy, watching her.

He does not wear a quicksuit, or any other form of

protection that Mieli can see, sitting on hot basalt, leaning back.

'Did you find your goddess?' she asks, almost laughing at the absurdity of the sight.

'I did,' the boy says. 'But it seems that you lost yours.'

Mieli closes her eyes. 'What is it to you?'

'I was not entirely honest with you. I'm not a pilgrim. You could say that I'm ... management. And I take an interest in whoever passes through here, whether they decide to join us or not.'

'She let go of my hand,' Mieli says. 'She did not want me to come. I can't follow her.'

'I didn't think you would. In spite of our reputation, we respect that. Or some of us do, in any case.' He walks to Mieli and offers her a hand, helping her up. With the suit's support, she manages to stand.

'Look at you. That won't do. See, this is what you get when you wear flesh and come here.' Suddenly, the suit is flooded with a cool sensation, fresh nanomeds, Sobornost ones. The pain turns into a full-body tickle.

'To be fair, your friend was not entirely honest with you either,' the boy says. 'She had been speaking to one of my sisters for a while now, about coming here.'

'What can I do?'

'Don't give up,' the boy says. 'I learned that a long time ago. If reality is not what you want it to be, change it. You should not accept anything blindly, not death, not immortality. If you don't want to join her, you can go to my sister and ask for her back. But let me warn you, there will be a price.'

Mieli takes a deep breath. Something rattles in her lungs. She finds that she is holding Sydän's chain in her hand, like a little piece of Oort, made of jewels and songs.

'I'll do it,' she says. 'Just tell me where to go. But why are you doing this?'

'For love,' he says.

'Love for whom?'

'No one,' he says. 'I just want to know what it feels like.'

After three days, Mieli finds the temple on the metallic plain, in the shield volcano's shadow.

Her limbs burn with fatigue. Her muscles and bones have almost completely healed now, and the q-stone armour helps, but hunger and thirst gnaw her insides, and she has to fight to take every step.

The temple is a labyrinth of stone, a seeming jumble of black rectangles and shards like building blocks discarded by a giant child. When she enters, it explodes into an intricate gallery where stone bridges and pathways lead in all directions. *Perhonen* whispers that the whole place is a projection of a larger, higher-dimensional object, a shadow solidified in stone. There, in the black rock, she sees silver flower markings, like the grey-haired boy said, and follows them.

After many twists and turns she finds the singularity in the centre.

It is a tiny thing, a star floating in a cylindrical room. Its Hawking radiation is so bright it floods her quicksuit. When she approaches it, the suit's outer layers evaporate.

*You should go back, Perhonen* shouts in her mind.

She takes another step, and is naked. The radiation that carries the thoughts of the goddess consumes her. Flesh turns into prayer. She holds up her hands. Her fingers burst into flame. The pain is so intense she has no words for it. And then there are no words or thoughts left at all, only burning red—

224

—that becomes the quiet murmur of a bubbling fountain. It is dark. The sky above is a velvet cloak, with tiny pinpricks. Apart from the sound of the fountain, there is a deep quiet, all around. The air tastes moist and fresh.

A woman sits on the steps that lead up to the fountain. She wears a white dress, diamonds around her neck. Her hair is an auburn mass of curls. Her face is neither young nor old. She is reading a book. As Mieli approaches, she looks up.

'Would you care for some wine?' she says.

Mieli hesitates and shakes her head. The goddess is not at all like what she imagined goddesses would be like: not a glowing, translucent being of light or a Titanic pillar of flame, but a woman. She can see the pores of her skin, smells her perfume.

Mieli reaches for *Perhonen*'s comforting presence, but there is nothing there, just a cold sensation down her back, an absence in her mind.

'As you wish. By the way, my hospitality does not extend to small machine things like your ship,' says the goddess. 'But you, please come and sit.'

'I prefer to stand,' Mieli says.

'Ah, spirit. I like that. What is it that you want, child? I embrace all souls who come to me, but not all of them go to such lengths to see me.'

'I want her back.'

The goddess studies her quietly, a faint smile on her lips.

'But of course you do,' she says. 'You haven't had it easy: too many losses in a lifetime too short. Growing up a stranger in the land of silent ice and vacuum wings.' She sighs.

'What would you have me do? I am no zoku genie who could study your volition and do what is best for you.

Otherwise, I would ease the pain of your loss, or perhaps take you to my gogol Library and let you say goodbye properly. Or make a raion and run a vir of the best possible future you two could have had together.

'But I am none of these things. What you want from me is mine. I am Joséphine Pellegrini. I am an avatar of my *guberniya*, and I do not give things away for free. So the question is, what will you give me, little girl? What will you give to get your Sydän back?'

'Everything,' Mieli says. 'Everything except death.'

# 21

# TAWADDUD AND THE AXOLOTL

Sumanguru finishes. He looks at Kafur quietly. His eyes burn in the eyeslits of his mask.

'Well?' Tawaddud says. 'Had you heard it before?'

'I accept the payment,' Kafur says. 'Although I would very much like to hear the ending. Perhaps Lord Scarface has saved it for later?'

'True stories do not always end,' Sumanguru says.

'Truly spoken.' Kafur stands up. 'Tawaddud, dear child, what you ask is not easy. Zaybak the Axolotl has gone to the desert, and is far from athar's reach. To entwine you need athar, to carry thoughts, to bind minds together. But old Kafur is crafty, Kafur is wise, he knows how to ride the wildcode wind.' He laughs softly.

'What do you mean?' Tawaddud asks.

'There are many things I did not teach little Tawaddud. If you want your voice to carry to the desert, you have to let the desert come to you.'

Images of Alile flash in Tawaddud's eyes. 'Is that what you have done?'

'Kafur has drunk the potent wine of stories too deep, it's

true. But it is the desert where stories come from, and that is where you will have to go to find an end to yours.'

'What is he talking about?' Sumanguru whispers.

'If I want to reach the Axolotl, I need to expose myself to wildcode,' Tawaddud says.

The Sobornost gogol touches her shoulder. 'He's mad. Let's get out of here. We will find another way.'

'I have bottled desert jinni who eat wildcode,' Tawaddud says slowly, touching her doctor's bag. 'I have used them to treat Banu Sasan. It could work if we do it quickly. And the Seals in my body are strong, my father made them. It could work.'

Sumanguru's eyes widen. 'But—'

'It's my decision.' She steps forward. 'I'll do it,' she tells Kafur.

The Master of the Palace of Stories bows to her. 'Old Kafur is glad,' he says, 'that somewhere, under the mask of the daughter of the Gomelez, you are still his Tawaddud.'

Deep down in the guts of the Palace, there is a room full of coffins. They are Sealed, emblazoned with the golden spirals and twists that shine brightly against the dark stone.

Laboriously, Kafur opens the lid of one of them. An athar interface flashes into being above it. Inside is a tank shaped like a human body, filled with water, and a breathing apparatus with a black tube like an umbilical.

'You need silence to listen,' he says.

She puts down her bag and takes out three bottles. 'First this one, then this, then this,' she tells Sumanguru. She makes him repeat the Names he must speak.

'This is crazy,' he says. 'You don't have to do this. It's black magic. Five minutes, and I'll get you out. I can take you to the Station, we can clean you up—'

Tawaddud holds up the Sobornost mind-trap. 'You have your magic, Lord Sumanguru, and I have mine.' She removes her robe and her mutalibun bodystocking and lets them fall to the ground. The chill radiating from the coffins makes her bare skin crawl, and she shivers.

Kafur takes out a clear glass bottle, filled with sand.

'Do it,' Tawaddud says.

Kafur opens the bottle and pours the contents over Tawaddud. The sand runs over her skin like a caress. As it touches her, it starts to glow. It feels like the fog-hands in her garden, long ago.

She lies down in the coffin and presses the breathing mask against her face. In an instant, the water becomes the same temperature as her body. Then the lid slams shut, and Tawaddud is alone with the desert.

At first, she feels heavy and weightless at the same time, floating in silence. After a while, the voices start: a thousand whispers, in languages she does not understand, dry and soft like rustling leaves. *Is this what Abu talked about? The voices of the desert.*

Then the lights come. It is like looking at the other Sirr Abu showed her, except she sees the whole world. She is floating in the heart of a galaxy, a vast spiderweb of light, bright pinpoints joined with threads that loop and spiral and intertwine.

*Zaybak,* she whispers. *Come to me.*

Her voice joins the muttering chorus around her, and her words are repeated, an echo of an echo of an echo in the bright net.

Something responds, and her heart jumps. Tendrils of light snake out and curl around her. She looks up and there is a glowing being floating above her, as if in an ocean, a kraken of light, regarding her with curious childlike eyes. One of its tentacles brushes her, briefly, and she feels an echo of terrible longing. Then it is gone, speeding into the gaps of the network like a wisp of smoke.

*Zaybak, where are you?* she calls again.

Something else answers, this time. A shoal of elongated things, snake-like, moving like whips, without eyes but with sharp, sharp teeth. They twine around her limbs, cold and slippery and tight. *Wild jinni who smell a body.* She shouts a Secret Name, but it has no power here; they scatter from her but keep circling, waiting.

*Zaybak!*

There are more jinni, things that look like chains and tori and strange loops that swallow themselves, thick around her, hungry for embodiment, coming closer with each circuit. She tries to feel her body, tries to find the lid of the coffin so she can call to Kafur and Sumanguru and get out. But she has no voice, no flesh.

A wind comes, scattering the desert things, blowing through her and into her and around her, a touch and a kiss and a voice at the same time, and suddenly she remembers steam rising from the tombs in the City of the Dead, after the rain.

*The Axolotl.*

Tawaddud.

*I missed you.*

I missed being you.

A pause.

Why are you here?

*Alile. Show me why.*

Regret. Shame.

*Show me.*

A journey through the desert, searching for purpose. Story gardens where the Aun live. Bliss and emptiness.

Return to the city. Masrurs, they are called, jinn insurgents: they speak of protecting the desert. Their words ring true. They say they are swords of the Aun, whose task is to rid the desert of Sobornost machines. They promise redemption. Battles. Courage. Meaning.

A muhtasib comes. He claims things are changing. Sirr will give names to Sobornost machines, so the Aun do not destroy them. There will be no more desert. No more stories. He says we can stop it. He will give the betrayers of Sirr to us, if we give him our stories.

*So that's why Alile died.*

She did not die! If you know the secret, the desert does not kill. Whisper them the secret of the flower prince, and you take them with you to the desert. They become a story, like us, like the Aun, live for ever inside the wildcode. She is here, Tawaddud. Sirr itself could be here. Without the Sobornost. You could be here. Come with me. Let me tell you the secret again. It is beautiful and bright. We can be together forever.

*Forever. There was a story, told by a dark man. Two women on Venus: one did not want for ever.*

We don't have to be that story. We are Zaybak and Tawaddud.

A pause.

*I am Tawaddud. I am a different story now. Isn't that what you told me? You are too old and strong. You were right. I want to be Tawaddud.*

I am sorry. It is so easy to be what we were.

*I know. It's all right. But tell me: what did the muhtasib ask for in return?*

A Name. A Secret Name Alile knew.

*Did you give it to him?*

No. Shame. Betrayal. It was a trick. Alile told me. The muhtasib worked for the Sobornost. She knew him. I fled to the desert with her, to keep the secret safe.

*Why would the Sobornost want to hurt Alile? She was going to give them what they wanted.*

She knew the secret of the Jannah of the Cannon. They want it more than souls.

*Who was it? Who was the muhtasib who betrayed you?*

A serpent of fire.

*Abu Nuwas.*

The name bites deep. It almost pulls her out of the entwinement, but the vast soft thing around her that is the Axolotl draws her back in.

*We have to tell them.*

You *are* stronger now. You should come with me. What do you care of secrets and the Sobornost and Sirr? What have they ever given you?

*Let me go.*

Come with me!

*I can't. Don't make me.*

Come!

*No,* Tawaddud says, opens her eyes and closes the Sobornost mind-trap around the Axolotl.

The coffin lid opens. She comes out of the water like a newborn baby, coughing. Her eyes hurt. Her skin crawls and feels dry and hot. She touches her face: there are hard ridges under her skin. She lets out a small sob.

Warm hands touch her shoulders. A voice whispers Secret Names. The wildcode vision is still with her, and suddenly her skin shimmers with tiny jinni, hungry triangles eating wildcode. Their touch is like cool water, poured all over her. Then they cover her head, and the chill makes her gasp. But it only lasts for a moment. She turns to look at her doctor—

—and sees a fiery serpent.

Abu Nuwas smiles sadly. He stands in the coffin room, holding a barakah gun, flanked by hulking jinn thought-forms, clouds of spiky black smoke. Sumanguru struggles in their grip. Next to him is Rumzan the Repentant, spindly hands crossed in front of a faceless face.

'Thank you,' he says, picking up the Sobornost device floating in the coffin. 'A mind-trap? I didn't think you would go so far, Tawaddud. But your efforts are very much appreciated. I have been looking for this fellow for a long time.'

'You bastard,' Tawaddud hisses. 'Where is Kafur?' She stands up, gritting her teeth against the chill. 'This is his Palace. He is not going to let you get away with this.'

A wet cough. Kafur drapes a robe around Tawaddud's shoulders. She recoils from his touch.

'I'm very sorry, little Tawaddud. Old Kafur was offered a better price. And Lord Nuwas has always been a very good customer.'

'Come along now,' Abu says. 'The night is young. And I did promise you a dinner at my palace, did I not?'

## 22

# THE STORY OF THE PELLEGRINI AND THE CHEN

She finds the master of the Universe on the beach, throwing rocks into the sea. He is wearing a child's face. This is an old memory. Did he choose it for her? This is not where they first met. And it is very different from his usual virs, abstract spaces of language and purity.

'It's very nice,' she says. The boy looks up, eyes wide, fearless but without any sign of recognition.

What is Matjek playing at? It took her such a long time to get ready. Going through her Library, finding a memory of who she was when they first met, a hundred-year-old woman in white, but looking no older than forty, with just a hint of fragility in her step, a hat and sunglasses hiding scar tissue, golden rings in tanned fingers.

'I'm not supposed to talk to strangers,' the boy says.

She kneels on the sand next to him.

'I would hope that I'm not a stranger to you, Matjek,' she says.

The boy looks at her, brow furrowed in concentration. 'How do you know my name?' he asks.

'I am very old,' she says. 'I know a lot of names.' What

234

kind of game is Matjek playing here? The wind tugs at her hat, and the sand is warm under her toes. Plankton lights up in her footsteps, like stars.

'What are you doing, Matjek?' she whispers. Suddenly, age returns to his eyes.

'I'm trying to find something,' he says. 'Something I lost a long time ago.'

'It's a disease, isn't it?' she says. 'Trying to cling on to lost things.'

He looks at her, with a cruel humour in his eyes. 'Yes. Yes, it is.' He pokes at the sand with a stick. 'I know why you are here. They are killing you, aren't they?'

'Yes,' she says. 'Anton and Hsien never trusted me. But we can talk about that later. It's such a beautiful vir.' She thinks it best to pay him a compliment when he is in such a sullen mood.

The boy Matjek gets up and throws a stone into the sea. It skips a few times, then disappears into the waves. 'It is not *enough*,' he says, with fury in his voice, Matjek's old rage at everything that is wrong with the world.

'I can't help you. I can't intervene right now. We are too weak to risk a full-blown civil war. The zoku are watching and waiting. I know they look weak – but remember what the Kaminari did. We need to keep up the illusion that we are stronger than them. I will not risk a civil war to save a few of you.'

'What exactly are you doing here, Matjek? Wrapping yourself in memories? This is not like you.'

He laughs. 'The innocent inherit the Kingdom of Heaven. Would you have believed that innocence is key to the Kaminari jewel? To think how I always found Christianity ridiculous. Trust me, if I find what I'm looking for here, everything will change. In the meantime, I ask you to survive. That is what you do best in any case, isn't it?'

'You would let me die? Is that how you pay me back for all these years? You would have me become a ghost, just because it's *convenient*?'

The vir dissolves around them. Matjek assumes his Prime aspect, the voice of a billion gogols, the Metaself, the keeper of the Plan, the Father of Dragons.

'I will sacrifice every Sobornost gogol, every conscious mind in the System, to make the Plan come true. But you never understood that, did you?'

His voice is strangely gentle. In other virs, other pellegrinis and chens are having the same conversation. How much easier it would be if she could truly share his mind, to see what goes on in his head. But that way lie Dragons.

Instead, she laughs. 'It seems that you have become a slave to our own convenient fictions. How endearing. But then you were always a dreamer. Why don't you dream us a new world, Matjek – a world without Dragons and entropy and zokus? Let me know when it arrives.'

In the virs below, from their god-view of the firmament, they watch the other outcomes. Violence. Love. But mostly, resentment.

'Don't come to me again. I know what you tried to do with the Experiment and the thief. You are on your own. I'm sure you will manage just fine.'

She withdraws, severing the links between her temple and his *guberniya*.

'You never did want to grow up,' she says.

# 23

# TAWADDUD AND THE THIEF

Abu and Rumzan take them to a viewing gallery near the top of the Ugarte Shard. The walls and floors of his palace are white and stark. Without athar glasses, Tawaddud sees only flickers of what is invisible: dense mandalas and geometric shapes decorating every surface. The wide window has a view of Sirr at night, dominated by the golden flame of the Station. She stares at it until it feels like it's going to fall down, and the rest of her world with it.

'My father knows we are here,' she says. 'You are finished.'

'Dear Tawaddud,' Abu Nuwas says. 'You may be able to lie to your jinn clients, but I can see right through you.' He taps his brass eye. 'Literally.' He shifts the gun in his hand, pointing at Sumanguru.

'You might want to know that this is not Sumanguru of the Turquoise Branch. There is someone else lurking beneath his ugly face: a thief and a liar called Jean le Flambeur.'

Tawaddud looks at Sumanguru. The other face that she has glimpsed before is fully visible beneath the scars now, intense eyes, a sardonic smile. He raises his eyebrows and shrugs. 'Guilty as charged.'

'What shall we do with you? I suppose it doesn't matter. Accidents do happen near the wildcode desert, after all. And we have time to discuss that. Please, make yourselves comfortable. We are still waiting for someone to join us.'

He gestures, and foglet chairs appear, transparent, curved shapes, floating in the air. He sinks into one, a leg over one knee. Gingerly, Tawaddud sits down facing the gogol merchant.

'Why?' she asks.

'I told you. Revenge. Because I hate this place. Because of what Alile and her friends did to me. Yes, it was her; she bought me from the entwiner. She used me to find the Jannah of the Cannon and then left me in the desert to die. I told her the Name that opened it and she took it from me.'

He squeezes the mind-trap in his hand, making a fist.

'Well, I survived. I came back. I went to an upload temple first, but the hsien-kus could not undo what was done to me, to wash the desert away, not until they made Earth theirs. I found other ways to serve them. They were kinder mistresses than Alile, and far more generous.

'But it's not just about me, Tawaddud. You have seen it, too. Sirr is rotten: it makes monsters to survive and feeds on souls. We live in dirt when others in the System build diamond castles and live for ever. Don't your beloved Banu Sasan deserve better than that?'

*It's not like that,* Tawaddud thinks, remembering the Axolotl's words. But she says nothing.

'The Accords mean nothing. They have been a convenience for the Sobornost, nothing more. They were burned by the Aun, but they are ready now: what do you think the Gourd is for? When your friend here,' he tosses the mind-bullet into the air and catches it, 'tells me what I want to know, there is

238

no need for the hsien-kus to take things slow. Earth will be uploaded, and I will have my reward. I will be made whole.' He smiles sadly. 'I wish I could say I'm sorry.'

*Tell them lies they want to hear.*

'You can never get it back,' Tawaddud says. 'What she took from you, you can never get it back. But you can find something else to replace it. Believe me, I know. Without the Axolotl, I was hollow, I was lost. But then, I met you.'

Abu looks at her, human eye gleaming, his mouth a straight line. Then he starts laughing.

'For a moment, I believed you. You did touch something, something I thought I no longer had.' He shakes his head. 'But you just used me to play your father. The body thief named you right. You are the Axolotl's whore. Why do you think I was so interested in you in the first place? Because that's what everybody calls you. When he gave me the slip, you were the obvious route to him. His weakness.

'So don't look so sad. We both got what we wanted. But enough of that. I do believe my other guest is here.'

A door opens, and a hsien-ku in a black Sobornost uniform walks in. She gives Sumanguru a curt nod.

'Lord Sumanguru – or should I say Jean le Flambeur? Apologies for arriving slightly late. My branch prides itself on punctuality.'

I watch as Abu Nuwas hands the mind-trap over to the hsien-ku. Tawaddud is corpse-pale and shaking. *Poor girl. I will make this up to you somehow. I promise.*

Except that the worst is still to come.

'We owe you thanks, le Flambeur, for alerting us to the existence of a primordial Chen gogol in the first place,' the hsien-ku says. 'It will be excellent currency to keep him off our backs while we move against our sister, who I believe is your current employer, am I correct? Perhaps there is an opportunity for you to offer your talents to us instead.'

I run through the options in my head. A voice is suggesting that perhaps misplaced loyalty to Joséphine at this juncture is not such a good idea. But then there is Mieli and my debt to her to think about – and I doubt the hsien-kus would be able to do anything to the locks inside my head.

'I'll consider it,' I say. Tawaddud stares at me, wide-eyed.

'It is only now that we dare to move openly: obtaining the gogol is far more important than our relationship with Sirr. Once we have dealt with our sister – with the help of our brothers the vasilevs – we will be back. And then there will be no need to dance to the whims of the gogol merchants. We will make Earth live again.'

'By killing it all over again,' I say.

'Words spoken by the flesh. Perhaps that is what our sister finds attractive. What is your answer? Will you serve us? If your answer is no, you have outlived your usefulness.'

'How do you think you are going to catch me?' I smile, thinking of my escape route.

'Oh, we are not going to catch you. We are scholars. But as it happens, our brother the Engineer created a gogol specifically for catching you. It should be on its way here as we speak. The Hunter, we believe it is called. Sasha always liked a bit of melodrama.'

*Shit.*

Abu Nuwas gestures with his gun. 'Could we get on with it, please? My mercenaries are ready.' The jinn, Rumzan, wavers restlessly next to him.

'Of course,' the hsien-ku says. She lifts up the mind-bullet between delicate fingers. No showmanship like what I did in the aviary: besides, I was just bluffing to get Tawaddud to entwine with the bird. This is the real thing.

'What are you doing to him?' Tawaddud whispers.

'Mind surgery,' I say through gritted teeth. 'They are going to torture him. Trying to get the Name out of his mind. Aren't you?'

'It is regrettable but unavoidable,' the hsien-ku says, a sad look on her broad face. 'Like most things are.' I can only imagine the turmoil going on inside. Thousands of iterations of the Axolotl-fragment being created and tortured and destroyed, a feeling far too familiar to me.

Tawaddud starts screaming. She collapses to the floor, twitching, tearing at her hair. *Of course. She must feel it through the entwinement.* Abu Nuwas gives her one glance, then looks away.

'For scholars, you can be real bastards,' I tell the hsien-ku.

'I will give it to you!' Tawaddud shouts. 'Stop it! I'll give it to you!'

Her world is made of agony. The Axolotl part in her mind flickers and dies, flickers and dies, like a hot needle pushed into her brain again and again and again.

'I will give it to you!' she hears herself shouting.

It stops. *I'm sorry, I'm so sorry,* whispers the Axolotl, far away.

She wipes snot and spittle away from her face and takes a deep breath. Then she cries out the Name of Al-Jabbar the Irresistible and becomes Rumzan the Repentant.

I cover my ears when Tawaddud shouts the Name. By now I have a fairly good idea about how it works. Extreme fractal compression of some kind, a self-referential loop inside a story, forcing the target brain to iterate it all over again, bootstrapping a new mind inside it into existence. How it is possible, I do not know. Even encoding pictures in such dynamical maps takes a lot of computational power, and doing the same for a human mind seems like something that is firmly in the realm of the transhuman.

No matter how it works, it works quickly. Rumzan – or Tawaddud – rams sharp thought-form fingers through the throat of the hsien-ku in a shower of crimson. Abu Nuwas is just fast enough to fire the barakah gun before the creature turns on him. It explodes into inert white powder. Tawaddud screams one more time and lies still. The mind-bullet rolls across the floor. I dive down and grab it.

But hsien-kus are hard to kill, and the death of this one is like trimming a fingernail. As the gogol's body dies, it sputters out the Name, torn from the Axolotl's mind. It shimmers in the athar and rings in the air. Abu Nuwas's eyes glaze over as he drinks it in.

As his gun hand wavers, I pick the still form of Tawaddud up and run. Sparks fly in my eyes as I push the Sobornost body to its limits. Tawaddud on my shoulder, I smash the diamond tool she gave me against the gallery window, as hard as I can. Pain shoots up my arm but the glass shatters like ice. Holding on to Tawaddud, I leap through the fragments, into the void beyond.

The Anti-Name echoes in my ears as we fall towards the blue and golden night of Sirr, far below. Its beauty takes my breath away.

But it's nothing compared to the warm amber glow of the ancient angelnet, when it finally catches us in a soft embrace.

*

Tawaddud's head feels like a shattered jinn jar. She lies on a cold, hard surface. Everything hurts.

She opens her eyes and sees the dark mouth of a barakah gun. Sumanguru – Jean le Flambeur – is pointing it at her face. He is smiling sadly.

'There is nothing personal about this, you understand,' he says. 'I think you know about wanting to be good. Unfortunately, I don't always have the luxury to follow through with that.'

'What are you doing? Where are we?'

'Please speak very, very carefully. If I hear the beginning of a Name, I will have to fire. That trick with the Name and Rumzan was very good. For future reference, it is a great idea to attack embodied Founders. It confuses them every time. We are in an old upload temple near the Station: I'll be needing some Gourd bandwidth in a moment.'

Tawaddud swallows. Her mouth is dry.

'Who are you? What do you want? Why are you doing this?'

'I want you to know that I am very sorry. You didn't deserve any of this.'

'Why … why are you apologising? Just let me go.'

'This was my fault, you see. I came to Earth to find two things. The Jannah of the Cannon was one of them. But it was going to be far too difficult to find it. I'm a thief, not an archeologist. So I made sure that the hsien-kus knew there was something in there they would desperately want: it was going to be much less trouble to steal it from them when they found it. They thought I let it slip, sent a careless message.' A smile flickers on his lips. 'I didn't think they would use a local agent like Nuwas, but then I must admit I did not really understand Sirr.

'It was a bonus that they actually sent me here to go after the Axolotl.'

Tawaddud feels empty and weak. She closes her eyes. There is the faintest echo of the Axolotl in her head, somewhere far away.

'I trusted you,' Tawaddud whispers.

'I told you, you shouldn't have,' le Flambeur says. 'Hush now. No talking. I just have some business with your boyfriend, and then I'll be on my way.'

He spins the mind-bullet between his fingers deftly, like a magician.

What the hell do you want? whispers the Axolotl.

'I want the secret, the one you got from the Aun. That's what I really came here for. The algorithm for turning minds into stories. The same thing you used to make all the other body thieves. But be careful. Any more tricks, and Lady Tawaddud here will become noise in the wildcode. Or I may decide to use the hsien-ku tactics: I can do mind surgery too. Your choice.'

Let him shoot, the Axolotl says in Tawaddud's mind. Let him shoot. We can still be together.

'It's too late,' Tawaddud says. 'It was always too late.'

When it's done, I give them both a bow. Then I plug into the Gourd communication systems in the upload temple. The scan beam comes down from the temple's dome, a shower of white, cleansing fire. I leave Sirr in a burst of modulated neutrinos. An eyeblink later I'm in my old body in the main cabin. I stretch: it feels strange after days in Sumanguru's massive frame.

*You are a real bastard, Jean,* the ship says.

'I know, but sometimes that's what it takes.' I pass it

the algorithm – a bizarre image the Axolotl imprinted in my mind, encoded in what I can only assume is a recursive Penrose tiling.

'Give this to the pellegrini and tell her to test it on a few gogols in the Gourd systems. I've seen it working firsthand, but just to be sure. And I think it's going to require a *lot* of computational power.'

*Sir, yes sir. Anything else?*

'I have some good news and bad news. The good news is that everything is ready, as long as Mieli gets into that jannah. Is she in Abu Nuwas's fleet?'

*Yes.*

'Good.' I squeeze the bridge of my nose. 'I need a drink.'

*Why do I have the feeling that I'm not going to like the bad news?*

'Yes, well.' I take a deep breath. 'The Hunter is coming.'


Tawaddud sits alone in the upload temple with the mind-bullet for a long time. When the Repentants find her, she is holding the barakah gun against her forehead. They take it away. When she falls asleep in her cell, she can no longer remember if she was going to to pull the trigger.

## 24

# MIELI AND THE SOUL TRAIN

Mieli watches the progress of the soul train from the sky. It is a silver worm glinting in the sun. The updraft carries her up lightly, and if it wasn't for the constant chatter of Stanka the ursomorph, she would almost be enjoying herself.

'—and then they came at us with some re-animated *tanks*, would you believe that, old drones they dug up from some military base, and Tara detonated them in a sequence that spelled FUCK YOU in the sky, poor bastards—'

While she can see why the Teddy Bears' Roadside Picnic Company's groupware matched them together as a combat team, sometimes she wishes the outcome had been different.

The train is sleek, all analog tech, made by Sirr craftsmen to give as little as possible for wildcode to infect. It always comes anyway, but it takes longer for the ancient nanotech to dig into simple machinery than smartmatter or more complex systems. Mieli herself is covered in Seal armour: words, flowing on her skin and face. It makes her wings look like pages of a book.

'Are you listening, Oortian?' Stanka says. 'I said I hope we see some action today.'

The ursomorph mercenary is a fierce sight with her spiky enhancements visible, riding on the roof of the train. She has a point. They are approaching the Wrath region where a lot of Sobornost ships fell, twenty years ago. There have been several attacks here by anti-Sobornost jinni, and Mieli is not sure what to expect. She has been through a few skirmishes, and so far they have been quick and confusing. Unlike in Sirr, the wild jinni in the desert can be vast and powerful, like living storms.

The wildcode desert confuses her. Seen from above, on visible wavelengths, it does resemble a desert: mountains, valleys and here and there a cluster of abandoned buildings. But in the spimescape view, or in what the people of Sirr call athar, it is like looking at the surface of the Sun. Aerovore formations like protuberances, tiny nanites moving in complex patterns. Matter assembled into large unnatural configurations by invisible forces. She saw a patch of the desert full of tiny smiling faces, painstakingly assembled from individual grains of sand, propagating through the landscape like a flood.

'It's like inside my cubs' dreams here, sometimes,' Stanka said when they talked about it. 'You get used to it eventually.' Stanka's people had been hit badly by the Protocol War: she left her offspring asleep back in the habitat inside their home asteroid. While they hibernated, she tried to win them a better life by working as a mercenary.

The desert makes many things difficult, including communication. Mieli can barely keep in touch with *Perhonen* through their neutrino link. The ship is moored in the Teddy Bears' makeshift base in the Gourd, trying to get in touch with the thief and negotiating its way through the complex Sobornost systems with the help of the pellegrini – whom the thief has apparently managed to insert into the hsien-ku infrastructure in the sky.

Mieli does not know who they are working for – one of the muhtasib families of Sirr – but it does not matter as long as they are provided with Seals. The souls, stored in Sirr-made jars and transported in the trains, also belong to them. Mined from the hidden jannahs beneath the desert and the hardware in the Wild Cities, they are either sold to Sobornost or put to work as jinni slaves in the city to earn their freedom.

She prays to Kuutar and Ilmatar every night, begging their forgiveness for being part of such dirty work. She asked Stanka how she could do it, one night.

'It's easy,' the bear-woman said. 'I think of the cubs.'


As they approach a valley between two gigantic Sobornost craft – oblasts that now look more like mountains, overgrown with strange, twisted trees and bushes – Mieli swoops down.

'We should slow down,' she tells Stanka. 'Too many opportunities for ambush.'

'Don't be silly. I doubt we'll even see a chimera after the beating we gave them last time—'

There is writing in the desert, in huge letters. There is a tickle in Mieli's forehead when she looks at it. An alarm goes off in her head. *Body thieves.* She instructs her metacortex to blank out the message in the sand and prepares for combat.

'What do you make of that?' she transmits to Stanka. She calls for recon support, deploys two Fast Ones from her backpack. Tzzrk and Rabkh dart forward. The mercenary companies deploy the fast-living creatures as scouts and native guides. For her, using quicktime makes it easier to communicate with them.

'... serpent queen...' mutters Stanka in her ear. Her voice sounds strange. And then the ursomorph is standing on her back legs and firing her heavy cannon at the train tracks ahead.

The boom of the weapon mixes with the groan of twisting metal. A fountain of sand and rubble erupts in front of the train. The momentum of the huge silver vehicle carries it into the rain of rock and dust, and for a moment Mieli thinks it's going to make it through. Then it twists, slowly, thrown up by the broken tracks like a snapped silver whip. The cars tumble over each other, ricochet from the walls of the valley, kick up dust. Finally, they come to rest in disarray, like a child's toys tossed aside. The bear-woman screams incomprehensible words in Mieli's ears.

Powering up her combat systems, Mieli dives down, just as a jinn storm of dust and glinting sapphire comes down the side of the old oblast ship. *I'm getting paid to protect the cargo. Let's just hope the backup gets here in time.*

She fires attack software at the storm, with no effect. She powers up her multipurpose cannon reluctantly – with a wildcode infection, she'll only get a few shots in – and puts quark-gluon plasma charges in the storm's path. Dust and sand and nanites fuse into a sharp rain of glass.

A crowd of chimera animals inside the storm swarms over the train, sleek, catlike creatures with a glinting sapphire carapace and sharp, sharp claws. Mieli dispatches the Fast Ones to call for backup from the Teddy Bears and lands, hard. She gets off one batch of q-dots that take out the first swarm of the sapphire cats like a scythe. Then her weapon goes hot. She tosses it aside and goes for hand-to-hand with a q-blade. She runs the microfans in her wings as hard as she can to disperse the foglet storm raging around her.

Then Stanka comes at her from the ruins of the train.

A swipe of a diamond-clawed paw throws Mieli aside like a rag doll and tears one of her wings into tatters. Then the ursomorph is upon her, pinning her down, enhanced teeth going for her throat. Her q-enhanced muscles scream as she gets her legs beneath the bear woman's bulk and kicks as hard as she can. There is a surprised look in the ursomorph's eyes as she flies into the air.

Mieli rolls, grabs the multipurpose cannon, squeezes the trigger, praying. The weapon gives her one more shot. An x-ray laser blast takes off half the bear's torso, and the rest rains down on top of her.

And then the rukh ships and the Teddy Bears are there, driving away the storm.

The mercenary camp is a cluster of muhtasib-sealed temporary bubble buildings between the Wrath area and the Wall, a few kilometres from Sirr. On the evening of the battle of the train, Mieli is taken to see the commander. Odyne is a skeletally thin woman from the Belt, living in a medusa-like exoskeleton, made bulky by the thick layers of Sealed material around it. Her narrow face inside the globe-like helmet makes Mieli think of the fish in Grandmother's spherical lake in Oort.

Odyne is sitting with a middle-aged portly man in lavish Sirr robes and rises to greet Mieli when she enters. A heavily armoured mercenary in mutalibun robes stands on guard behind them.

'Please. Sit,' Odyne says.

Mieli has been through extensive debugging by the company's combat muhtasib, and her skin is still tingling. Odyne looks at her, tendril-fingers knotting together.

'You have done well, Mieli,' she says. 'In fact, well enough that I would like to introduce you to our employer. This is Lord Salih of the House Soarez.'

The man acknowledges Mieli's presence with a barely perceptible nod.

'My thanks,' he says in a flippant tone. 'I understand that you played an important role in protecting my property. A warrior woman, how remarkable. My mother would approve.'

'A comrade died for your property. A truedeath: backups do not work here,' Mieli says. 'She left cubs behind. I'm sure they would appreciate your gratitude more than me.' *When this is over, I'm going to make sure they are all right*, she thinks.

Odyne waves. 'Yes, yes, that is very noble of you, Mieli. The Company protects its own, have no fear, and Lord Salih has been very generous. However, there is another reason I have asked him here today.'

Salih raises his eyebrows.

'I regret to inform you that our arrangement is coming to an end,' Odyne says.

'What?' Salih sputters. 'You are in breach of contract!'

Odyne sighs. 'As it happens, we have reason to believe that the business we are presently engaged in will cease to be profitable in a very short amount of time. You'll recall that our contract includes protecting your own person from any harm that might befall you or Sirr, from the desert *or* Sobornost. You may be surprised that, strictly interpreted, this dictates some drastic actions from our part. Mieli, please kill Lord Salih and make sure you thoroughly destroy his brain.'

Mieli hesitates. It is a dishonourable thing to do. But the Mieli she has become here would not hesitate, and this is a man who trades in gogols—

Lord Salih's head disappears in a burst of flame.

'Too slow,' Odyne says, a zoku q-gun floating next to her head. 'You will have to be faster in the service of our new employer.'

'Dear Odyne, you will excuse me if I regard hesitating before executing her employer a positive quality,' says the mercenary, drawing her hood back. A brass eye stares at Mieli. 'You will have plenty of opportunities to demonstrate your talents where we are going.'

'Mieli is one of my finest warriors,' Odyne says. 'Although she does seem to be having an off day.'

'I am Abu Nuwas,' the man with the brass eye says. 'Pleased to meet you.'


The mercenaries sail over the wildcode desert in rukh ships, huge vessels kept aloft by swarms upon swarms of the chimera birds in vast blue clouds. The Teddy Bears have been joined by at least ten other companies, and the posthuman warriors carried by the vessels number in the thousands.

Some of them fly under their own power, in gliders and other analog craft custom-made to survive the hardships of the desert. Abu Nuwas's two flagship galleons, *Munkar* and *Nakir*, are surrounded by a halo of Fast Ones. Their shadows race below them in the desert as the sun sets.

Mieli stands on the bridge of *Nakir* with Odyne, Nuwas and the other mercenary commanders. The lights of the Fast Cities dance in the distance, and the surface of the dark sea that used to be the Mediterranean has an eerie green sheen. They have lost a few craft already to sudden jinn storms, driven away by Nuwas's muhtasibs, but the fleet pushes forward.

*Mieli?* comes *Perhonen*'s voice suddenly.

*Thank Kuutar*, Mieli whispers. *Where have you been?*

*In touch with the thief. He knows how to get to the jannah. But so does a man called Abu Nuwas.*

The ship fills Mieli in on the thief's activities in Sirr. A conflict with hsien-kus and and the local authorities, and getting a girl into trouble. *Why am I not surprised?*

*He thought you were going to be in a position to—*

*I am really going to kill him this time*, Mieli says. *Abu Nuwas has a whole damned army. It's not like I can just slip into the jannah he digs up unnoticed and get our gogol.*

*He said you would be pissed off.*

*Well, he was right. Bastard.*

*Apparently, he got the other thing he needed from Sirr. It's up to you now, he says.*

Mieli sighs. *Of course it is. Can you get me any imagery of this region?*

*It's all pretty weird over there. On Old Earth, you would have been flying over Turkey now. Lots of good places there to bury something.*

*Whatever it is, it's not going to stay buried for long*, Mieli says.

*What are you going to do? I'm sorry about this, Mieli, I wish I could do more to help. I'm in touch with the pellegrini, she has been doing something in the Gourd—*

Mieli swears. This is not what was supposed to happen. The thief was not supposed to get involved in local politics, he just needed to get the location of the jannah. It was going to be a matter of sneaking away from her unit, retrieving the gogol and and transmitting it up to *Perhonen.*

*Let me talk to him*, Mieli says.

*I hate to admit it, Mieli, but this did not go as well as I expected,* the thief says. *I was outmanoeuvred by a one-eyed merchant. If you think the situation down there is too difficult, perhaps we can cut our losses. It might be possible to use what I got, to get into Chen's mind more directly—*

*But you would still need the Founder codes for that.*

*Yes, I suppose so,* the thief says. *And we don't have much time. It sounds like there is going to be a straight-out war between the hsien-kus, vasilevs and the pellegrini sometime soon.*

*War,* Mieli says.

*Damn,* the thief breathes. *I'm just seeing your feed now. You would need a whole army to get to the jannah now. Leave it, Mieli. It was my fault, I screwed up. We'll find another way.*

*An army,* she whispers.

*What are you talking about?* the thief asks.

Mieli ignores him, closes her eyes and prays to the pellegrini.

## 25

# TAWADDUD AND THE COUNCIL

The next day, before they bring her before the Council, Dunyazad comes to see her in her cell, a tiny cube-shaped room, where the air is hot and thick with Repentants. Before Duny enters, she stands at the door and watches her for a long time. She is formally dressed in a Gomelez muhtasib robe, dark cloth embroidered with Secret Names. But to Tawaddud's surprise, she is not wearing her qarin jinn jar around her neck.

'Do you know why I became a muhtasib?' Duny says.

Tawaddud says nothing.

'Because I wanted to protect you from this.' Duny speaks a Secret Name, and then Tawaddud is in her sister's head.

She watches the city from her tower. This is the first duty of the muhtasib, always: the other Sirr where the jinni live, watching the flow of Seals and sobors, listening to the pulse and the breath of the city in the athar. Nieve is there with her, of course, painting the night city for her stroke by stroke, whispering to Repentants who bring her information, racing along wires and patches of athar untainted by wildcode, to show Duny the shadow of reality.

After a night spent in the tower she always feels like the Other City is the real city: this is where she adjusts things, reaching into its virtual image, touching a node, feeling it in her grasp, between the fingers of Duny/Nieve, embodied both in the shadow and the flesh.

She thinks about Tawaddud and her love of monsters, of things she does not understand, wonders if her sister understands the monstrosity of the muhtasib and their dual nature. One part rooted in the brain, the self-loop that remembers the games she played with her sister up on the Wall, and the Nieve part, the part she carries in the bottle around her neck, the soul that races through the night and yearns for a body.

Her father gave her to the entwiner when she was seven. Too old, the man said, stroking his beard. Why now? It will never take root.

Her father's hands rested heavily on the man's shoulders, jinn rings pressing into the flesh of his neck. She is a Gomelez, her father said. She must have a qarin. His voice had a trace of anger that echoed with the fights he had had with her mother. Duny would sneak in to listen when they fought, using the words Chaeremon had taught to make her silent. Tawaddud slept all the way through it, always.

A few more months, her mother said that night. I cannot let them go yet.

It is time, her father said. It is already too late. He paused. Perhaps one would be enough. Can you choose?

How can I choose?

Foolish woman. The qarin is not a thing of evil. It is a sign of glory, of power, a new soul. It gives you strength to serve the city.

But there is more to it, her mother said. It changes you,

they say. I have seen you with Chaeremon. You become different.

I'll do it, Dunyazad said.

Her parents looked at her.

My mouse, my flower, you do not know what you are saying, her mother said. You should go back to bed. Mother and Father are talking.

I heard what you said. I want to do it.

Her father looked at her seriously, with dark eyes that he got when thinking deeply. Then maybe the decision is made for us, he said.

Nieve the jinn comes back to her like a touch of the chill, and she is again a different being, the one who feels the ragged fragments of wildcode in the athar, a mind extended into the foglets of the air, the cool shell of the Seal in her own cells. She is not just Dunyazad the child, but a cloud of fireflies around her, and the memory feels foolish, suddenly. This is where she belongs, this is why her father brought them together, this is why the entwiner made her temples burn with the helmet on her head, made her dream of Nieve, made Nieve dream of Dunyazad.

How did she ever doubt that it was right?

'It is not always right,' Dunyazad says. She holds her jinn jar in her hand.

'I never knew,' Tawaddud says slowly. 'Why tell me now?'

'Because they are going to throw you off the top of the Shard and Father is going to go along with it, to get his precious vote through. Even when there are alternatives.'

'The zoku,' Tawaddud says.

'Yes. I can see you have been talking to Sumanguru, or whatever his name really is.'

'Why them?'

'Because I don't *like* who I am with Nieve. It wasn't like with your Axolotl. We are all monsters, Tawaddud, us muhtasibs. They graft us and jinni together and make new beings and do not care what it does to us. I want to find a different way. I hoped you would understand, that I could get you out of your shell, to help me. Instead, you embraced the madness of your Axolotl and became a killer.'

Tawaddud shakes her head. 'It's not like that.' She tells her sister the story of Sumanguru, and Abu Nuwas, and what they discovered. Duny listens carefully.

'So, if Abu Nuwas reaches the jannah, none of it matters anymore,' Tawaddud says. 'The hsien-ku will stop playing nice. It will be a Cry of Wrath times ten. And this time, they will win.'

'I believe you,' Duny says. 'You are a beautiful liar, but you have never been able to lie to me.'

'So, what are we going to do?'

'This could play in our favour. This could give me the leverage to propose an alliance with Supra City, to get a zoku embassy established here. But we need proof. Otherwise, they will never believe us. Nuwas is far too influential. Is there any way to link him to the murders?'

'The Axolotl did not know how it was done. He gave Nuwas his story, and then he woke up in Alile's mind. No one would listen to him anyway.' Tawaddud squeezes her temples. 'I wish I could *show* them.'

'No one would accept an entwined testimony either, not with the Axolotl involved. And it's just too perfect, with you as the scapegoat. The black sheep of the Gomelez family who has been working with the Devil himself, to bring down Sobornost and all that it represents, because her mother died in the Cry of Wrath.' Duny pauses. 'The bastards could not have planned it better. But it's not all lost. I can get you out of here. I have contacts—'

'I need to try, Duny. I need to testify.'

'All right,' she says and embraces her, long and hard. 'I will be there, too. I will speak for you. Perhaps it will be enough.'

The Great Observatory sits on top of the Blue Shard, above its waterfalls and palaces and muhtasib buildings with their azure walls. It is a lenticular structure held aloft by arches that rise from the top of the Shard and bow towards the city. Tawaddud has never been there. The carpet guides Tawaddud, Duny and their Repentant guards to a modest entrance on the building's upper surface.

The Observatory galleries are a historical relic, large spherical spaces, with pentagonal windows, and a circular balcony bisecting them. Secret Names are engraved in gold on every surface. Mosaics guide the eye to the observation windows. The harnesses where the muhtasib used to sit with their glasses and athar telescopes are still here, but now only wooden life-sized dolls are suspended from them.

The Councillors wait for them in front of the large pentagonal windows that open to the wildcode desert, a jagged landscape of fallen Sobornost technology, now overgrown with windmill trees and nameless plants, chaotic geometry broken only by the rails of soul trains, heading towards the mountains in the north.

There are six of them. Cassar's face is like stone. He is flanked by Lucius Aguilar, his old supporter, dour and thin-faced. A jinn thought-form hovers around a plain Council jinn jar. *Mr Sen*. House Soarez is represented by a short-haired woman, Councilwoman Idris. Ayman Ugarte, a powerful man whose face is covered in Seal tattoos, gives Tawaddud a hard stare.

And then there is Veyraz, Veyraz ibn' Ad, of House Uzeda. Her husband. When he sees Tawaddud, his eyes widen. He gives her a look that she has been dreading for four years, full of hate and jealousy. Duny takes her place next to their father, who nods at Tawaddud and then wrenches himself up from his chair laboriously, spreading his arms.

'We have been chosen by the Council to question you, Tawaddud Gomelez. You are accused of assisting the jinn Zaybak, also known as the Axolotl, in the murders of Councilwoman Alile Soarez and the Sobornost envoy Sumanguru, of the Turquoise Branch. This is not to establish your guilt, which is already apparent to the Council, but to present the people of Sirr with a full account of your crimes before the Aun.' His face is red. 'Before we begin questioning, you may speak.'

Tawaddud swallows. Her mouth is dry. *No more pleasant lies,* she thinks.

'We are fools, all of us, all of Sirr,' she says. 'We are selling our blood for wealth, and think it makes us rich. But we are pale and tired and weak—'

'Are you mocking the heritage of your own House, woman?' shouts Veyraz.

Cassar holds up his hand. 'Let her speak.'

'But she is clearly—'

'Let her speak!'

Tawaddud looks down. She feels their eyes on her. The speech she rehearsed for so long in her cell feels muddled and empty.

'We cannot live without blood. We cannot survive on empty wealth, thinking we can make Sirr-in-the-sky live again. There is another power in the sky now, and its thirst will never be quenched.

'I am not guilty of the crimes I am accused of. But there are things this council needs to hear, and I will leap from the Shard and embrace the desert, if that will make you listen.'

Her father looks at her, with a strange look of anguish on his face. Suddenly, Tawaddud remembers where she saw that expression. They were cooking together, on one of the long quiet evenings after her mother died. Instead of following the recipe, she put in a liberal mixture of spices, cumin and marjoram, because it felt right.

'That is what you need to get food to do, to tell a story,' Cassar said. 'Even if you need to use a few forbidden spices.'

Duny is looking at her too. For a moment, Tawaddud remembers what the city looked like through her eyes, a muhtasib's eyes.

*To tell a story.* The circle and the square. No wonder it seemed so familiar.

'He used the city,' she whispers. She looks at the Council. 'I can prove that Abu Nuwas the gogol merchant conspired to murder Alile Soarez.'

It takes a lot of chaos and confusion and jinni dashing through the Observatory, but eventually, they all watch Sirr on a large athar screen. The circle and the square are there, in the dance of the nodes, in the flow of sobors and Seals, the whole economy of the city telling a children's tale for those with the eyes to see.

Idris Soarez exhales.

'The amount of capital needed to do this – it's staggering. Embedding a body thief's story in the financial system of the city, to be seen by only one muhtasib in a single sector – madness.'

'Effective madness,' Duny says. 'Everything my sister says is true. The foundation our city is built upon is crumbling. The age of gogol trade is over.'

'I still think there is room to discuss this openly with Sobornost,' Lucius Aguilar says. 'Get them to admit that they have openly dealt with and corrupted a muhtasib, that—'

'What Councilman Aguilar does not appreciate is that we have not really been dealing with *Sobornost*,' Duny says. 'We are dealing with an eccentric aunt in the Sobornost family. The full might of Sobornost turned against us will mean our end, and when they come, it will be over in hours, if not in minutes.'

'The first and only thing we have to do is to stop Abu Nuwas from getting to that jannah,' Tawaddud says. 'He has a mercenary army in the desert, on its way there.'

Mr Sen's thought-form, a flame-bird, wavers. 'It does look like the Nuwas family has spent great amounts of sobors essentially hiring all the mercenaries they could get their hands on. It is not possible to mobilise a similar force at such short notice.'

Visions of what the Axolotl showed her in the Palace of Stories flash in Tawaddud's mind. Rivers of thought, castles made of stories. The eyes of a girl in a dirty dress, burning like embers.

'Sirr does not need an army,' Tawaddud says, turning to her father. 'We have the desert. Father, it is time to speak to the Aun.'

# 26

# MIELI AND THE LOST JANNAH

A part of Mieli watches Abu Nuwas stand in the prow of *Nakir* and speak strange words. Below, the wildcode desert smiles and moves in response. It reminds her of the Lakshmi plain on Venus, huge things moving beneath Earth's crust.

'My lords,' Nuwas says, 'ladies. I give you the Lost Jannah of the Cannon.'

But another part of her is in the pellegrini's temple.

'Mieli,' says the goddess, smiling. There are stars in her auburn hair. 'It looks like you have failed in yet another task.'

'I have not failed yet,' Mieli says. 'It is just that I need to become something else to accomplish it.'

'And what is that?'

'An army,' Mieli says.

In the other place, outside her head, a city is rising from the dust. A storm boils beneath the mercenary fleet. The wildcode desert recognises the Secret Name Abu Nuwas has spoken. Blue-tinted towers, palisades and walls rise from the spiral of white chaos. A hot wind comes, waste heat vented by the desert nanomachines. It makes the air boil and twist.

The rukh ships struggle to stay still. Muhtasibs strain their wills to control the chimera creatures. Below, streets and buildings appear, angular letters written by a vast pen.

In a temple, far away, a goddess starts laughing.

'What are you asking, little one? How would I even grant your request?'

'I know you have inserted yourself into the Gourd systems. All that hardware above Earth. Use it.'

'And reveal myself to the hsien-kus?'

'The hsien-kus and vasilevs are going to come after you anyway. If they get the chen gogol, they are going to blackmail your lord and master to stay out of their way.'

'An interesting theory,' the pellegrini says. 'Of course, it has one flaw: no one blackmails Matjek Chen.' She touches her lips, suddenly. 'Although… you have just given me an idea.'

She turns to the singularity of her temple. 'Perhaps it *is* time for me to move more directly against those who would destroy me.'

Mieli bows her head.

'You do understand that our technology will not survive in Earth's atmosphere for long? That you are condemning those other selves of yours into a painful death?'

'I am not afraid of death,' Mieli says. 'So none of us will be.'

'Very well,' the pellegrini says. 'I am pleased. Perhaps you are growing up after all.'

She touches Mieli's cheek. The goddess' ring is cold against her scar. 'It is only now that I'm taking your gogol,' the pellegrini says. 'No matter what Jean might tell you, I am not cruel. And you do remind me of someone I knew a long time ago.'

Then she is gone and Mieli is back on the bridge of *Nakir*, watching the Lost Jannah of the Cannon below.

Mieli steps forward and places a q-dot blade across Abu Nuwas's throat.

'I claim this jannah in the name of Joséphine Pellegrini of the Sobornost,' she says.

Abu Nuwas stares at her with his one human eye.

'Who the hell are you?' he asks.

'I am Mieli. The daughter of Karhu of Hiljainen Koto, the beloved of Sydän of Kirkkaat Kutojat.' She points at the sky with her free hand. Up in the dark blue of evening, between the arcs of Gourd, there is a cloud that flashes golden in the sunset light. 'And so are they.'

There are machines within the Gourd, built over decades by the hsien-ku, gogol factories and smartmatter moulds and picotech fabbers. The pellegrini tells them to make angels.

The metacortex in Mieli's brain lights up, becomes more than just a layer on top of her frontal lobe, a metaself. She feels the echoes of her other selves, moving with a unified purpose, a goal, exchanging rapid bursts to synchronise differences between mind-states, spreading their wings and diving towards Earth.

They enter the atmosphere in their thousands, smartmatter armour flaming in the re-entry. Already, they feel the kiss of wildcode that brings death, but that is what they are here to embrace.

They sing songs of Oort as a choir as they fall.

Mieli's viewpoint on the bridge of *Nakir* shatters into a kaleidoscope. The words of Oort arrive before her other selves do, by a fraction of a second, a thunderous roar from a thousand throats.

The fractal angel storm cuts through the mercenary fleet like a blade. Rukh swarms evaporate before synchronised cannon fire. *Munkar* veers to one side.

'This is a place of the Aun,' Abu Nuwas shouts as the ship sways. 'Your machines will be eaten. Without the Secret Name, they will never let you in.'

'I told you my name,' Mieli says. 'That had better be good enough for them.'

She pushes the muhtasib aside and dives towards the jannah, joining the battle song. The wildcode desert rises to meet them.

They fight their way through the desert city. They take out wild jinni with codeweapons, destroy chimera beings with plasma and fire. The jannah itself turns against them. A tower becomes a nightmare worm. A mieli takes it out by detonating her fusion reactor in its mouth. The combined force of their wings creates a pillar of dust that hides the mercenary fleet above.

The deaths of her other selves are hammer blows in Mieli's mind. The hot twisting burn of the wildcode. The tearing claws of chimera beasts. The pure white of a fusion explosion. The quick sharp self-destruct that some choose, before the wildcode turns them against their sisters. Mieli is there through every last moment, every final darkness, and there is a strange joy in each one, a purity that makes her feel like a brass bell, ringing.

*This is what I was made for. This is what I am.*

In the end, the Lost Jannah of the Cannon is silent, full of fallen angels and shattered sapphire and dead towers like broken teeth. A domed building in the centre remains, a beautiful structure with an arced entranceway.

*Remind me to never make you angry again,* the thief says in Mieli's head.

'Get ready,' she says. 'You are going to have your prince soon.'

Flanked by her other selves, Mieli enters the building.

There is a metal disc on the floor beneath the dome, ten metres in diameter. There are three figures waiting for her in front of it. There is a man in green, a strange glowing creature that looks like an octopus made of light, constantly shifting shape – and a little girl in a sooty dress and a wooden mask.

'You have come for Father,' the little girl says. 'Our brother told us about you.'

Mieli blinks. The figures do not show up in spimescape, but they appear fully real. She can see the grains of the wood and the flaking paint in the girl's mask.

'*Perhonen*, are you getting this?' Mieli whispers.

*As far as I can tell, you are alone down there. Except for all the other Mielis, of course. The pellegrini has access to all the Gourd ghost imagers now. The jannah is directly below you, at the bottom of a long drop through a salt rock layer, almost a kilometre deep. There is a really big chamber down there, and lots of other stuff – geothermal power sources. Lots of chemicals, boron and hydrogen and radioactives.* A layered representation of the underground facility flickers in Mieli's field of vision as the ship speaks.

'Are you going to try to stop me?' Mieli tells the desert ghosts. 'It's not going to go well for you.' She still has almost a hundred remaining selves – battered, wildcode-ridden, armed only with makeshift weapons and flickering, failing q-blades – but they are all battle-ready.

'We should ask you for a true story,' the girl says. 'But we already know yours.'

Then the three are gone, leaving Mieli with a strange, yearning feeling. She shakes her head.

'Let's get this over with,' she says.

With the help of her other selves, she cuts away the metal, revealing a cylindrical shaft. She descends slowly on her wings, lighting up her armour to illuminate the passage.

It is hot at the bottom. There is a round chamber with a ledge around its base, hardened terminals in the walls, ancient touchscreens and ports for jacks that haven't existed for centuries. Mieli lets her software gogols loose on them, pushes q-dot tendrils into the guts of the ancient machines.

Then she is inside the jannah's vir, and everything is bright.


Mieli is standing on a beach.

It is not exactly like the hard physics-based virs that the Sobornost use, but something softer, more dream-like. Mieli stops to look at the sea: she has never seen one like it. The blue expanse seems endless, and her gaze gets lost in it for a moment. Its soft crashing on the sand feels soothing after the madness of battle.

There is a boy playing near the water, building a sand-castle. He looks up when Mieli approaches. A smile lights up his tanned face.

'Hi,' Mieli says. 'What are you doing?'

'I'm building a castle for my friends,' the boy says.

'Why don't you introduce us?'

'This is the Green Soldier,' the boy says, holding up an old plastic warrior, battered by salt water and the sun. 'This is the lightkraken.' He points at a blob of transparent putty in one of the towers, with a cartoon face. Then he picks up a little doll made from sticks. 'And this is the Chimney Princess. The Flower Prince should be here, too, but I can't find him. He likes to run away, sometimes.'

'Nice to meet you all,' Mieli says. 'But what is *your* name?'

'Mom told me not to speak to strangers.'

'And do strangers ever come here?' The boy reminds Mieli of Varpu and her leaps of logic.

'No,' the boy says uncertainly.

'Then I can't be a stranger, can I? My name is Mieli.'

The boy considers for a second. 'I'm Matjek.'

'How long have you been here, Matjek?'

'I came in the morning, with Mom and Dad. They just left and said that I could play a little longer. It's almost time to go home, but not quite.'

Mieli swallows. *Can I really take him out of here? Out of a childhood memory? The thief claims he will never know. We can leave him running after we are done, for ever if need be, it will be all right, he will never tell the difference.*

*That's the kind of thing Sobornost always says,* she thinks. But I just fought side by side with my other selves and won, and they all died willingly, just like I would have done. Perhaps Sobornost are not wrong about everything.

*And even if they are, you are the only one who can take me to Sydän, little Matjek.*

'It's time to go, Matjek,' she says. 'Your mother and father are worried.'

'But I haven't finished building the castle.'

'Don't worry. It will still be here tomorrow.'

'Promise?'

'I promise,' Mieli says.

She holds out her hand to the boy. Together, they start walking away from the sea.

She is back in the metal shaft. Above, there is fire and thunder. Her metaself flashes her a series of staccato updates. Nuwas's mercenaries are attacking, and her other selves are defending the entrance against them. She checks her systems. A copy of the jannah is running in her metacortex. She starts the ascent, spreading her wings.

'I've got the package,' she tells *Perhonen*. 'I need extraction.'

*The pellegrini got us a Gourd orbital hook we can deploy. Just hold on.*

She rises past the circle of her other selves and salutes them just as the tendril from the sky crashes through the dome and carries her up and away.

## 27

# THE THIEF AND MIELI

*Perhonen* and I watch in awe from orbit as Mieli fights an army by herself. Around us, the Gourd boils with conflict: we barely made it out of the Teddy Bears' station alive. The pellegrini copies I seeded the ancestor vir with have activated, and are taking on the hsien-kus everywhere. The surface of the vast Sobornost structure seethes like a disturbed anthill. So we go up, to a Lagrange point, hiding amongst the technological debris there, calculate a trajectory to pick Mieli up. *Perhonen* is in full stealth mode, getting ready for the Hunter – although there has been no sign of the bastard yet.

I taste the story in my mind. It feels like a loose tooth. It wants out, wants to be told. *Almost there,* I tell it.

*I still don't like this, Perhonen* says.

'Any other suggestions are welcome, but it *is* getting late in the game. Mieli's stunt was impressive, but it's going to bring the whole Sobornost down on our heads. I doubt even Chen can afford to ignore what's going on.'

*No kidding,* the ship says and shows me the spimescape view. *He's only a couple of hours away. It just appeared. It had some sort of massive metamaterial cloak before that.*

There is a new star in the sky. A *guberniya* is approaching Earth, one of the major Sobornost megastructures, moving. It is using a Hawking drive, lighting up half the Solar System behind it. A halo of countless raions and oblasts surrounds it. It has been coming for days. The pellegrini is gambling with high stakes, inviting him. Clearly, Chen wants something very, very badly, and he's not going to be subtle about taking it.

For a moment, my gut goes cold. I fab myself two fingers of whiskey. Drinking it wakes up an older voice in my head, a wiser voice. *The scale does not matter,* it says. *It has never mattered. A con is a con, a heist is a heist. Even gods fight stupidity in vain. Or, to put it another way, the bigger they are, the harder they fall.*

*Mieli has the gogol,* the ship says. *She is on her way up.*

I swallow the rest of the whiskey and let it burn in my throat.

'Let's pick her up. The show is about to begin.'

The familiarity of *Perhonen*'s main cabin and the feeling of its systems enmeshing with her mind almost makes Mieli cry. The thief watches her breathe it all in for a moment, and grins.

'Now you know what it feels like to die a thousand times,' he says. 'Not my favourite experience in the world. But you got the job done – and everything else is in place. Let's see the goods.'

Mieli holds up the mind-bullet she has copied the Matjek gogol into. "Here he is. He is … on a beach. He is very happy. It was hard to leave.'

'The afterlife designers of the old upload corporations were pretty damn good,' the thief says. 'We can admire it later. Just give it here. I'll be in and out before he knows it.'

*We are expecting company, Perhonen* says. *Chen and the Hunter, not necessarily in that order.*

'I'm afraid things are going to get a little difficult for the people of Earth,' the thief says. 'They don't deserve this. But before you get pangs of conscience, this really was not our fault. It was an anomaly that they were able to survive this long, just that crazy wildcode thing. The way things are going in the System, it's going to come down to the Sobornost and the zokus, and once we are done with this job, we are at least going to be free to choose sides. No offence, but I'm not including Oort on my list. A bit too chilly for me. Or too hot, with the saunas. Now, hand the kid over so we can make retirement plans.'

Mieli hesitates. *Happiness. Just before going home.* Surely, that cannot be the Founder Code of Matjek Chen.

'There is something you are not telling me,' Mieli says. 'What exactly are you going to do to him? It's not the Code, is it? It's not even something he knows. He's a child. Innocent. What are you going to do to him?'

'You really don't have to worry about it,' the thief says. 'It's going to be fine.'

Mieli grits her teeth. 'I just fought half the mercenaries of the System and the whole wildcode desert to get this. Don't push me, Jean. I told you I can make you talk if I have to.'

*Mieli, maybe he is right, Perhonen* says. One of its butterfly avatars tickles Mieli's cheek. *Maybe you should let him do his job, that's what he is here for. We need to move. I can't keep us hidden when that* guberniya *gets here.*

'Not you too,' Mieli whispers. 'I told you. I don't want you to protect me. If I make mistakes, they are mine to make. Now, thief, *tell me what you are going to do with this gogol.*'

'Mieli, you do realise this is Matjek Chen we are talking about? Do you *really* care about what is going to happen to him?'

Her scar burns with rage on her cheek, like a fiery tear. She gives the thief one look with all her anger in it.

'All right,' the thief says, massaging the bridge of his nose. 'I'm going to tell him a story. It's not going to hurt. But it's going to insert me and the pellegrini into his mind. That was another reason we needed to go to Earth. I had to find out how to do that.'

'You are going to *become* him? You are going to wear his skin?'

'I wouldn't put it that way, the whole entwinement thing is far more complex than that, you should talk to this woman called Tawaddud—'

'The woman you had arrested for murders she did not commit?'

'Never mind, that was a bad example—'

'You are going to steal his consciousness? His soul? His self?'

'I would say it's more like *borrowing*—'

'No. Absolutely not. We are not going to do this. This is where I draw the line. You will find another way.'

'I don't see what the problem is,' the thief says, exasperated. 'We know what Chen wants – a childlike version of himself. So we are going to give it to him. *Your* job is done. It's my show from now on.'

'The answer is no. We do something else.'

'Something else is what I tried *last time*, Mieli. It got me arrested and I died more deaths than you can imagine. Your doppelgänger experience down there was nothing compared to what I went through. I'm never going back. And this *will* work. I'm doing it not just for me, I'm doing it for you, for Sydän. *Perhonen* told me the story—'

*You did what?* Mieli screams at the ship in her mind.

*I'm sorry, Mieli, he had to know so we could—*

Mieli shakes her head. 'It doesn't matter. My people – we don't do this. We have—'

'Your *people* do not augment themselves with a metacortex, let themselves be uploaded into Dilemma Prisons, kill gogols with ghostguns built into their hands or with lasers from orbit, am I right? Do they turn themselves into *entire armies* and then just *let their other selves die*? Face it – you have crossed a line, we both have, and there is no coming back.'

'That's not what Jean le Flambeur would say,' Mieli says.

'Perhaps I am not Jean le Flambeur.' The thief covers his eyes with both hands.

'Look, the stakes are high. The pellegrini needs this. It's the only way out for both of us. And that's not all. If what I saw in the Box before you broke it is true, then the System itself is not going to be a happy place if the chen gets what he wants.'

'Perhaps it would be better to die before that,' Mieli says.

Then the pellegrini is there, a white figure standing by the thief's side.

'Stop this tantrum right now, Mieli. We are going to go ahead with Jean's plan. Or have you forgotten what happens when you disobey me?' She raises her hand. Her ring glints, sharp and bright.

Mieli closes her eyes.

*This is why I had to die a thousand times. To be here and not be afraid anymore.*

'Now I see what you both are,' she whispers. 'You are just

the same. You will never change. If you change, you will die. And you will always be afraid of the Dark Man.'

She can feel the pellegrini unfolding in her head, a dullness spreading into her limbs.

'I'm sorry, *Perhonen*,' she says.

Then she screams a fragment of the song that made the ship, the last note she sang, the song of ending. *Perhonen*'s systems respond and send a cry across the System.

*Jean le Flambeur is here.*

She watches the pellegrini letting the thief loose from his chains, trying to escape. The thief stares at her, blank-faced, tears in his eyes.

The Hunter comes. Beams of light cut through *Perhonen*. The knife-things are everywhere. One of them hovers in front of Mieli, its point sharp like the final note of her song.

*I'm sorry too, Mieli, Perhonen* says. *I always loved you more than she did.*

The ship's EM field grabs her. The acceleration is black light in her eyes. And then the Dark Man kisses her hard.

All my constraints are gone, but it's too late. The Hunter comes fast and furious, this time. I watch Mieli disappear, and feel a strange sense of relief. Then I'm too busy being burnt alive.

*Get us out of this and you will be free,* Joséphine whispers.

*Perhonen!*

*Burn, you bastard.*

*The atmosphere. The Hunter can't handle the wildcode.*

*Neither can we.*

*Let's take our chances. Please?*

The ship fires its antimatter engines. We dive into the blue globe, enveloped by a swarm of Hunters. I watch the clouds and the seas and the continents as white light takes me apart, cell by cell, atom by atom—

## 28

# THE PRINCE AND THE MIRROR

'And that's how I got caught the last time,' the thief says, leaning back on the sand. The dream vir's sky is full of images: Earth ablaze with white fire, the Gourd torn apart around it, the *guberniya*'s huge diamond eye.

'The Hunter came, and here I am.' He looks at Matjek. 'That's exactly what I would have told the other Matjek in the jannah, you know. You might as well drop this charade. Trying to be more innocent is not going to get the Kaminari jewel to accept you just like that.'

'Being innocent suits me,' Matjek says. 'It was a good excuse to go through my Library. And your story was a wonderful attempt to hack into my mind. Unfortunately, I have a *very* good metaself that has been looking out for any signs of a le Flambeur self-loop.'

'It must have been a blow to your ego to be rejected by the Kaminari jewel,' the thief says. 'The zokus have their eccentricities, but they did hit on something with the whole extrapolated volition thing. Calculating the effects of your wish on the maximum happiness of the whole zoku. I guess no gogol of yours so far has met the criteria the jewel has.'

'We'll see,' Matjek says.

The old woman comes to them with tired steps. Her face is lined and wrinkled, ancient and withered, but there is a proud look in her eyes.

'Gloating does not suit you, Matjek,' she says and sits down on the sand wearily. 'You *are* being very careful: a vir within a vir within a vir. Still, you might have some trouble with the creatures they call the Aun.'

'When it comes to the Aun, I have certain advantages,' Matjek says. He frowns. No matter what he told the thief, he hates being young-old: the kaleidoscopic awareness of all his other selves in the *guberniya* around them is always there, waiting to pull him back to give them commands, to tell them a story of themselves. He is the Prime, after all, the Self of the chens.

'There is a reason why sobortech is so very vulnerable to the Aun,' he says. 'Stories. The hsien-kus never figured it out. The Aun insert themselves into gogol brains. Minds are their native environment.'

'And how do you know that?' the thief asks.

'Because I made them. Or at least set them free. They were never very grateful. Just like I made the Dragons, who have no self-loop, no eudaimon. It's convenient to deploy them to fight my older creations, don't you think?' Matjek laughs. His other selves show him images of Earth. He feels like he has just kicked an anthill, a nasty sort of pleasure that makes him feel a little bit guilty. But it is made all the better by that.

Joséphine looks at him in horror. 'You sent *Dragons* to Earth. They will eat *everything*. There will be nothing left.'

'They will deliver my past self to me. They can have the rest, for all they care.'

The thief runs his fingers through sand. 'You know, Matjek, I am curious. What *is* it that made you into such a bastard? You never told me in Paris.'

'Are you still trying to get my Founder Codes, Jean?' Matjek says. 'I assure you it won't be that easy.'

'Actually, I'm really just dying to know. I've told you a story. Perhaps you could entertain us with one. Mieli seemed to genuinely *like* the old you. I want to know what happened.'

'Death,' Matjek says. 'Death made me angry.' He tells the dream vir to make his words real. Why not? He has all the time in the world.


## The Story of Little Matjek and Death

Matjek is fabbing a leg for his imaginary friend when his mother decides to take twenty minutes of holiday.

He likes playing in the rooftop garden. Beyond the glass walls, the tops of the high buildings remind him of being in a forest. Sometimes they let him go to a park, escorted by security drones, but it is never the same. And it's the perfect place to play with his friends. When they are cooperative, that is.

The lightkraken does not like the way the transparent limb extruded by the handheld fabber's beak looks, and expresses its displeasure by dancing angrily in the air. Its tentacles whirl around like a glowing carousel.

'Stop it!' Matjek tells it angrily. 'Or you are not going to have a body after all.' The kraken gives him a disapproving look with its sharp ink-dot eyes. It is the eldest of all of Matjek's friends so of course it has to be the first one to come through. But there are more on the other side, waiting for their turn: the Chimney Princess and the Green Soldier and the Flower Prince. It might not be a bad idea to teach the kraken a lesson, Matjek thinks.

'Hello, Matjek,' his mother says.

He looks up. When she is off work, she always looks like a stranger. Her face moves, her fingers are not twitching as if playing invisible keyboards, and even her eyes are still as if there is no data coming into them except what she sees. And she always looks so tired. Matjek's mother is a small woman, and she does not have to bend down far to give him a hug. In spite of the warmth in the rooftop garden, her skin feels cold.

'What are you doing?' she asks. He looks at the fabber. There is something wrong with it: it is sputtering out gobs that look like large boogers. Probably he should not have fed the tree branch into it. But the Chimney Princess wanted a face made from painted wood.

'Nothing,' he mutters.

'Tell me,' she begs.

'You are not going to have the time to listen,' he chides her.

'Little kvetinka, I have almost half an hour,' she says, eyes dull with fatigue. She tousles his hair, like she always does. He does not want her to notice he is wearing the beemee again, so he brushes her hand away.

'It's just you are early,' he says. 'I wasn't finished. It's important.'

'Shall I go away?' she asks, a hurt look on her face. 'You can continue if you want.'

'I guess it's all right,' he says. Her face lights up. 'It looks very exciting,' she says. 'Can we do it together? Is there anything I can do to help?'

'I'm making bodies for my friends,' he says.

'Baby, we talked about this,' her mother says. 'They can't have bodies. They are not real.'

Of course he knows that the lightkraken and the others are not real in the same way he is: he asked the watson to explain to him about imaginary friends and paracosms. The idea that they would all fade away as he got older just seemed *unfair*. So he has been tuning the beemee to the parts of his brain the watson says they live in, to help them to get out. But he decides it's not a good idea to tell that to his mother.

'Yes, they are,' he says firmly. He pushes out his lower lip in a way that tells his mother that the conversation is over. She is smart enough to pick up on it and sighs. 'Whatever you say, dear. Can we play with them, then?'

'No,' he says. 'They don't like you. They went away.'

She looks around. 'I'm sorry, sweetie. What can I do to make it up to them?'

She has the haunted look in her eyes that means that she is already thinking about work. Matjek asked the watson what his mother does but did not really understand the answer: quantum hedge funds and corporate avatars and doing what the shareholders vote for you to do. It sounded a bit like having imaginary friends except letting them control *you*, instead of the other way around.

'They want to see Daddy,' Matjek says.

'Your father has promised to spend time with you tomorrow,' his mother says.

'I want him *now*,' Matjek says. His friends join him in an angry chorus inside his head.

'He is only going to be able to make it tomorrow, sweetheart. He is very busy with his show.'

It's like there is a bell ringing in Matjek's head, suddenly. The bell that wakes up the Flower Prince.

'Now. Now. Now.' He purses his lips and looks away from his mother.

'Mommy's holiday is almost over, sweetie. Are you sure we can't do something together?'

'I want Daddy,' Matjek says. His mother sighs. 'All right. I'll call him.' She looks pale. 'I'm going to have to get ready for work now, sweetie. Be good.' She almost touches his hair again, sees his expression and pulls her hand back. Then her ghosts take over and she walks away, giving him one more look before her eyes fill with flickering numbers.

*You were mean to her,* the Chimney Princess chides him, brown eyes sad in her wooden face beneath her lopsided crown. She sits on the grass and smooths her sooty dress.

'That's the only way she listens to me,' Matjek says. He looks first at his waiting friends, then at the sputtering fabber. He kicks at it. It spits out one more misshapen clump of plastic and circuitry and dies.

'Son,' says the Green Soldier. 'There is no point in being upset if you are not prepared to do something about it.'

Matjek looks at the Soldier's craggy face. He is crouched on the ground, leaning on a tree, a rifle across his knees.

'What should I do?' Matjek asks.

'Let's go find your dad,' the Chimney Princess says.


Matjek is not allowed to look at his father's beemee feeds. But he has already figured out how to pretend to be his mother. The watson shows him a timeline of his father's activities. Like all big beemee stars, there are whole fan communities around tracking him, distributed computing engines running Bojan Chen recognition software. The watson condenses discussions for him:

*But is it not just a glorified form of pornography? No, it's poetry of experience. He could be anywhere, he could be anyone. That's what you pay him for, making the mundane extraordinary.*

Lots of the beemee stars do extreme things: benji jumps, hot air balloon rides. The big stars go for having sex in a drop capsule during an orbital dive from a space station. But Matjek's father is credited with turning the beemee-experience transfer via transcranial magnetic stimulation – into an art form. To be seen through Bojan Chen's eyes is something special.

Still using his mom's password, Matjek queries the watson for his father's calendar. He is not far. He is going to be in a park in the city, looking at wet leaves. So that's the location. The problem is getting there.

'How can I sneak past the watson?' he asks his friends. 'I'm not going to get very far. Mom will find out. And then there is no point.'

'Don't worry, son,' the Green Soldier says. 'You just leave it to us.'


The doors open for him. The security system does not see him. He takes the elevator down, the one that usually opens for Mom or the guards, through the three hundred floors. The Chimney Princess whispers to him all the way.

*Now, right. Now, left.*

Thousands of people, in a shopping centre. Ribbons of light and images in the air around them. Shop windows sending avatars to materialise in front of them, telling them about toys and games. A camera drone whizzes past him, then swings around. Soon, there are several of them. He whispers to the Flower Prince and they fall down to the floor. Then he runs, the Green Soldier guiding his steps.

It takes a long time to find the park, but if the calendar

was right, there is still time. And there, on the bench, looking down, is his father. Shouting, Matjek runs to him.

Matjek's father pushes up his goggles, swirls his red cape aside and grins at Matjek. There is glitter around his eyes. His thick blond hair covers his beemee. He swoops Matjek up in his arms.

'Matjek! What are you doing here?' He uses the formal tone that means he is on the beemee feed but Matjek does not care, he is having too much fun.

'I came to find you,' he says.

'That's great. Sit with me.' He pats Matjek on the back.

'Have you been reading?'

'No,' he says.

'You should, it's different from beemee. Harder work, but more rewarding.' He grins at Matjek.

Then his eyes widen. 'Is that ours?' he whispers, not to Matjek, but to someone else.

There is a tiny dragonfly hovering in the air, all gleaming black plastic and metal, a couple of metres away. Its eye lenses are bright.

'They saw me in the shopping centre,' Matjek says. 'It's kind of pretty—'

There is a clap of thunder and a burst of white heat. Matjek's father throws them down to the ground. Matjek hits his head and feels his father's weight falling over him, crushing all the air from his lungs and the light from his eyes—

He wakes up in the garden. Everything feels distant and strange, like a dream. His mother is there, and she seems bigger, somehow. She is not wearing her work face.

'Can you hear me, little one?' she says. He nods.

'What happened?' he asks.

'Somebody tried to hurt your dad.'

'Why would anyone want to do that?'

'Lots of people want to *be* your dad, sweetheart. That's what he does. And somebody wanted to know what it would feel like if he died.'

'What does it feel like?'

'I don't know, Matjek. And you shouldn't worry about that either. Sleep now.'

The lightkraken is there in his room, keeping the room bright and safe from monsters, but it is a long time before Matjek can sleep.

It's not difficult to get the watson to show him the beemee feeds.

He is

on a beach with his body straining thin fabric in strange places, a cocktail in hand, looking at black shining bodies, smell of chlorine, long fingernails tinkling against glass as he takes out the little umbrella to drink, the sun a hot blanket on his back—

looking at a burning candle with a scalpel in his hand, cutting and the pain is like the skin on his back but magnified, as if focused into one point by a magnifying glass—

a dog running in grass panting panting panting through the spray of the lawn watering system, wanting to bark—

But none of these things are what he is looking for. There are darker corners of the beemee web, and if the watson does not let him in there, there are other ways. He tells the lightkraken to find it for him. It knows exactly what he wants – it used to be a part of him, after all – but it is faster, much faster, and he barely has time to blink and it is already there.

Death

is a hospital ceiling with flaking paint and a Virgin Mary statue clasped between his hands that are like tree roots—

a sip of cognac, right before he loses everything he used to be, and as the alcohol and poison blaze in his belly, he is suddenly so afraid—

a thundering chaos and shards of rock hitting his face and a heavy helmet on his head and then a roaring sound and warmth and then the cold and dark—

He cries, at first. But after a while, the tears leave him and what remains is anger. It's not fair. It's not fair that it should be like this.

His mother does not understand. How could she? In the land of the Princess, no one has to die. She has not been there.

And that's when he knows what he has to do.

It's not that he needs to bring the lightkraken and the Princess and the others to this world. It's the other way around.

He sits in the garden for a long time, thinking about it. It feels like there is something inside him, bigger than he is.

They have gathered around him, the Prince and the Green Soldier and the Princess, and the little lightkraken dancing in the air. They say goodbye, and vanish. The Princess comes last. Her hair smells of smoke and her smudged lips beneath the wooden mask are dry when she kisses his forehead.

'I'll come back,' he says. 'I promise.'

Then he packs his bag, puts the beemee away and leaves to fix the world, before his mother's next holiday.

*

'There you have it,' Matjek says. 'Thank you for your company, but it is time for me to wake up and meet myself. The more innocent one you so kindly delivered to me. We will open the jewel together and make things right. And then no one will have to die.'

'No one will have to die,' echoes the thief. In the evening light, his features start changing. They flicker through all of Matjek's faces, all contained within each other, an infinite corridor of mirrors.

'You did guard yourself well,' they say, in a chorus that rises like an angry sea, and suddenly it feels like his own mouth is speaking the words as well.

'But you did not listen. I told you in the beginning. I told you in the end. I am not Jean le Flambeur. You see, the name Joséphine here gave to the Hunter was not the thief's.'

'You should really be more careful with the things you make, Matjek,' Joséphine says. 'Little boys should not play with fire. And you should know me better than to think that I would bet all on one gambler, even a high roller like my Jean. I needed an ace in the hole. So I made sure there was one, hiding inside him.'

'All-Defector,' says Matjek's mouth, but his head is already full of mirrors.

'All-Defector,' the thing echoes. And now its voice is coming from behind him, dusty and papery and whispering, and Matjek knows that if he just turns around and looks he is going to finally wake up—

# 29

# TAWADDUD AND THE AUN

It is only Tawaddud, her father and Dunyazad who go to the desert, clad in mutalibun robes, rukh staffs in their hands. They leave the city through the gate of Bab, the gate of the treasure-hunters.

They walk in silence across the rough terrain of the Wrath, the angular shapes of buried Sobornost machines, until the proper desert begins. The Shards are a vertical starry sky behind them, against the evening blue.

'This is the story of Zoto Gomelez, the father of my father,' says Cassar finally.

'When Sirr fell, the Aun came to him. The Chimney Princess. The Green Soldier. The Kraken of Light. The Flower Prince.

'They told him that they used to live in the flesh: they were copied painfully from mind to mind, ghosts and shadows, hardly any awareness but what their hosts gave them. They would find tricks to ensure that they were remembered. Promises of immortality and the heavens. And so they prospered for a time, and were called gods.

'But when the humans made fire and wheels and electricity

and started to make immortals of their own, they had to hide in stories. The Goddess. The Mentor. The Shapeshifter. The Trickster. And they knew that when they were found out, they were going to die.

'Except that, before the Collapse, there came one who set them free. The Prince of Stories. The One in the Jannah. And in the world of uploaded minds, after the Collapse broke all old things, they came into their true power.

'They made Earth their flesh. Wildcode is a part of them. They move through it like shadows, and hear it when we whisper their names, see it when we write them in the Seals.

'They told Zoto that they could take his people amongst them, to turn them into stories. But Zoto had a wife, and did not want to live without flesh. So he made a deal. He would allow the Aun to see the world through human eyes again, through the people of Sirr. They would learn the Secret Names and shape their world and stay safe. And in return, they would give the Aun something they had not had for a long time: worship. This is the secret of the Gomelez.'

'So, how are we going to speak to them?' Tawaddud asks.

'Tell them your story,' Cassar says, 'a true story. They are always listening.'

He spreads his hands wide, as if embracing the desert.

'I am Cassar Gomelez,' he says. 'I loved my wife so much I turned away from my daughter who bears her face, because I could not stand to look at her for the memories she would bring. I almost gave my city away because I was so afraid to lose it. I made my other daughter carry all my hopes and dreams. I am Cassar Gomelez, and I would speak with the Aun.'

And then they are there, written into the air: the little girl in a mask, the old man in green, and the thing that shifts and glows and dances.

'What do you seek?' asks the Princess, the Chimney Princess, the Princess of Stories.

'A boon,' Tawaddud says.

'The price is always the same.'

Tawaddud nods. She sits down on the sand and pulls her robes closer to her against the wind. She smiles at her father and sister. 'This might take a while,' she says.

She takes a deep breath and begins.

'Before Tawaddud makes love to Mr Sen the jinn, she feeds him grapes.'

The story takes a long time to tell, and when Tawaddud finishes, there is a strange, bright star in the sky. The winds have risen, and in the horizon, there is a glare, a tall, burning pillar of flame.

'We accept your gift,' the Princess says. 'What is it that you would ask of us, daughter of Zoto Gomelez?'

'I ask you to save my people from the Sobornost, from the eternal undeath of the gogols. Rise up against them, like you did before. Set us free, and we will honour you.'

'It is too late,' the Soldier says in a gentle, gruff voice. 'It has already begun.'

The sky is stitched with falling meteors. The new star is now bigger than the moon, and on its surface, Tawaddud sees the rough features of a face, not a kindly Man in the Moon but something older and colder. The earth beneath their feet shakes.

'They are eating us,' says the kraken in a small, sing-song voice. 'We are powerless against them, empty ones, dark things that are many.'

'It is not such a bad thing to end,' says the Princess. 'We are tired and old. And all stories end.'

'You promised us a boon,' Tawaddud says. Tears run down her cheeks, mixed with sand. 'Can you not give us the choice of Zoto again? Can you not take us away?'

There is a boom in the distance, and then a hot wind blows over Tawaddud, filling her eyes and mouth with sand. *It can't end like this,* she whispers. *It is not supposed to end like this.*

Then the Chimney Princess gives her her hand, small, strong fingers around hers, and helps her up.

'Our brother has returned to us,' she says. She is smiling behind her mask.

The wind rises again. A man in a dark suit and blue glasses stands before her.

'There is always a way out,' he says.

# 30

# THE THIEF AND THE STORIES

We fall and burn in the *guberniya* dawn.

The white incandescence of the Hunter is gone, and yet I remain. I feel strangely light, like an old man of the sea was gone from my back. I almost start laughing, until I see wildcode twist my hands sapphire claws. The Hunter components are dead, too, taken by Earth's powers-that-be, drifting around like dead insects.

*Perhonen* tries to brake with her wings. They catch fire and are torn away.

'I'm sorry,' I whisper. 'I was wrong.'

*So was I*, the ship says.

The wildcode is everywhere now. The ship's systems are full of white noise. Its hull twists and curls like burning paper as we fall. Earth reaches for us like a giant's hand.

The butterflies are all around me. It is hot in the cabin, and they catch fire, tiny candles, flame and dust. I reach for one and close my jagged hand around it.

As the avatars burn, they form a face, the face I saw in the tiger's vir, a pretty girl, skin like snow.

*You get out of everything, Jean,* she says. *Tell her that I love her. Look after her. For me. Promise.*

'I promise.'

She kisses me, lightly, a butterfly kiss. Then she is gone. Ashes fall on my face. I close my eyes.

In the end, there is a sound that fills the world, and then only black.


They are like serpents of light, all around me, woven into each other so it is hard to say where one ends and another begins. They are old. They wear many faces. And I know them, or a part of me does. The Flower Prince.

The girl from the ancestor vir is there. She takes off her mask and kisses me on the forehead.

*Welcome back, brother.*

'Bastards,' I tell them. 'Why did you not save *Perhonen* as well? She deserved it more than I did.'

*We could not see her. We can only see ourselves.* There is a grief of ages in her voice.

'Damn it. It's not fair.'

*When was it ever fair? It doesn't matter. We will go back to Father and be with him for ever.*

The old thing inside me wants to say yes. To be with the Prince of Stories again. But something pulls me back. *Perhonen.* A promise.

*I keep my promises.*

Whatever the serpent things are, I am something else. I remember reading a book in a cell. I remember a door opening. That's when I was born, out of the crystal stopper. A creature made from *La Bouchon de cristal*, a boy from the desert and an old god.

294

*Come with us. Come with us, brother.*

'My name is Jean le Flambeur,' I say. 'And we have work to do.'

I smile at Tawaddud.

'I'm sorry,' I say. 'I got you into trouble. I tend to do that.'

To her credit, she seems to take my sudden appearance in a stride. *Tawaddud Gomelez, a lover of monsters.* 'If you want to make it up to me, you had better find a way to save my city,' she says.

'Chen is using things called Dragons,' I say. 'It's going to take some drastic measures. I think there is a way to get everybody out. But you might not like it.'

Cassar Gomelez gives me a look I've had from many fathers. 'My daughter now speaks for our people,' he says, placing a hand on Tawaddud's shoulder. 'She decides.'

'It may require a … transformation.'

'Do it,' Tawaddud says. 'Zoto Gomelez said no. We say yes. All together.'

I shape my wish into a thought and give it to the strange beings who claim to be my brothers and sisters. They whisper together for a moment with voices like hissing sand. Then the one called Princess nods.

The world goes mad.

The storm of wildcode rises and washes over Sirr. When it reaches Tawaddud, she feels herself being lifted up, expanding, becoming a part of the hurricane of jinni. She watches with a godlike eye as the city turns into sand, as the heavens rain dragons upon the Earth.

The Aun come and take the minds of Sirr, turn them into stories, compress them into a form that is like a seed that can bloom in any mind, an eternal life in the space of a book, between blue covers like *The Book of Nights*. And as the book closes, she feels the Axolotl and Dunyazad and her father there next to her.

Chen's Dragons are eating wildcode and jinni and everything that makes up the bodies of the Aun. But there is one place on Earth they are not going to touch.

It turns out there is a reason why they call it the Lost Jannah of the Cannon.

A 150-kiloton thermonuclear explosive device in the midst of reaction mass, under a giant shell, an impact shield of boron. A hardened vir running inside a Wang bullet of steel, a 3000-ton projectile with a full-blown spacecraft inside.

The vir inside is tiny, but stories do not take up much space. The only running minds are a boy called Matjek and me. It was him who came up with the design. It is a bookshop, bright and airy, with inviting shelves and nooks and crannies for reading.

Before we launch, he takes a book from one of the shelves, with a blue and silver cover. He looks at the first page and then closes it.

'I want to read it,' he says. 'But I can never remember the stories in my dreams when I wake up.'

'Something tells me that this one is different,' I tell him. And then I press the red button in my head.

We sit together and drink tea as the jet of plasma underground takes us up, thousands of Gs and ten times the escape velocity. We are past the Moon before Chen realises we are gone. Then I deploy the solar sails and take us to the Highway.

Mieli is still out there. I made a promise to *Perhonen*, and

I plan to keep it. I am small again, barely more than human. But that doesn't matter. I just need help from a few friends, and without Joséphine in my head, I know where to find them.

There is a smile on my lips as the prince and I steer the ship of stories towards Saturn.

# Epilogue

Joséphine Pellegrini watches the All-Defector sitting on the beach. The thief disguise is gone, like a discarded skin, and now the creature wears the childlike shape and the serene smile of Matjek Chen. But there is no trace of the Prime in his eyes: only infinite hunger remains. She shudders, turns away and looks at the sea.

'I always thought you were going to take me, too,' she says.

'I'm going to take everything, in the end,' the All-Defector says. 'But I still need you.'

He is holding the Kaminari jewel in his lap, like it was a rock he picked up on the beach, space and time in the form of two hands in prayer. 'Chen was wrong. There was a reason why it did not open for him. It was made to open for you.'

He holds the jewel out to Joséphine. She looks at it: the ultimate zoku jewel, the secret of the Spike, the key to Planck locks. She accepts it hungrily. It opens like a flower in her hands.

Something white flutters to the sand. Joséphine picks it up. A small rectangle, made from paper. A calling card.

She reads out the text written on it with a beautiful cursive hand.

Jean le Flambeur
Gentleman-Burglar
Will Return when your Zoku Jewels
are Genuine,

it says. And then it, too, is gone, dissolving like a dream.

Mieli is alone in the dark. She watches the *guberniya* arrive in orbit around Earth and the tidal forces it creates. Its presence alone tears the Gourd apart and makes the blue globe's white clouds boil. It is raining black things down on humanity's home, von Neumann machines or worse. Continents change shape and a dark shell spreads over the marble of the planet.

*Chen is eating Earth,* she thinks. So much for Sirr and all its stories, so much for the lost jannahs.

'See what you did?' The pellegrini seethes with rage inside her head. 'I'm going to tear you apart for this. No Sydän for you, ever, no death, no *alinen*. I told you I'm not a gentle goddess. When my sisters come for me, I will—'

'Do your worst,' Mieli says. 'I don't work for you anymore.' She steels herself for the pain. A part of her looks forward to it. She deserves it, for Sydän, for *Perhonen*. Perhaps even for the thief.

Something glints in her field of vision. A blue oval, smaller than her hand. Even in the vacuum, it smells faintly of flowers.

*The zoku jewel.* Perhonen *shot me out with the zoku jewel.*

It whispers to her, and the pellegrini's voice becomes like distant rain.

*Take me home,* she thinks at it. *Take me where I really belong.*

The jewel glows brighter. Everything is still for a long time. And an eternity later, there is a ship, a zoku ship.

Strange beings surround her. Glittering wheels, with faces in the middle, rings of jewels like miniature solar systems. They look like angels or figures from tarot cards. They remind Mieli of someone.

'Mother,' Mieli says and drifts to sleep, perfectly happy, in the moment just before it's time to go home.

# Acknowledgements

This was a tough one, for many reasons. So thanks first and foremost to Simon Spanton for his sharp editorial eye and enduring faith.

Willing or unwilling victims of thought thievery include Andy Clark, Douglas Hofstadter, Maurice Leblanc, Jan Potocki and the thousand nameless storytellers of *The Arabian Nights*.

As for people with names, ones I owe a sincere thank you to include:

My agent John Jarrold for being a solid rock and a foundation of advice, as always.

Sam and Lesley, for friendship and support during interesting times.

Esa Hilli, Lauri Lovén, Phil Raines and Stuart Wallace for discussions, careful readings of early drafts, candid feedback, comments and bug-hunting.

Writers' Bloc – including Alan Campbell, Jack Deighton, Morag Edward, Bram Gieben, Mark Harding, Gavin Inglis,

Helen Jackson, Jane McKie, Stefan Pearson, Charlie Stross, Andrew Wilson and Kirsti Wishart. Special thanks to Andrew Ferguson for introducing me to the Axolotl.

Antti Autio  for his flowing Finnish and keen eye for details and plot holes.

Sabrina Maniscalco for friendship and quantum physics discussions.

Jakko Ojakangas for musical inspiration.

Darren Brierton for first exposing me to philosophy of mind, and Sami for being a tough sparring partner on related topics (as well as a good friend).

Anni, Antti, Eino, Panu, Sanna, Lauri, Jaakko and Tuija for hospitality and friendship.

My parents Mirja and Mauno, for making sure there is a timeless place called home.

Zuzana, for the best true story I could wish for.